"YOUR SCALP IS HANGING ON THE BULLETIN BOARD, JOSH."

"It's about Condor, isn't it?" Josh asked.

"No, I didn't hear a word about Condor, whatever it is. There's an ongoing project assigned exclusively to you. And the orders didn't originate in DIA. They came from outside."

"From where outside?"

"The executive branch, down through the Joint Chiefs. The executive—the President of the United States."

Josh was staring out the window, trying to make sense of that incredible revelation, when the flat blue cigar of an attack sub surfaced a few hundred yards offshore and began to disgorge men in shiny orange rubber boats.

As his belly tried to cram itself into his throat, he realized that, whatever it was, it was bigger than he'd even *begun* to imagine. . . .

SYSTEMS

A Novel
by

W. T. QUICK

A SIGNET BOOK

NEW AMERICAN LIBRARY

A DIVISION OF PENGUIN BOOKS USA INC.

This book is dedicated to Desmond Mong Seng Tan, for all the right reasons.

Acknowledgments

I would like to acknowledge the work of Dean Ing who, to the best of my knowledge, first described the Club under the guise of the Cold Gas Launcher in his book *Firefight 2000* (Baen Books, 1987). Also, thanks are in order to Ben Bova, who created Moonbase and graciously threw it open to those who wished to write about it: Certain aspects of Moonbase are incorporated in Kennedy Crater. Finally, hats off to the killer duo of Mary Ann Murphy, proofreader and copy editor without compare, and Bill Stoshak, who has kept my battered computers running, provided loaners and good advice, and generally been an excellent fellow. My heartfelt thanks to all of you.

Chapter One

He opened his eyes. Pain blasted across his face. At first he thought he was blind. Bloodshot haze throbbed where his brain said vision should be. After a time the crimson fog diminished, and faint, vaguely human shadows appeared. Something cool touched his forehead.

"Joshua? Mr. Tower? Can you hear me? Can you see?"

It was a woman's voice—soft, reassuring, and unfamiliar. A professional voice. He tried to put things together. Pain. A woman's soothing voice. Concern.

Finally he had it. A hospital. There must have been an accident of some kind and he'd been injured. Now he was in a hospital. He tried to shape words, but he'd misplaced his lips, his tongue.

"I think he's aware," said the feminine voice. "Maybe he can hear us."

"Don't push it," a masculine voice rumbled gently. "We don't know about nerve damage yet."

"No. I checked for response, but it's too early to tell. Later, maybe. I'm going to put him back under now."

He heard a hissing noise and felt a dull pressure beneath his right ear. Hypospray? Suddenly it didn't matter. The bloody clouds receded, turning gray and slow.

One last thought.

Julia . . . Julia?

The waiter flicked up their menus like a man raking in cards, bowed slightly, and turned away. Tower fumbled in the pocket of his suit, found the lumpy shape, and took it out. He handed the small package across the table. Julia looked away from his face as she worked the distinctive Cartier bow with long, graceful fingers.

"Josh, my god! A diamond ring."

She was in her early thirties, almost ten years younger than him. Her hair was the real black that few achieved without artificial means, falling smooth and straight to her shoulders, framing a face that was all cheekbones and wide, gray-black eyes. She wore a simple white dress that exposed her shoulders. He thought she was the loveliest woman he'd ever seen.

He luxuriated in the chill smoke of her voice and wondered what strange karma, what unknown bonanza of luck, had gifted him with her. Silently he mouthed the syllables of her name. *Julia.* The three syllables sounded like chimes in the bell of his skull.

She raised her eyes, and he wanted to laugh aloud. His spine ached with happiness so pure it was almost pain.

"You always wanted a ring," he said. "I couldn't think of a better time."

The perfect blue-white solitaire glittered like a mislaid star on her hand. He watched her lips, her eyes. "Do you like it?"

She nodded slowly.

"Hey, don't start crying now. This is the happiest moment of my life. It's only a diamond. A little thing. You're giving us a son."

Slowly her fingers crossed the space between them and came to rest on his cheek. The jewel glinted at the corner of his eye in silent premonition.

The world rolled slowly.

"I love you."

"I love you."

It was dark when he woke up. His vision had returned. The throbbing, bloody haze across his eyes was gone, taking the pain with it. Now he felt cold and frightened. Random synaptic connections tried to kick-start memory, but the mnemonic engine wouldn't catch. For the moment he was stuck with the present. He shivered. His bones told him the past was a pit, the future hell.

After a while he slept again.

"What should we call him?" he asked.

Maxwell's Silver Hammer was one of the oldest restaurants in San Francisco. Patrons fought to make reservations weeks in advance, hoping for a Bay-side table with a view of the great tankers sliding into port. Tower called in every minor favor he had and gimmicked entrance on two days' notice. He thought about the cost only peripherally: two weeks' pay for a single meal. Cheap at twice the price, he decided, watching the chandeliered light dance in her thick, night-shaded hair. Their first child deserved a parade. He was sorry he couldn't do better than diamonds and dinner.

"Josh," she asked, "what did you think when I told you?"

He grinned. He wanted to reach across the table, knock over the fine crystal, and take her in his arms in front of the shocked stares of other diners. "I thought it was about time. Didn't you?"

A faint shadow crossed her face. "You did? I wondered. . . . Sometimes you seem so distant. As if . . . I don't know. It's hard to tell what you're thinking. Did you know that?"

He realized she was serious. It was a failing of his. He assumed that his own feelings were so pervasive she shared them automatically.

He started to speak, then shook his head. "I wish you could read my mind. I wish that was possible. Then you would know. Can't you feel it? Really?"

The shadow went away and her features relaxed. The peculiar gray-black shade of her eyes lightened somewhat, and the beginning of a grin tickled the corner of her lips. She glanced at the bright stone in the ring. "You can also be very persuasive."

"I could prove it, I guess. Right here on the table,

if necessary." He made sweeping motions, as if to clear the linen, the china, and make a bed right there.

She shook her head and smiled. "We'll call him Joshua, of course. Drink your champagne."

He felt light on his face before he opened his eyes. For a moment, wild vertigo gripped him. He was lost in a morass of dread, without the guideposts of memory to direct him. Hospital. Accident. Fear. It was all he had.

What had happened to him?

He sat bolt upright, his eyes stretched wide, his lips cracked around a shout.

"Hey. It's all right. You're okay."

Her face was a stranger's but comforting. A strong, youngish face with lines beyond its age. A face that had seen things, faded blue eyes full of knowledge. Short, neatly cut blond hair protruded in a gold rim beneath her starched white cap. She wore a white uniform that fitted her well-formed body closely. The room was full of machines that made breathing noises. He smelled sharp chemical incense, the odor of pain.

"You're a nurse," he said.

She nodded. "Call me Kelly. Nurse Kelly." She put down the magazine she'd been reading and rose from her chair. Briskly she checked the readouts on a monitor at the foot of his bed. He watched her movements. She looked down at him. "You're awake, then. You made it. I wondered there, for a while." She watched him carefully. Her face was quiet and serious.

A dull, pounding ache surged behind his eyeballs. The light seemed very bright. Slowly, he turned his head and saw a window. Outside, the day was blue and clear. A few cauliflower clouds ambled across the sky, and a hill, crowded with toy-box houses cream and turquoise and jade, slouched down and away. A flat blade of the Bay glittered knifelike in the hazy distance.

He tasted his lips. The skin was dry and scabby.

"Here. Wait a second." She turned to a table and lifted a pitcher. After a moment she raised his head with one hand while she gently placed a water glass to his mouth. "Go slow," she said. "It's been a while."

He was astonished at how powerfully these small, mundane things affected him. A woman's touch, the taste of water. There was something potent about helplessness, something attractive. Deep inside his skull a knot of darkness chittered, but another part of him, equally insistent, pleaded acceptance: Relax, sink back into the pillows, let somebody else do it. Let anybody else take responsibility.

She moved away, still watching his face. "Okay. Try again. By the way, you are a very lucky man, Mr. Tower."

He moved his tongue and words stumbled out. "When . . . can I see my wife?"

Kelly stared at him silently. He watched faint wrinkles form at the edge of her blue eyes. Something huge and empty opened its mouth and yawned inside him.

"My wife . . ." he tried again.

Slowly, she shook her head.

The maw widened; he fell into it, screaming.

They had to walk down Russian Hill to the taxi platform.

"I want to fly. I feel like flying. How about you?"

Julia glanced at the uniformed doorman and held tightly to Tower's arm. The champagne had spread a flush across the bridge of her nose. "Flying. Aren't we doing that already?"

He stared into her face and felt an answering grin shiver across his teeth. "The real thing, lover. An air taxi back to Marin. How about that?"

She frowned thoughtfully. "So expensive . . ." She spoke slowly, enunciating each word, and he realized she was more than a little drunk.

"Who cares? We're not broke. There's three of us now, and this night won't ever happen again. Unless . . ." The thought stopped him. "Are you all right?"

She squeezed his arm more tightly. "I'm fine. You

worry too much.'' She took a deep breath. ''Hell, yes. Let's fly.''

The night was full of the smell of bending grass, oleander, mist, freshly turned earth. Dark gardens in bloom. They stepped down to a shifting sea of fog. Overhead, ancient streetlights popped and sizzled. Neon tapestries lit their way. The stars were muffled.

Their heels made sharp, pistol sounds on cracked concrete. They laughed and walked on.

''You have a lot of surgery left,'' Kelly said flatly. ''Your face, for instance, is a mess.''

He knew it was a game of some kind, but his abraded memory gave him no clue what kind of game it was. There was a pull to it, as if he were expected to answer, but he had no answers. The question and the answer were the same. Julia was dead.

''Not going to say anything? Listen, buddy, I've got better things to do than hang around your room. I run this whole ward—just me, all by myself.'' She paused, glancing at the encircling machines. ''A little mechanical help, maybe.''

He stared at her. What did she want? For a moment he almost had it, but it ghosted away when he tried to concentrate. Lots of things did that now. All he had were a few facts, small spiky hard things that ripped where he touched them. Accident. Julia. Dead.

Was there more? He was terribly afraid there was.

The air-taxi platform was on the Wharf, where the cable-car turnaround once had been. He was just old enough to remember those cars, rickety and roaring with happy tourists, swooping from the hilly peaks like runaway metal dreams. It was late; the Wharf was nearly deserted. The platform rested on a calm pool of golden light next to dark water, its circular guide ring floating like a halo overhead. It was a shame the cable cars had gone, but he understood. Air taxis were noisy. The turnarounds were relatively isolated and thus good places to shelter the new technology. San

Franciscans didn't want the expensive peace of their priceless condos disturbed.

They walked up a short, wide flight of steps to the main area, holding hands like children. He scanned sleek oval shapes that rested like complicated eggs in their chromed baskets. The silver Hyundai-USX star logo glittered on each taxi like a tiny birthmark.

"Good. I was afraid all the twin taxis were gone."

"What?"

"You know. A four taxi costs more. Maybe we could squeeze into a mono. What do you think?"

She laughed. "There's three of us, remember."

"So a twin taxi is better. Don't want to crowd us. We're a crowd already." He felt slightly lightheaded, and he couldn't decide if it was happiness or champagne. Maybe both.

He saw the street warrior before she did. Old reflexes died hard. He turned to face the shambling, slope-shouldered gargoyle who lurched from a darkened corner, his hand outstretched.

"Hungry," the man growled. His eyes were manic pools. His arms flexed and rippled beneath a glowing patina of high-charge electric tattoos.

"Josh . . ."

"Don't worry, Julia. I'll just talk to him. You go over to the taxi stand."

He felt her hand slide away. "Be careful," she said.

Be careful. She always said that. He knew part of it was fear for him, but a portion was for herself, as well. Security meant a great deal to her. She'd been terrified of his old job, of the possibility that he might not come home some night. He shook his head. That was all over.

Nevertheless, a weird kind of exultation came as both his hands were freed. He stepped forward, meeting the forward movement of the panhandler.

"Hey, buddy, what's up?"

"I'm hungry," the larger man said. "You got any money? I bet you do. So you give it to me, okay?"

Tower understood. It looked like a simple conversation—he hoped it did, for Julia's sake—but it was a

strong-arm job, plain and simple. To this thug he probably looked like easy meat. His slender body didn't
hint of a threat. He knew this gorilla saw the mask of
what he tried to be: a small, brown-haired man with
gray-blue eyes, wearing a suit, living a quiet, ordered
life. The thug saw prey.

Once, in another life, he'd found that useful.

The man's huge, broken-knuckled fist came up to
Tower's chest, and Tower took the fingers in a gentle
grip. Something prickly and tense coursed through his
muscles. He moved his hand in a certain way and
watched the surprise in the street monster's eyes turn
to glittering pain.

"Hey." The man's vice was soft with agony. "I'm
just . . . let go."

"You're just hungry," Tower agreed quietly.
"Right?" He stepped back and reached into his
pocket. "Here. Go somewhere and eat. Somewhere
else. You understand?"

The man took the money without looking at it. He
kept his eyes on Tower's face as he backed away.
"Sorry, mister," he mumbled. "I'm sorry."

Tower watched him until he reached the foot of the
steps, turned, and started running.

"What did he want?" Julia asked.

"He was hungry. I gave him money." Consciously
he willed forgotten memories to subside. He hated
what he'd once been, what Julia had saved him from.
He didn't want her to see the spectral remnants of
those times on his face.

"Two taxis," he said. "Red or blue. You pick."

He smiled, and after a moment, she did.

"At least you're talking," Kelly said. "You don't
have much to say, but you're talking."

Her words bounced off him like soft birds, drifting
without meaning. "I don't remember. I don't remember the accident. Did I tell you that?"

"Uh huh. You did. And I told you that's normal.
You suffered major head injuries. Concussion. Maybe
some nerve damage. It will heal. Whether you remem-

ber . . .'' She shrugged. "Maybe you won't. Maybe you won't want to. That happens, sometimes.''

He was propped on a cloud of pillows. Some of the machines were gone. Maybe he was getting better. She moved around the room, picking aimlessly at bits of plastic, at screens, at enigmatic metal boxes.

A slow thought began to crest behind his eyes. "I want to remember,'' he told her. As he spoke, he knew he'd crossed a bridge he hadn't even suspected was there. She turned and stared at him.

"Your choice,'' she said.

He punched in his home address quickly. The twin taxi's computer confirmed a flight window within ten seconds. Tower turned to his wife. "Now we fly,'' he whispered and leaned over to brush her cheek lightly with his lips. He turned back to the console, noting the flight specs: a twenty-second boost, followed by a minute of free fall, and finally another twenty seconds of brake time. Simple ballistic trajectory, the army part of his mind informed him. Forty miles in less than three minutes.

"Like a roller coaster,'' Julia said. "Josh, are there any roller coasters left?''

"Of course there are,'' he said absently. Then he realized what she was trying to say. She was frightened.

"Julia.'' He swiveled toward her and took her hands in his. "I forgot. You've never ridden in a laser cab before.''

Her eyes gleamed in the dark. She shook her head.

"There's nothing to be scared of, darling. These things are absolutely safe. Even if something happens to interrupt the beam—wait a sec. Do you know how this works?''

"It flies,'' she said simply.

He laughed. "Well, yes. But not like an airplane. No wings, right?''

She glanced out the window on her side. "No. No wings.''

"Look up.''

Obediently, she tilted her head. "What am I looking at?"

"Nothing, really. You can't see it. But in orbit up there is a mirror, a big one. The Consortium built it. It's part of what pays the dividends on our Consort stock. Anyway, in a few seconds a ground-based laser is going to shoot a beam up into that mirror. Then the mirror will focus it and shoot it back down to us. Right here."

She thought about it. "Seems like a roundabout way of doing business."

He nodded. "Just like the real world. Anyway, when it gets here, we catch the beam on a grid—you can't see it, it's in back—and boom! Off we go."

"Boom?"

"Well, more like a real loud hum. Or a fast string of firecrackers. We'll wake up the neighbors when we get home."

"Mrs. Sansibutti . . ."

"Do her good."

"You don't have to deal with her."

"Thank God," he said and touched her ear with the tip of his tongue.

"Stop that."

"No."

The beam hit. They boosted.

Kelly wheeled his chair out onto the balcony. In the morning sunlight, the flesh of his hands was yellowed and translucent. He stared at the map of scars and veins there. *What did I do to my hands?*

"Too bright?" she asked.

"No." He was silent, watching the hills throw their cargo of colored boxes at the sky. "Why can't I remember, Kelly? I have bits and pieces, right up to . . ." He stopped, a faint sheen of moisture on his forehead. He shook his head. "She didn't die in the crash."

"No. She was still alive when the crash team brought you in. But there was too much . . . damage. We couldn't save her."

Tower's lips twitched. A tic began to dance beneath his left eye. Kelly moved past him and stood at the edge of the balcony, her back to him, gazing out over the city.

He looked down at his hands. "Yes," he said at last. "I wish you could have saved my son."

She turned and faced him. Her eyes squinted. "What did you say?"

Tower suddenly felt himself on dangerous ground. Something in her faded eyes warned him. He felt loose, confused, like a high-wire artist about to take a wrong step. "My son," he said. "We were going to have a baby. That's why we went out that night."

"Oh, Tower. We didn't know. When we pulled up her records . . ." She shook her head. "No mention of pregnancy. She hadn't registered the fetus. There were no signs. It must have been very early."

He still didn't understand. "She wanted to tell me first. She . . . what difference does it make? You weren't able to save her."

He knew the emotion. He'd seen it before. It was pity.

"If we'd known, we could have saved *him,*" she said.

Without realizing that he did so, he counted down the seconds. When he reached twelve, the twin taxi's engine shut off. Deep inside his skull, a tiny worm of unease lifted its head and looked around.

He glanced at the console. Glowing green numbers still advised a twenty-second burn. Twelve seconds. Thirteen, fourteen.

The night rushed by with the sound of muted thunder. "It's beautiful, isn't it?" she said. "Why didn't you ever take me before?" He thought she sounded very happy, very relaxed beside him.

Fifteen, sixteen.

He reached over and checked the fastenings of her safety web. Gently, he placed her hands on the grab rings. "Now," he said carefully, "I want you to hold on to these. Hold on tight."

"What? Is something wrong?" Her eyes went suddenly wide.

"Hold on tight," he repeated.

He reached for the panic button.

Nineteen, twenty . . .

He lay in the dark and stared at the ceiling. Around him the machines breathed softly. His eyes felt hot, scratchy, as if something were burning from the inside of his skull outward.

Why hadn't she registered the baby?

The thought circled endlessly, biting its tail. He felt his fingers curl into claws. Why?

"Can't you feel it? Really?"

The words dropped like molten coins into his consciousness. Her face. Her eyes. Had she answered?

Yes. She had. But the short pause before her words was the real answer. She'd been afraid. Afraid he wasn't ready for a child. Afraid he didn't love her enough?

Afraid. Underneath it all, she'd been afraid of him.

"But I love you," he said aloud. His words echoed off the machines.

He closed his eyes.

Had she thought about abortion? Was that why? Two weeks into pregnancy it was simple enough. She waited and didn't register their son. The cells split and grew inside her womb and she waited. For what?

Permission?

"I'm a datahunter."

Kelly looked up from the terminal at the end of his bed. "What?"

"It's what I do. I'm a datahunter."

"Okay, I'll play. What's a datahunter?"

He tried to marshal his thoughts. "I look for information. I work for the big conglomerates, and when they want to know something, I find it for them."

Her shoulders moved. "Is that hard? I thought computers knew everything."

"They do—sort of. Picture a library full of books.

A big library. Lot of information there. But you have to be able to find it. The world's like that. Computer files contain an incredible amount of data. The world is drowning in information. Some hidden. Some locked up. Some of it is simply forgotten. A computer can't find what it doesn't know how to look for. It needs a template. Maybe a key to unlock another computer. Maybe anything. That's what I do. I make templates. I grind keys.''

Her blue gaze pinned him. "Is this important?"

He shrugged. "I want to know. I have to know what happened. The part I can't remember. I have to know why.'' How could he explain his guilt to her? He had blacked out and missed Julia's last moments. Why hadn't she told him about her pregnancy right away? And then at the end, he hadn't been able to help her. Had she forgiven him? Was she sorry? Did she love him? What had been her final thoughts, her final words? He had to know. Even if there was nothing to know. He had to know that, too.

"Tower—Joshua. That sounds a lot like an obsession starting to grow."

His lips curved. It hurt to do that. He wondered what his expression looked like to her. "Whatever gets you through the night."

"Right. You dream a lot, did you know that?"

"No. No dreams."

"You don't remember. That doesn't mean you don't dream." She lifted one hand. "These machines don't lie. When you sleep, lots of rapid eye movements. That means dreams."

"Okay, then I dream. But I still don't remember. There must be some kind of drug that will help me."

"Oh, yes. Several drugs. But you're a sick man, Josh. We don't know what would happen. Physical damage. Mental damage. We just won't take the risk." She paused. "Maybe there's a reason you don't remember. Listen to your body. Your mind. Could be they know better than you do."

He shook his head sharply. "There's a record. Somewhere, there is a record of what I want. You don't know. If I don't have it, I can find it. Like I said, it's what I *do.*"

She sighed. It was the first time he'd ever heard her do that. "Josh, I don't know—"

"I want a terminal in here. Can you get me that?"

"Of course. But the doctor—"

It felt right: "Screw the doctor," he said. "Get me a terminal."

"Josh, what's wrong?"

He summoned strength from his other life. You could never let others see fear. It was contagious. Fear killed.

"There's been some kind of malfunction, but don't worry. I'm going to hit the parachute. We'll be okay." He peered out the window at the dark. The taxi must have already peaked its shortened trajectory and was coming down now. Had they cleared the Bay?

Down below, the earth gleamed brown and rolling in the moonlight. No water. His chest relaxed a bit.

"Might get a little bumpy," he said.

Her knuckles were tiny white dots in the darkness.

"Okay, hold on now."

He pushed the button. The flowing silence was shattered immediately by a heavy *whumpf* as the chute exploded above them. The taxi bounced like a yo-yo at the end of its string.

Julia made a tiny frightened sound.

"It's okay, baby. It's okay."

The movement slowed, stopped. They drifted down, silent.

"See," he said. "I told you we'd be all right."

He was still counting silently. Almost a minute into the trip. He wondered where they would land. Somewhere in Marin. He hoped it wouldn't be on top of a house or in a remote place where they would have to hike to safety.

"It will be a little rough when we land," he told her. "Maybe even pop the crash balloons. That's okay. Nothing to worry about."

"Oh, Josh. The baby—"

"No, it will be fine. I promise."

High overhead, the orbiting mirrors received a jumble of failure messages. Frantically the onboard computers struggled to correct misaimed beams, responding to hundreds of power-down bulletins.

The glitch that had disrupted the entire installation for no more than ten seconds had passed. The computer swiftly refocused a web of light, snatching clusters of air taxis in silent flight. A few taxis had panicked and were broadcasting chute-out messages. These the computer ignored. Chute beacons were allowed to land unpowered. It was too dangerous to focus on those taxis, for fear of damaging the chute itself.

One taxi was two days overdue for maintenance. A relay had failed. Its beacon broadcasted no chute as it settled like a giant moth beneath a great white wing.

Tower watched the ground come up. A hundred meters, fifty, forty . . .

He wrapped his right arm around her and squeezed. She was shivering. "It'll be over in a second, baby," he whispered. "Then we'll go home."

A high-power emergency beam burned through the thin layer of cumulus above them, racing to spear them from the sky. The lance of focused light caught them and shredded their chute like so much dandelion fluff. Unbalanced, the small machine tumbled, flipping the receiving grid away from the power beam.

The earth rushed up, screaming.

In the silence of the night, green letters and numbers scrolled across his terminal. His eyes felt gritty. So much news about a small accident. Only a few had been injured; only two dead. One from a heart attack.

He understood systems and wasn't surprised at the rest of it. Politicians fought for position. Big corporations jittered. The stock market heaved and shuddered. There was an immense amount of money involved, as public confidence in the safety of all transportation networks went nervous and soft. Somebody, he supposed, was making a great deal of money. Somebody usually did.

Somewhere in this morass of data was what he sought. Taxis were monitored constantly. It was just a matter of finding out who monitored them and where the information was stored.

It would be tricky. With all the publicity, files would be closing. Classified tags would appear. Data would be shifted, hidden.

The snake of need uncoiled behind his eyes. Had she forgiven him his nameless sins? Had she said ''I love you''? Or had it all been silence? He realized something had come loose inside him and was whirring madly. That seemed right, too.

Patiently, his fingers danced across the touchpad of his terminal. It would take time—but that was all he had.

All the time in the world.

Chapter Two

Kelly walked him to the front steps of Mercy General. They paused at the top, and she squinted against the bright sunlight. "The rules say I should have wheeled you out in a chair."

He nodded. Her expression was worried. He wondered why. "I didn't thank you—"

She shook her head quickly. "Then don't. You don't have to. It's my job. Like you said, it's what I *do*."

The sudden fierceness of her tone startled him. He didn't understand. Down below, on the street, a solar taxi honked impatiently. Tower hefted the plastic bag that held his belongings, his medicines. He pointed his head toward the taxi. "I've got to go now."

She stuck out her hand. He took it and was surprised at the strength of her grip. She pumped his hand once, then stepped back. "You should have let them fix those scars on your face."

He couldn't explain that to her, so he simply nodded. "Well . . ."

"Take care of yourself, Joshua." Her faded eyes seemed almost clear in the daylight. She had freckles across the bridge of her nose. He'd never noticed that before.

It seemed he should say something, but he couldn't think what. "You too," he said at last.

Her gaze flickered once. She nodded then, and without another word, she turned and walked quickly back into the building.

What was that all about?

The taxi honked again, a long, raucous sound. The

question faded. He began the long trip down, and back.

Back home.

A group of Mystic Vudu converts were clustered on the boarding platform in front of the northbound BART bullet train. With their spiky, polished hairdos glittering beneath the harsh lights of the station and their jerky chatter, they reminded him of a covey of exotic birds.

"Here, take this," a boy said, thrusting a pamphlet into his hand. He stared blankly, shook his head, and stepped around them. Once on the train it was quiet. He had the car almost to himself. Slowly he moved to the rear and settled himself in a thickly upholstered seat next to the window. He closed his eyes.

It was very easy to do. He found himself slipping into the state more often. Just shut everything out and drift. But always the random thoughts coalesced, like the insects homing on a corpse.

Julia . . .

A soft chime sounded. Pneumatics whooshed as the doors slid shut. A moment later the train rose above its magnetic rail, and acceleration pushed him into his seat. He opened his eyes.

The train rushed up a slight incline and out into the open. Automatics darkened the windows slightly in response to the bright sunlight. He looked out. The city whipped past, a blur of color and movement. He'd always enjoyed the ride before. He'd taken this train hundreds of times, knew its route as well as the fingers on his hands.

Hands. He stared down at the fresh scars. His hands were different now. He felt as if he were packed in cotton, insulated from the reality of the present. Had the trip changed, as well?

They burst out onto the New Golden Gate. He'd never seen the old one, shattered by the Great Quake of '92. He'd only been four years old, but faint impressions of the disaster still persisted. There had been shortages and, of course, the Crash. He remembered how worried his dad had been. They'd had to move three times, each move to a smaller, less attractive place. Something had died in his father during those few years. Later, he'd become a monster.

The choppy water of the Bay sparkled with light. Far out to the west, a low bank of fog humped like a hill of pearls, moving closer. Absently he wondered if it would cool things off. Probably. Have to make sure the house central processing unit was programmed for the weather change. Most people used standard programs in their machines, but he liked to tinker. He couldn't remember if he'd changed the heating program or not.

The train braked sharply for Sausalito, paused a few moments, then rose and charged north again. Even with all the stops, it was only a twenty-five-minute ride to his station, forty miles away. The train was laser powered, just like an air taxi. Far overhead a bank of mirrors gathered light from orbiting solar-power generators or caught it on the rebound from ground-based lasers and fed it back to hungry engines on earth.

Limitless power, he thought. We live so well. Even our parents, steeped in the high-tech whirlwind of their times, could never have imagined the wealth.

He shook off his musings and watched the brown hills flow by. None of it mattered. None.

He rested his cheek against the cool window glass. The gentle vibration of the train flowed into his skull and scattered his thoughts. He let his eyes fill with scenery, with stands of pine, and finally with the flat, dusty green of vineyards. At last the grapes thinned out and the hills grew darker, more foreboding. Overhead the sun was a hot dime in the sky.

Two more stops, he thought, and then home.

Crazy. Yes, it was crazy. Nothing else to call it. If he had to put a name on it, what he sought was forgiveness from the grave. His lips curled slightly. That was crazy enough, but even crazier . . .

Perhaps he didn't deserve it.

What had she said?

He felt the slight change in velocity as the train slowed for his station. After a moment he lifted his face from the glass and looked around, but nobody was watching. He was alone.

She's *dead*. He coughed so hard he thought he wouldn't stop, that he'd retch up the hard, sour ball from deep in his gut, but when the spasm passed the little knot of obsession was still there.

Slowly he stood up, moving like a man twice his age. He walked down the aisle to the door and stepped out to the open-air platform. A wall of pine trees at the back of the station bent gently in the soft breeze. He smelled their familiar, pungent odor.

Home, he thought. I'm home.

He faced the small terminal. In the darkness of the remodeled laundry room he called an office, the glowing green figures on the screen were hypnotic. At times it seemed as if he'd fallen into their endless rows, like a modern-day Alice tumbling down a glimmering high-tech hole.

The numbers beckoned. His fingers moved. Slowly, patterns emerged. His training, even a sort of basic bone knowledge, told him all things were systems, and in systems rested order. The puny terminal at the hospital had given him hints, but it lacked the power and sophistication to attack really big databanks. Now, with his own tools, he began to make progress.

He rubbed his chin, surprised to feel a wiry growth of stubble. How long had he been here? Time had taken on a funny, elusive quality. He ate, slept. Sat in front of the terminal. Day and night had become a blur.

He brushed his fingers across the touchpad and watched a parade of red letters scroll suddenly down the screen.

Another alarm. The fourth in ten minutes. Somebody was protecting heavily what should have been low-security data. He cleared the screen and checked the bank he'd been raiding. Condor Securities. His research said it was a small holding company that owned bits and pieces, specializing in low-level securities trading. Nothing big. Yet this was the third time he'd followed a trail here, each time with the same result. Heavy data security, cut-outs, intruder traps. So far he'd eluded the traps.

But why would Condor find it so important to know who came looking? He recalled a similar setup from his army days and shook his head.

It couldn't be like that. No way. Not like that.

Carefully, he began to plan one more attack.

His little shingled house perched on the side of a low hill facing a ridge of similar hills across a broad, thickly wooded valley. Tower stood on the balcony that fronted the upper part of the house and watched the sun turn flat and red beyond the distant ridge. Below, a few wispy fingers of mist smoked above the woods. It would be a cool night.

Nine empty plastic beer cans were lined up in perfect order on the railing of the balcony. He drained the tenth can, then placed it unsteadily next to the others.

"Happy trails," he said to nobody in particular. Something chittered in the brush below, and a mournful hoot rang out of the darkening shadows.

He turned and went back through the double doors into the living room. Here dusk had turned to night. He swung his arm up for the light pad and heard glass break. Something wet and greasy covered his palm. Finally his fingers brushed across the small panel next to the doors, and two lights behind the brown sofa came dimly on. He saw that he'd knocked out one of the glass panes in the door and cut his hand.

It was not a large room, but there was a comfortable, airy feeling to it. It had been Julia's favorite place, and everything about it showed her touch.

Across the brown sofa stretched a bright splash of color—a Navajo blanket they'd purchased on the Arizona vacation two years before. She'd worried that it wouldn't fit, but now he couldn't imagine it anywhere else.

Two polished wooden ducks floated on the glass top

of the coffee table. He'd found them in a junk shop
and brought them home and she'd laughed. She called
them Heckle and Jeckle, despite his efforts to convince
her they were a different sort of bird.

The chrome and wicker rocking chair she'd bought
him for Christmas gleamed beneath the sofa lamps. It
looked inviting. He went over and sat down and began
to rock. The chair made soft *scretch-scretch* sounds on
the carefully waxed wooden floor.

It was no use. Everything reminded him of her. He
sawed back and forth and waited for her to walk out
of the kitchen with a pair of drinks. It didn't happen.
He stood up and went to the kitchen himself and
opened the refrigerator. A number—he tried to count
but lost track—of beer cans still cluttered the bottom
shelf. It didn't seem like much else was there. He'd
been planning a trip to the grocery before the . . .

He popped another can and closed the refrigerator
door.

He drank steadily all the rest of the evening, turning
the evil kernel of his discovery until it went soft and
fuzzy in his mind. A little after midnight he opened
the doors to the balcony and stared at the moon. Then
he went back into the living room and jerked the
Navajo blanket from the sofa. He dragged it out and
threw it over the railing, watching it flutter down like
some crippled night flyer. He turned and swept the
carefully arranged beer cans away. Then he went inside and found the ducks.

He was never, for the rest of his life, able to recall
what he did after that.

"Josh. Hey Josh, wake up." Rustling sounds.
"God, what a mess."

At first he thought it was a nightmare. He felt cold.
His head felt soft and puffy. He tried to raise his right
arm, and that hurt so much he let out a short moan.

"You okay?" Somebody pulled at his shoulders.
That hurt too. Then the tugging hands went away and
he slumped back down.

Something wet and cold slithered across his face.

He tried to turn his head, but the chill damp thing persisted.

"Go . . . way."

"Come on, wake up. Open your eyes, you dumb . . ."

It was a thick, rasping voice. A man's voice, and familiar, although at the moment he couldn't quite pull a name out of the fog.

"Wake up, damn it."

A hand tugged hard on the back of his neck, tilting up his head, and his eyelids popped open. A pair of eyes the color of unpolished jade, framed by a bush of curling gunmetal eyebrows, stared into his own. The hand in front of the eyes held a wet towel.

"Oh . . . Jesus." Even his voice felt weak.

"Right." The eyes receded. "I thought you were dead. Then I got a whiff and knew you were okay. You smelled too bad to be a corpse."

Now he began to make out a shape. Big, bearlike. Moving closer. "Come on, let's get you up on the sofa."

Strong arms grasped him around his chest and heaved. The sudden movement made his stomach clench like a fist. He wondered what was wrong. He'd never felt so plain-ass sick before.

The sofa came up and hit him in the butt. He grunted heavily and sprawled backward and down. Even with his eyes wide open, there was something wrong with his vision. Things were pink and shadowy, and his eyeballs felt like tiny bits of glass were embedded in them.

"I'm sick."

"You sure are. You are just about the sickest son-of-a-bitch I've ever seen."

Something clicked inaudibly inside his skull and the world came back with a malevolent rush. "Uh . . . Link. What are you doing here?"

Now he could see the man. He tried to sit up, but his stomach did another drop-the-elevator trick, and he put his hand over his mouth.

Lincoln Foster's nicotine-shredded voice was full of cheerful disgust. "Arrived just in time, buddy. That's what it looks like to me. Now, do I drag you into the john so you can puke, or do you think you can ride it out here?''

As he forced himself to puzzle out Foster's words, the nausea slowly began to recede. "No, I'm okay. I think."

Foster stared at him, his eyebrows raised and quivering like a brace of furry rodents. "You're not okay, friend, but maybe you'll live. In a few minutes that may not seem like a blessing, though. How about some coffee?''

His stomach teetered on the end of the three-meter board again. "No. No coffee."

"Right. It'll be ready in a minute. You sit right there."

Sit? He squeezed his eyes hard shut. What does he think I'm going to do? Fly away?

Kitchen noises drifted across the room, and after a while, he could smell the sharp, woody-acid smell of coffee perking. The aroma made the thought of drinking it sound more plausible.

By the time Foster had returned, bearing two large mugs, Tower had managed to sit up unaided.

"Go on, drink it. It'll do you good."

Tower concentrated on holding his mug steady. It took both hands, and even then, the coffee jittered like a lake in a windstorm. He sipped slowly, grimacing. The coffee was hot enough to burn.

Foster stared at him across the coffee table from where he sat in the rocker, tilted forward, his elbows balanced on his massive thighs. He sat flat-footed and drank his coffee in silence.

Finally Tower put his mug down, placed the heels of both his hands on his forehead, and rubbed. "God . . ."

"I don't think He had anything to do with it." Foster paused, frowning. "Joshua, what got into you last night?''

"What do you mean?"

"Have you looked at this place?"

Tower started to shake his head, winced, and settled

for moving his eyes instead. After a moment he inhaled sharply. "Oh, god *damn.*"

"Uh huh."

Directly across the room, both glass-paned doors stood wide open on the balcony. One was partially off its hinges, and both had missing panes. There was a litter of broken glass in one corner. An overturned chair rested on the crushed remains of a floor lamp. Streaks of dried blood marked the polished hardwood in front of the doors. Tower looked at the back of his hands and realized where the blood had come from.

"Must have been quite a party," Foster said. "Good thing you didn't slip while you were punching all those windows out. You might have got an artery instead of a few knuckles scraped."

Tower looked at the damage, his face going smooth with amazement. "Did I do that?"

"Got me. You remember inviting anybody else?"

Tower shook his head. Slowly.

"Didn't think so. Listen, friend, the next time you feel that urge coming on, invite me. Probably you won't feel any better in the morning, but I guarantee there won't be as much damage."

There was something surreal about the conversation. Tower couldn't quite figure it out, but there had to be something strange about this neighborly chat in the midst of the wreckage of his living room.

He gave up and finished his coffee in two swift gulps. "I think," he said carefully, "that I'm about to be sick."

"If I remember, the john's that way. You need any help?"

Tower shook his head. He heaved himself up and began a controlled stagger across the room. Foster began to stand up.

"No," Josh said. "I'll make it. On my own."

Dimly, he thought that might be the biggest lie of all.

When they'd moved into the house Julia had decided the bathroom was too small, and in an effort to give the illusion of size, she had covered the walls and the sliding panels of the bathtub with mirrors. Josh flipped on the light and was immediately surrounded by an army of himself. His mouth fell open. Somehow, since he'd been back, he'd managed to avoid looking in a mirror. He couldn't remember how he'd done it. Maybe he'd used the john in the dark. He certainly hadn't done any shaving. The scraggly-bearded, jaundiced death's head that goggled back at him was almost unrecognizable. Under the pitiless light, he stared at what he'd become. Always slender, he was now a scarecrow, his clothes wrinkled rags, his face livid with two long, curving scars, his eyes sunk in swollen yellow bags.

His clothes looked familiar. He thought for a moment, then realized they'd been fresh when he first put them on. The day he left the hospital. How long had that been?

The figure in the mirror swayed gently, like a cut tree just about to fall. Slowly he knelt. The tiles were hard beneath his bony knees. He lowered his head to the water in the toilet bowl. It smelled cold and full of chlorine. He opened his mouth and waited. Nothing happened.

The thought of sticking his finger down his throat was a kind of barrier he simply couldn't cross. He crouched there for a long time, his shoulders shaking, and made sounds that might have been sobs.

After a while he stood up, dry-mouthed, arid as a stick. He took off his filthy clothes, wadded them into a bundle, and threw them on the floor. Then he stepped into the shower. When he was done he walked naked into the bedroom, opened the closet, and took out a clean pair of sweats. He pulled on socks and running shoes. Then he went back to the living room.

"Where are you going?"

"Out," he said. "I'll be back."

"You're going running?" Foster shook his head in disbelief. "You're a better man than I, pal."

"Just wait. It won't take long."

Foster watched him cross the room and open the

front door. He raised the mug in silent toast. After the door had slammed shut, he placed a hand over his eyes and squeezed. It had been a long night and he was tired.

Along with the house came shared ownership of almost eight hundred acres of woods in the valley. A group of neighboring homeowners had formed a syndicate to purchase the land in response to the threat of development. A hotshot from the city had wanted to hang a string of bubble-condos there, but the syndicate had managed to outbid him. Now the area was virginal, crossed by a narrow, fast-running stream and webbed with overgrown hiking paths. In the center a rude dam bridged the stream, creating a fiddle-shaped pond. Children liked to play there.

He found the head of a path and started to jog. His head buzzed. It was still early enough that a thin layer of mist lay over the land, shielding it from the long rays of the sunrise. He pushed one foot in front of the other, his breath rasping in his chest. After a while a cold sweat broke out on his forehead, and the shadowy trees seemed to spin. He pounded on, counting a silent cadence, waiting for it to happen.

Suddenly his legs went shaky under him and he lurched to the side of the path, coming to rest on a thick bed of pine needles. He fell to his knees, then went down on all fours. Without warning, it all came up. When he was done he felt purified, as if more than rancid beer marked the spot. Shakily he stood. Now he could smell the sharp odor of pitch, and dark, damp earth. In the distance the brook roared softly over rock. A single jay cried hoarsely.

The sun came up. He turned and ran easily back along the path. Maybe there was coffee left.

He felt disconnected and simple, pounding one foot down in front of the other, loping like an animal back up the path. He'd left something ugly behind, under the dark morning trees, and now he felt lighter, almost floating.

His thoughts turned to what he dimly remembered
from the night before. Something had sent him spiral-
ing into the dark well of booze and violence. He
couldn't recall it, not any details, but he didn't worry.
His notes remained, and the records of his investiga-
tions were carefully filed on the bubble memory of his
computer storage drives. As he ran, he touched those
vague recollections carefully, like a man who leaves
his dentist probing a source of pain with the tip of his
tongue.

Julia's death had been cheapened. He understood
that much. If what he suspected was true, their accident had been a mere by-product of something much
larger, uncaring and evil. He sought a comparison,
thought of Japanese lives destroyed as an afterthought,
mishaps to the conscious nonaccident of Hiroshima.

A squirrel exploded across the path in front of him,
chattering and scrabbling at the soft pine-needle covering. He smiled suddenly. His life had been destroyed
and now he could rebuild it. The foundation would be
bloody and uncomplicated. Vengeance was always that
way.

Overhead, the sky turned from gray to clear blue as
the morning sun burned away the mist. Foster could
help. Would help. The thought of that steady, ursine
man waiting back at the house cheered him. Maybe he
was in over his head, but nothing was too big for his
former commanding officer.

He smiled gently as he recalled those days. He'd
been a spy, and Foster had been almost a father figure
to a young man so full of explosive anger that the covert world was a welcome balm. Death was tranquil-
izer. Somehow the older man had understood, had
taken him under his massive wing and turned him into
a killing engine whose switch only he truly understood.

Foster had left the service first, lured by the money
call of business. Later, when Tower met Julia, her only
condition was that he also leave the shadowy under-
world of deception and betrayal, and because of her
he was ready. Foster had helped even then, showing

him how to set up his datahunter business and providing him with the contacts he'd used to get started.

He knew he thought of Foster as a father and understood why. Even in the most terrifying, desperate hours of his childhood, when his life had been a terrible survival game with the man who shared his blood, he'd always believed in the idea of a father. Instead, he'd had the man without the dream. Foster had become the dream.

Foster even looked like some massive, Yahweh-type figure. His body resembled that of a retired pro wrestler, big and sloping, with the beginnings of a bulging gut, the legacy of his fondness for anything alcoholic. He'd kept all his hair, grizzled now to iron and snow, and winglike, expressive eyebrows over eyes the color of a green mountain lake on any winter morning.

Foster would help him, as he always had. He was grateful. He would need help. Against something like Condor, he'd need all the help he could get.

He pounded on beneath the morning heat as time unwound into the day. Only a few birds saw his face, and they didn't care. They could only call and fly.

"You look better. That's not saying much." Foster cradled his mug in one sausage-fingered hand, regarding him narrowly over the rim. "Maybe it's a good thing I came over."

Tower watched his own hand quiver lightly as he reached for his coffee. His running sweats were soaked, dirt-stained on the knees, and torn at one elbow. "Why wouldn't it be?" he said. "If I had a best friend, I guess you'd be it."

Foster shrugged. "Funny way to put it. But you've always been a little strange, a little off. I came over to see if there was anything I could do. You know."

"Uh huh. Link, did you ever lose anybody? Anyone that you really cared for? Loved?"

"Like Julia, you mean?" He paused. "Yeah, I lost somebody." His dark green eyes went slightly unfocused, then snapped back. "Nothing I want to talk about, really. It doesn't apply here. But I did lose somebody. Help any?''

Tower felt the hot buzz of anger ripping away inside and knew he couldn't handle it any longer. Slowly, pausing every few minutes to sip cold coffee, he told Foster about Julia and about the unborn child she'd carried.

Foster sighed heavily and stared at his fists. ''Rough. That's rough as a cob. I knew about your wife, but not about the kid. Makes a difference. At first, when I saw you and saw this place, I figured you'd flipped. But maybe not. I can't say . . . I don't know if I'd be any different than you. What I mentioned—losing some-body—taught me that. You can never be sure.''

Tower grinned. The expression felt odd, unfamiliar. ''There's a nurse in San Francisco. If she knew what I was trying to do, she wouldn't have any doubts. She'd reach for a hypo right away, then call for the head wreckers.''

''You mean finding out what happened after the crash?'' Foster stared at his knuckles a moment, then set his mug down on the coffee table. ''I understand that. It's like a book. You can't put it down till you finished the last chapter. If it was something really weird—but it's not. You know enough to pull up that information. And you're right. It probably does exist somewhere. Most things are monitored these days. For damn sure something like those laser taxis are.''

''That's what I thought. And maybe you can help me. I think I know what happened to me last night. Why I got the way I did.''

''What's that?''

''I found something. I'm not sure what. I can't re-member. They still have me taking a lot of stuff, and it probably doesn't mix too well with a case of beer. It's just a feeling, but pretty strong. I kept running into dead ends. Traps, major security, stuff like that. I think I broke through, though. And I found some-thing.''

''Like what?'' Foster stared at him intently.

''Like maybe it wasn't an accident. Like maybe Julia

dying was, but only if you think people dying from fallout after Hiroshima was an accident. You know what I mean? I think somebody planned that glitch.''

"That's pretty strong, Josh. You sure about it?''

"Of course I'm not sure. Not right now. But I'll check my notes, take a look at the stuff I stored on my machine. I do remember one thing, though.''

"Better than nothing, I guess.''

"Yeah. You ever heard of something called Condor Securities?''

Foster paused, his eyes half shutting with concentration. "Condor . . .'' Finally he shook his head. "No. Rings no bells.''

"It's got something to do with it.''

Foster stood up. "Well, let's go take a look. Your office still in the same place?''

Tower nodded, then slowly pushed himself up from the sofa. "I don't think I'm nuts, but I'd like a second opinion. Yours would be fine. After all, you taught me most of what I know about this racket.''

"But not everything I know.'' Foster smiled suddenly.

"Why I asked,'' Tower agreed. His voice was somber.

They walked down the long hall past the master bedroom and the bathroom and finally came to the last door. The sun, now halfway up the sky, cast a prismed bit of light on the carpet from glass wind chimes Julia had hung in front of the window at the end of the hall.

"In here,'' Tower said as he pushed open the door. He paused.

After a moment Foster stepped closer. "What's the matter? Something wrong, Josh?''

Wordlessly, Tower stepped aside. Foster stuck his grizzled head around the doorjamb. Then he turned and stared at his friend's stricken face.

"Son-of-a-bitch,'' he said.

The interior of the tiny room was a shambles. Both terminals were smashed. Tower's gigabit memory bub-

ble was in three pieces, its core nothing more than
shining sand on the carpet. Shredded paper covered
the desk, which listed crazily on three legs. The metal
wastebasket against the far wall was on its side,
dented, and it spilled a thick swath of black and gray
ash.

"What the hell?" Foster said. "Why'd you do
this?"

Tower's eyes were empty as ghosts. "I don't know,"
he said.

Foster shook his head slowly. "If this was your evidence, your back trail, you aren't ever going to find
anything, buddy."

Tower's eyes didn't change, but his jaw went tight.
"Condor," he said. "Condor Securities. I've still got
Condor."

"If it means anything."

"Oh, yes," Tower said. "It does."

Chapter Three

A sudden surge of wind hummed around the corner of the house and rattled the double balcony doors. Tower leaned on his broom and stared wearily at the rest of the living room. Next to the double doors was his accomplishment so far: a pile of glass, some splintered wood, and a shoal of crumpled plastic beer cans. He brushed his forearm across his brow and felt skin slick with sweat.

"Hot," he said.

"Not that bad," Foster replied, from where he squatted next to the sofa, feeling around for a beer can he'd seen go sliding underneath. "You're sweating booze, my friend. I can smell it over here."

Tower ducked his nose toward his armpit. "Uh! Me too. Maybe I should take another shower."

Foster's flat green eyes narrowed. "I've smelled worse. It can wait till we finish with this. You ever do any hunting?"

Tower shook his head. "Just men. And you know all about that."

Foster's face went smooth and blank. "Yeah." He seemed to shake himself without actually moving. "Anyway, I hunted bear once, up in Alaska before they outlawed everything like that. Got off a bad shot and only wounded the animal. We tracked her to a cave, finally killed her outside. Don't know why she went back to her den—no cubs or anything. Maybe some kind of instinct."

Tower nodded. He understood how a wounded creature might try to go home.

"So afterwards I stuck my head inside the den. You know what? Place smelled just like your house here. Gotcha!" Foster had managed to reach the elusive beer can at last. He fished it out and held it up like a trophy. "How long you been back here, Josh?"

The question surprised him. He rubbed his chin and decided his next session in the bathroom would have to include a shave. "I, uh . . . let me think. To tell the truth, I'm not sure. What day is it?"

"Tuesday."

"I got out on Saturday, so three days, then."

"Tuesday the twenty-third."

"That's right. They discharged me on the thirteenth, so . . ." His voice trailed off.

"Uh huh," Foster said. "Thought so. You've lost a week, haven't you?"

Tower felt his chest go weak and soft. "I have, haven't I? Maybe I am nuts."

Foster looked thoughtful. "You've been drinking a lot, Josh. And taking medicine. There might have been some kind of synergistic effect. Or maybe you were crazy. Whatever. You seem okay now."

He considered it, waiting for the helpless feeling to go away. So this was what it was like, not to trust your own body, your own mind. Time gone forever, memories lost, unconscious violence. "I don't know," he said at last. "I have to assume so, I guess."

"But it will be a while before it feels right. Listen, Josh, I've seen this kind of thing before. Trust me. It will pass, eventually. Be careful, though. Check everything for a while. And don't put too much stock in whatever you've been doing recently. It might just be phantoms."

Tower thought about Condor. "No," he said. "Not all of it." He remembered his broom, glanced up, and stared sadly at the pile of wreckage. "God. Maybe I should just burn the place down."

"Don't say things like that, even for a joke. You might not be over the hump yet. Why give yourself nasty suggestions?"

Tower shook the broom. "I didn't think about that. Nasty suggestions? You kidding?"

Foster pointed at the garbage. "I didn't do that, pal."

The computer room was the hardest part. "You finish the living room, okay?" Tower said. "I'll take care of my office. It's not big enough for both of us in there."

"Sure thing," Foster replied. "I'm about done anyway. Listen, buddy, we ought to go into town, you know. Novato, someplace like that, big enough for a hardware store. I can replace those glass panes in the balcony doors. That one closest to the lock on the front door I had to knock out myself."

"Yeah? How come you busted one?"

"To let myself in, of course. I found you outside, did you know that? You'd locked yourself out somehow. Stupid. You could have frozen. It gets cold at night, remember? I carried you inside. Took me the longest damn time to wake you up. . . ."

"Lovely. A lovely picture. Maybe I'm glad I don't remember."

"You have a talent," Foster said. "Give me that broom."

Tower took the larger trash can, a big green plastic affair he'd brought up from the garage, and dragged it down the hall. The tiny shard of prismed light had moved up the wall and now hung at shoulder level like a tiny butterfly. The sight cheered him.

He sighed as he stared at the wreckage. It seemed worse in the full light of day. The thoroughness of his rage astonished him. *What was I trying to do? What did I want to destroy?*

He shook his head. Whistling silently between his teeth, he went to work.

It took him almost an hour of slow, steady labor to clear away the wreckage. Even the furniture was smashed. When he finished, the trash can was full and the room nearly empty. Total loss, he thought. Nothing left.

A glint of light caught his eye from the corner. He bent over and picked up a piece of plastic terminal screen, still shiny, although half of it was splintered away. As he handled it he left a bloody fingerprint and realized he'd opened up the cut on his hand. He shook his head. After a moment he used the bottom of his sweatshirt to wipe the oily red mark away, before he tossed the screen into the trash. He glanced around. The room, once so familiar, was hard and alien. All his machines were gone. The white walls, dust shadowed in spectral furniture outlines, stared at him blankly as pieces of paper. Something about that seemed odd, but after a moment the feeling thinned and disappeared. He shook his head one final time. So much work to do.

He walked around the trash can and headed for the bathroom. There wasn't any depilatory—he didn't like the stuff—so he hoped there was still a charge in his razor. He didn't trust himself to use steel. Not the way his hands were shaking.

"Hot dogs and beer. I feel like I ought to be watching a ball game." Foster sounded unhappy, but he was chewing on hot dog number four.

"Sorry. There wasn't much in the fridge. Unless you wanted me to brew up some of the dried stuff."

"Uh, thanks, but no thanks. Can't stand it. All those chemicals."

"I didn't know you were a health nut. You know what kind of additives are in that hot dog you're inhaling?"

Foster removed the sandwich from his mouth and stared at it. After a moment he said, "Hell with it," and he finished it in two bites. "You got any more?"

"There was only half a package. I had one."

"Too bad. Maybe we ought to head into town. Pity you don't have regular delivery out here."

Tower shrugged. "One of the drawbacks to living

in the country. They keep saying they're going to run a route up this way, but you know how that goes.''

"We got to get those glass panes, remember? And you better make some kind of arrangements about a computer. You got any money?''

"Yes. Some, not a whole lot. My twenty shares of Consort, of course, and three more I bought a few years back. I had a couple of good contracts recently, so there's money in the bank. And . . . Julia's insurance, I guess. I haven't talked to anybody about that yet.''

Foster nodded. He exuded a kind of blowsy, good-old-boy practicality that Tower found comforting. It was hard to imagine him strangling a man to death, but Tower had seen him do it. Then he put a bullet into the skull of the third member of their team, wounded beyond help but still breathing. Operation Dawn Fire, that had been. . . .

"You going to sue the taxi people?''

"What?''

"I said—''

"I heard you,'' Tower replied. "I hadn't thought about it. It seems somehow like . . . I don't know.'' He shook his head.

"Go ahead, say it: like profiting from her death. It isn't, you know, but that's beside the point. If you plan to go poking around in a lot of other people's business, it wouldn't hurt if it looked like you had a reason. Other than your real one, that is. If that stink is real, you just might get some people very unhappy with you.''

"Let them.''

"Right. And the former spy hero will murder them with his bare hands. Have you glanced in a mirror lately? I wouldn't back you against a five year old.'' He shook his head. "A five-year-old girl.''

Tower squirmed against the seat of his rocker, painfully aware that the butt of his tail bone had little padding against the wicker seat.

"You look like a scarecrow,'' Foster added cheerfully.

"It will pass. I'm over the hump now."

"We'll see. Maybe. Anyhow, what I said still stands. Do you want to go into town?"

"Sure." He paused. "Listen, Link, why did you come out here? Really?"

The bigger man looked away, as if something interesting had landed on the balcony. "I don't know," he told the invisible visitor. "I saw Julia's name on the nets. Hadn't seen either of you in almost a month. Now it's too late. Maybe I felt guilty. Julia was a nice lady." He exhaled heavily and patted his gut. "Why? You don't want me around?"

"No, I didn't say that. I mean, I'm damn glad you *did* show up. But what about, uh, what's her name . . . Carol?"

Tower grinned. It made him look years younger. "It was Carla, you son-of-a-bitch, as you damn well know. I'm afraid the latest is now the last. Or previous. She moved out a week ago. Along with my wallet."

They stared at each other. Tower couldn't help it. Foster's face twitched, alternating between embarrassment and bitterness. Tower laughed before he could stop himself.

"Yeah, funny," Foster said sourly. "The old man gets hooked by another cheap date. Not so cheap, actually."

Tower's mirth finally bubbled down. "So you're kicking around that big house all by yourself again?"

Foster nodded. "Yeah. You know, Josh, maybe I should get an apartment or something. It's too tough, trying to keep a woman around just to dust that dump."

"Maybe they'd stay if you offered them a little better deal."

The big man shook his head. "You mean like you and Julia? Marriage? I'm afraid not. Three times is enough. It's just not for me."

"You've been married three times? I thought it was two."

"Who counts, after the first?" He slowly unfolded himself into an upright position. It was like watching a huge elevator bridge open over a river. "You want to go now? Or sit here and reminisce for the rest of the day?"

"I got it. I know what the rush is: I'm out of beer."

"And vodka, and gin, and scotch. Don't you keep any staples around here?"

"I guess not," Tower replied. And for a moment he almost felt happy. "Let's get to it, then."

The house computer terminal was in the kitchen. Tower turned and said, "What grocery do you use?"

Foster lounged against the refrigerator door. He shrugged. "Beats me. Whatever comes up, I guess."

Tower nodded. Julia had appropriated the shopping chores after an incident in which his own efforts had produced twenty different kinds of laundry detergent. "Men are so helpless with machines," she'd muttered at the time.

He punched the first name that popped into his head. After a moment one wall of the kitchen disappeared. In its place was the characteristically fuzzy outline of a holo field. Another moment brought a series of dancing grocery clerks—when had he last seen a grocery clerk?—singing loudly the virtues of Safeway. He remembered Safeway from when he was a kid, when suburban people still shopped in stores.

He quickly pressed the enter key and the dancing clerks disappeared. He scanned his terminal screen. The grocery's offerings appeared to be divided into sections.

He glanced at Foster. "I suppose beer, first." The other man grinned.

Tower checked the terminal, grunted, and switched over to voice mode. "Beverage," he said. Another menu appeared and he selected alcoholic, then beer.

The holo field showed a wall of cans. Brand after brand. Some of the cans blinked off and on. Some vibrated. One popped off the wall, opened itself, and began to pour.

"Jesus." He checked the screen and spoke the name of his usual brand. The holo field cleared, then filled

with the image of a single can of German Budweiser.
A man strolled into his kitchen, holding a can of beer
in one hand, and a heavy mug in the other. He carefully poured out the beer, which formed a perfect head
on the mug. He looked up and smiled sincerely. "Hi.
I'm Ed McMahon, Jr. What I'm holding here is a mug
of the best beer in the world. Looks good, doesn't it?"

Tower ordered two cases. Foster was laughing uncontrollably now as Tower struggled with the unfamiliar job. Finally he finished.

"You think you can do better?" Tower said as the
terminal obligingly printed out his completed grocery
list. He knew that his bank account had been debited
at the same time and Safeway had acquired that much
more cash.

"No." Foster shook his head, still grinning like a
monkey. "I would've never made it past beer. Did you
get a look at that singing pork loin?"

Involuntarily, Tower began to chuckle. Then laugh.
He tried to do an imitation of the strange waltz the
pork loin had done while piping, "Eat me, treat me,
I'm *real* meat." Foster dissolved at this, and they
ended up pounding each other on the back until the fit
passed.

"Julia knew how to turn all that crap off," he said
helplessly. But that memory sobered him. He frowned.
"I don't, I guess."

"I hope you can get a computer without all that
bullshit," Foster said at last.

"Well, I can try."

It took him a moment to select the proper store, and
two minutes later the last shred of hilarity evaporated.
"That's ridiculous!" Tower said. "A whole week to
put my order together, and then I have to pick it up."

"You weren't exactly buying off-the-shelf stuff,"
Foster pointed out. "A custom setup takes a while to
make."

"But a week? This is the twenty-first century, isn't
it?"

"What it is, is life," Foster replied. His eyes caught
Tower with an expression he couldn't quite make out.

In another situation, he might have called it pleading. "Did I ever tell you my three rules of life?"

Tower shook his head.

"Easy. Number one: Everybody wants to buy, but nobody wants to pay. Number two: Always follow the money. Number three: Whenever there isn't a reason, the reason is always money." For a moment, Foster's face was still and somber. Then he brightened. "Pretty heavy, huh?"

Tower felt uneasy. "I guess so," he said at last. "Come on. Let's go get the beer."

After he had finished painting his office, Josh took a shower and put on fresh sweats. He went outside, locked the door, then hid the key in a wooden planter filled with ancient geraniums. The moon rode low over distant, shaded hills. The air was clear as a Sunday bell, sharp as a sword. His feet crunched on the gravel shoulder of the road in front of his house. He paused a moment and stared up at the stars. His breathing made small, silvery clouds in front of his face.

"Nice," he said aloud. "Nice night for a run."

That he talked to himself no longer embarrassed him. Over the previous week, while he waited for delivery of his new equipment, he'd slowly begun to pull himself together. The cut on his hand had healed. He forced himself to eat three good meals a day, even though his old appetite was a forgotten thing. He did calisthenics in the morning, tai chi, exercises from his army days. And he ran at night, loping through the woods until exhaustion fogged his memories and he was able to sleep.

Now, standing in the quiet dark, he realized that his body, at least, would recover. He wasn't sure about the rest. Foster said that would come, too.

When? The night offered no answer. He shook his head, stepped down to the path, and began to run.

He paused for a moment, then moved off the path and leaned his back against the last big pine before the road. The moon was halfway up the sky now, fat and yellow and scarred. How long this time? An hour? Two? He didn't wear a watch when he ran, trusting his body to tell him when it was time. He panted heavily, waiting for his heartbeat to subside, feeling his muscles quiver with tightness. His sweat suit was soaked. He shivered slightly in the mild breeze, smelled the odors of black earth and green wood. It was very quiet.

Someone shouted.

His face came up. He knew he was about a hundred yards from the road. The voice had been near, a guttural, wordless cry of frustration. He leaned forward, straining to listen, but the sound wasn't repeated.

It didn't matter. He knew. There was nothing in the area but his house. He thought he'd been careful, before, when he'd cracked those databanks. But it wasn't kids out there. The cry wasn't from joy-riding teenagers. He hadn't been careful enough.

His nose twitched. Smoke. Something burning.

He closed his eyes.

When he opened them again he saw, through the scrub and small pines between him and the road, the first searching ripples of flame, fat and yellow in the dark.

They were burning his house.

He began to shake uncontrollably. Finally he wrapped his arms around the bole of the pine and squeezed until the joints in his shoulders made small popping sounds. He rubbed his forehead against the rough bark. His teeth were like a closed vice. Eventually the pain cooled him.

All my life, he thought. Forever. Some bastard has ruined things.

Now this.

His body felt cold and still. He wiped the smear of blood from his forehead and took a deep breath. The icy air filled him with a preternatural alertness. Shadows went sharp as knives. He began to work his way forward, his face toward the spreading flames.

Perhaps they had made a mistake. He would find out soon enough.

* * *

The jagged chunk of rock, about the size of a base-ball, felt cool and heavy in his fist. He crouched be-hind a low ridge of scrub just off the road. Nearly forgotten reflexes had come into play, and he avoided the road. If they were any good, somebody, most likely with a high-powered rifle and night eyes, was scanning the tarmac continually for movement. It was the way he would have done it.

Two hover cars were parked haphazardly on the far side, about fifty yards beyond the house. In the hot, sinuous light from the burning wreckage, he made out moving figures, cardboard cutouts against the flames. Several men. They kept moving, so it was hard to get their exact numbers. He guessed five, probably. With two cars, that left at least one unaccounted for. Most likely the watcher, the backup with a rifle. Maybe two, though. One at each end of the road, for a crossfire if necessary.

He recognized the setup. It was a killing field. But why burn his house? He tried to create their scenario. They came in the night, a whole fire team. It had to be around two in the morning. They would have infil-trated carefully, surrounded the house. They had enough men. Then a sudden smashing entry, expect-ing to find a single, disoriented victim thrashing to escape tangled bed covers.

Instead they'd found an empty house and a neatly made bed.

What then?

It depended on their instructions. Was it a simple kill, a wet contract, or did they have something else in mind? Interrogation, perhaps? He suspected that was the case. An immediate termination didn't need this kind of crew. A man or two in the hills with a rifle would have been enough. So they wanted to talk to him, open up their little chemical tool kits, maybe use their fists or a knife to help things along.

Why?

What answers did he have? And who was asking the questions?

Condor. He tasted the word carefully. What he knew

of Condor was fogged and groggy. A company. A small investment firm. Not the kind of operation that sent killer teams into the field.

So Condor wasn't what it appeared to be. It was something else. Viewed that way, it became obvious what he'd stumbled into. A cut-out company. A front for something, somebody else. And whoever that ghostly shadow might be, it had enough power, enough money to dispatch the execution teams.

Execution was intended now, he decided slowly. They wouldn't burn otherwise. They hadn't found their target, so they burned the house. It was a good tactic, designed to flush him out. It might even have worked, if he'd merely been out, visiting or drinking, and gotten word of the fire. Of course he would have rushed back and, by doing that, made himself a perfect target, They wanted to talk first, but if that wasn't possible, murder would be sufficient.

They couldn't have known about his recently acquired habit of nighttime running. One stroke of luck for our side, he thought, squeezing the rock tighter.

Now, where are those watchers?

Carefully, he began to move up the road, keeping a screen of brush between him and the fire. He passed the parked cars, paused, and scanned the darkened shadows for a sentry. Would they leave somebody to watch the cars? Possible.

He stared at the windshield of the second car and after a moment was rewarded. A faint ember flared and died in the interior. Stupid. The driver was smoking.

They must not take this very seriously. And why should they? Six men, at least, targeted on one grieving convalescent. A no-worry job. Or so they would have been told.

He grinned slowly. Then he moved on.

He scrambled two hundred yards further up the road. If the watcher was where he ought to be, he was in the hills above the house, far enough away to disengage quickly if necessary but close enough to watch the road and the area around the house. There was no reason to keep a sharp eye on the area *beyond* the action point. Or so Tower hoped as he inhaled sharply, then crouched low and scuttled quickly across the tarmac.

He rolled into the shadow beyond the road and let out his breath. Then he froze and lay unmoving for a full minute, listening.

He was acutely aware that he didn't have much time. Somewhere in a near-earth orbit one of the California Forest Service's satellites was noting the small, hot mote of his burning house on its infrared scanners. He was in a fire-danger area. The report would go priority, and within a few minutes he could expect an airborne fire team to swoop down on the blaze.

These invaders had to know that, too. He'd get one chance, and that was it.

He waited a few seconds more. Nothing happened. He didn't expect to hear a shot if he'd been spotted. The watchers would have silenced rifles. His first hint of discovery would most likely be a Teflon-coated bullet exploding in his brain.

Finally he began to work his way back to the cars.

He saw the glow again and this time noted a dim outline. The man was in the driver's seat. Tower crouched at the back of the car, close to the hover skirt, and felt around on the ground. Then he picked up a handful of gravel and tossed it gently along the side of the car. It made a soft, scraping noise.

After a moment he heard the door lock click. As soon as the sharp click had sounded, he moved around the car and went to the door.

He knew what was going through the driver's mind: What was the sound? An animal? The wind?

His senses would be alert. An alert man didn't step out of a car into a danger zone without being ready. Unconsciously, the driver would check his pistol, scan the area, then carefully open the door.

Tower didn't wait. He slapped the door-lock panel and rose in a single movement. The driver was still turning, his pistol half out of its shoulder holster, when Tower slugged him under the jaw with his rock.

The man slumped back, stunned; then he shook his head and bulled forward suddenly. Tower stepped aside as the man surged out of the car, exposing the back of his head. Tower hit him again, this time behind his right ear. The driver collapsed without a sound.

Swiftly, Tower crouched over the prone body, his fingers searching the man's clothes. He took the pistol in one hand and tried to tuck it in the elastic belt of his running suit, but the stretchy plastic was too weak to hold the heavy gun. Using one hand, he rolled the man over and worked his wallet out of his pocket. He flipped it open, but in the dim moonlight he couldn't make out anything.

Something slammed into the side of the car with a sound like a hammer punching metal. Tower rolled, wallet in one hand, pistol in the other. He scrabbled frantically around the rear of the car, working angles in his head. The watcher had to be about where he'd guessed to get off a shot like that. The angle was extreme, which was probably why he was alive to think about it at all. Now the car should be between him and the hidden rifleman. Keeping low, he scurried for the brush. Another bullet chunked into the earth close by, spraying him with bits of dirt. He kept on moving. The gunner had a problem. He was far enough away that there was an appreciable amount of time—a fraction of a second—between firing and the arrival of the bullet. Time enough for Tower to move.

Then he was in low scrub and climbing quickly. A minute later he was a hundred feet up, looking down on his house. He heard shouts, saw running figures. A small constellation of bright lights lofted over the far hills. The Forest Service fire team, he guessed.

He smiled softly, hefting the weight of the pistol. The backup rifleman was on the hill with him somewhere, but he ignored the idea of going after him. He'd be moving by now, heading down to rejoin his partners. This operation was over. Especially when they found the unconscious body of their sentry.

Tower moved down to the edge of the cleared area around his house. A big laser van landed and disgorged men in asbestos reflective suits carrying chemical bombs. They set off two of the devices quickly. A white cloud began to choke the blaze. He wanted to join them, but he waited. It was possible a final backup remained, his rifle pointed toward the fire.

He crouched down to watch, anger and frustration like acid in his skull. He remembered the wallet and held it up against the dying light of the fire and the momentary red and white strobes of the emergency vehicle. The laminated blue card he saw shocked him into immobility.

Overlaid across information giving the holder's name and other data were three large letters.

DIA.

Defense Intelligence Agency.

He stared at the dying embers of his home and wondered just what he'd gotten into, what he'd discovered that could send a detachment of his old army buddies out to kill him.

What *was* Condor? And what were his chances of staying alive long enough to find out?

Interesting questions.

He wanted some interesting answers. Soon.

Chapter Four

The sun baked down on the back of his neck. Sweat puddled in the hollow of his chest and dribbled across his belly. His thighs hurt from the awkward position he'd been holding almost an hour. He turned his head slightly.

His vantage point was near the base of the hill behind his house, looking up toward the spot where he suspected the sniper would be. He had a better grip on things now. If the ID he'd taken from the hit-team member several hours earlier was legitimate, then he was dealing with DIA. They would do things by the book. The book said to leave a trailing sniper.

It was a problem, but it wasn't insurmountable. He was armed now—and what he was armed with was somewhat amazing. Before he'd left the Defense Intelligence Agency he'd field-tested a prototype version of the weapon he now held in his right hand. That system—for it was a *system*—had been much larger and clumsier. Even so, when he'd first fired the thing he'd been shocked by its destructive power. The research boys had called it a Coldgas Launcher 40mm Recoilless Automatic Fire. That unwieldy name had been quickly shortened during the field tests: When Tower had seen what it did to a human skull—something very much like what happened to a ripe melon slugged full force with a baseball bat—he thought of a club, a long-distance club.

What was soon known as the Club was relatively simple. A capsule of extremely pressurized gas launched a very strange shell, one that was, in effect, a tiny ramjet. The gas thrust the shell from the barrel until the ramjet kicked in, propelling the cylinder of metal at enormous speed. The damage it did was incredible. What he'd taken from the luckless sentry was a much smaller version of the same weapon. He imagined the tiny shell impacting between his eyes and shuddered. Splat. No head.

The Club was an advantage, although he imagined whoever might be waiting for him would be similarly armed, perhaps with an even more powerful version of his own weapon. But the mysterious sniper would have to see him first, and this was why he'd waited, concealed beneath a rusty green canopy of dogwood, while his muscles knotted and his eyes blinked away rivulets of sweat.

He'd waited since dawn, when the Forest Service fire team had packed up and left. A few yards downslope the charred ruins of his house smoldered in the sun. His bedroom appeared intact, although it was hard to estimate the chemical damage done while extinguishing the fire. Nevertheless, under normal circumstances, he would have chanced reconnoitering. Now, though, he had to satisfy himself that it was safe.

A sudden bright spark of light jerked him out of his gloomy thoughts. He squinted. Yes, there again. About fifty yards upslope, a reflection, maybe off glasses or a ring or some unprotected bit of polished metal. He grinned. It was almost exactly where he'd expected it to be. Perhaps a tired sniper, shifting his position slightly to ease an aching back.

He extended the Club out in front of him and lowered himself to his belly. Then, on elbows and knees, he began to inch up the incline. He forced himself to breath regularly, in and out.

He wondered what kind of training they got these days. He wouldn't have moved and given away his position. But, then, he was fighting for his life. The other guy wasn't.

At least, he didn't know he was.

* * *

The underbrush looked impassable to the untrained eye, but Tower made his way through easily enough. The trick was to stay very low. The sort of shrubs and bushes that crowd California hillsides tend to grow a bit higher and further apart at the trunk than most people realize, so by staying almost flat on his stomach and inching along, he made good time. He wished he'd worn his watch, but when he glanced unconsciously at his bare wrist, his own personal body clock estimated it had taken less than half an hour to reach his new hiding place.

The sun was only a third of the way up the blue dome of morning sky; it was no more than nine o'clock—less than seven hours since his life had been turned around again. He hadn't allowed himself to think about it. The larger question of why the Defense Intelligence Agency, his old outfit, had taken such a sudden, murderous interest in him would have to wait. First, he had to make sure their original intent didn't get carried out.

Slowly he pushed a concealing branch of thickleafed jade out of the way. At this point on the hillside there were ledges of bare, brown rock only partially covered with shrubbery. He closed his eyes for a moment, then opened them, trying to pick out anything that didn't belong. At first he didn't see it. Then, on the second try, the anomaly showed up plainly.

One black leather shoe attached to about six inches of gray pants leg. The rest was concealed by a thicket of assorted brush, but the aerie was precisely where he'd seen the revealing flashes earlier, well situated to cover not only the area around his house but also the road in either direction.

The sniper might not know how to maintain a guarded ambush, but at least he knew how to pick a spot correctly. Josh sank back in his covering bushes and squinted thoughtfully. He had a decision to make. It was a hard one, because he'd gotten rusty. As a datahunter, safe behind the blank anonymity of a computer screen, he hadn't been called to decide life or death questions for almost ten years. Now two lives were at stake: the sniper's, and his own. As an either-or proposition it wasn't difficult. But there was a third possibility.

His primary concern was staying alive to the end of this immediate situation. But beyond that momentary problem lay the question of the future. He brushed sweat from his forehead and licked his lips. Somebody was after him, but he had so little information. What had begun as nothing more than a search for records of his wife's final moments had somehow escalated into a situation involving shadow companies, mysterious computer files, and now government agents bent on his destruction.

It would be nice to find out what was going on. The man on the hillside below would not know everything—DIA always operated on a strict need-to-know basis—but he might know *something*. It would, however, be much more difficult—and much riskier—to take him alive. That was a gamble. Was the hidden sniper's knowledge worth that extra danger?

He glanced at the ruin of his house. For a moment the smoking wreckage seemed to symbolize his own life. They had taken his wife, his unborn son, his home and his freedom. Even his memory. In their place they'd left him nothing but fear and a thirst for revenge. Now they were trying to kill him.

Slowly, he peered out again. The black shoe twitched slightly, then pulled up under the canopy of scraggly leaves. The man was patient, if nothing else. And suddenly he understood. Whoever wanted him dead would keep on trying. They could command the services of one of the most elite covert forces in the world. If he hoped to stay ahead of them, even with his own superb but out of date training, he would have to have information. Knowledge was as potent a weapon—even more so—than the deadly attack system, the Club, he cradled in his arms.

Only the blind luck of his newly acquired habit of night running had saved his life this time. He couldn't depend on luck forever. This would be a first step on the long road back.

Besides, he wanted to kill the fucks.

He began to slowly strip off his blue running suit.

The man under the low bushes exhaled with disgust. The bushes gave him some protection, but the heat had already caused him to sweat out the armpits of his gray suit, and he'd paid a nice little chunk for it. It didn't look to be getting any cooler, either. He moved his forearms slightly, to redistribute the weight of the Club that rested there. It was a sniper model, fitted out with a combination infrared and light-gathering scope, which made it somewhat unwieldy. He was used to that, however, and the awkwardness of the Club's size was more than compensated by its ability to reach out almost fifteen hundred yards to punch through four inches of hardened armor plate. Once he'd taken out a target at half a mile through nearly a foot of wood and concrete wall. The victim had literally not known what hit him.

He smiled faintly at the memory. Today wouldn't be like that, though. If the target showed this time it would be quick and easy. For a moment he wondered how the target had gotten to Starkey. Hit him with a rock, the squad leader had said. He glanced at the miniature comm unit on his wrist. Colonel Tagg, his team leader, had promised him relief by noon. Three more hours.

Most likely the target was long gone, grateful for his luck in knocking Starkey out, which left him free to break through their net and escape. Yet, the more he thought about it, the more he recognized a small flicker of unease. He'd gotten a couple of shots at the man, but he'd missed. That was disquieting in itself. Then he'd had the impression that the target had run *toward* him, up into the hills, rather than away from him. Not normal reactions for a man being shot at. And finally there was the matter of Starkey's Club. It was missing. The worst case was that the target had it.

Which was why, despite his overall discomfort, he

was staying buttoned up. Whoever the target was, he would have to come to him. And when he did . . .

The sniper caressed the stock of his own Club. He'd been graded an expert in his last seven ratings on the weapon. Even if the target did have Starkey's Club, he'd have to get close enough to use it. The sniper had no intention of allowing that.

He blinked. The air over the rubble of the house his team had burned the night before seemed to shimmer. Heat illusion, no doubt. Would the target be stupid enough to return to the house?

He hoped so. He wanted to finish up and go home.

He hated these rush missions, anyway.

It was hard to separate the elastic fibers of his waistband but, working slowly, Tower managed it. When he tied them together he had a stretchy cord almost fifteen feet long. It would have to do.

He raised his left hand. He could have used either, but he wanted his right in as good a shape as possible. The scabbed-over wounds on his knuckles were almost healed. He grimaced at what came next, but it was necessary. He raised his hand to his mouth and began to gnaw away the scabs, then to tear at the pink flesh beneath. It was unfortunate, but he needed a lot of blood.

The sniper's name was Higgins. He'd been DIA for almost five years now. He like it. When he was a child he'd been a bed-wetter and, later, had enjoyed torturing small animals. He had no idea this was almost a classic predictor for psychosis. He'd joined the army before he actually killed anybody, and the psych tests had picked him out. The evaluator who'd handled his records had finished and made a sour face. He'd turned to his partner and said, "Here's another one. God, what a cesspool."

His partner, a cool, blonde woman whom he desperately wished to throw in the sack but who, he secretly suspected, despised him, glanced through the file. "Automatic reject? Discharge him?"

The evaluator grunted. "This one? Hell, no. These sort of profiles are red-tagged for DIA. They'll know what to do." He grinned at her, feeling a sour satisfaction in his own cynical knowledge.

"We use scum like that?"

He nodded. "Ugly business, isn't it?"

She glanced at him out of the corner of her eye, a darting look that made him feel ashamed. "You might say that."

"It's an ugly world," he said glumly and tossed Corporal Higgins's chilling psych profile on the teetering pile of his out basket.

But Higgins knew nothing of this. He only knew that his superiors valued his peculiar talents, and had even trained him to make better use of them. More efficient use. He particularly enjoyed the times when he was allowed to debrief in the field. He had one of the trim leather cases in his suit pocket. It was full of interesting chemicals and he was very competent in their use. But he preferred to be creative. It was amazing what you could accomplish with common household tools—paring knives and cheese graters and food processors. Too bad the mission had gotten blown the night before. He'd been looking forward to debriefing the target. He wouldn't have had to worry about being neat—usually a consideration. This target was a wet and dry situation—suck him dry, then terminate wet. He wouldn't have been around to complain later.

Higgins had his own private motto: no pain, no gain. He sighed and checked the time again. Only a half hour. Seemed like a lot longer. It always did on stakeouts like this. The trick was to stay alert without getting jittery. He looked down the hillside. The rubble of the house seemed finally to have smoldered out. At least the haze of smoke that had masked the ruin was now gone.

Two and a half hours till noon. He could do that standing on his head. In fact . . .

The snapping crash behind him took him completely by surprise, as did the high, hysterical shout that accompanied it. The noise surprised, even shocked him, but he was a pro. He saw the flash of movement in the bush, the blue flicker of cloth, and triggered the Club on full automatic before he'd even rolled all the way over.

It really was a stupendous weapon. Its rate of fire was over a thousand rounds per minute, yet it had almost no recoil and was as silent as a kiss. He chopped the top of the bush to dangling green shreds and heard the *shh-thok!* of the shells pound into something more solid.

Five seconds later he hitched himself up. The bush was only fifteen feet away. The guy had been good to get this close, but not good enough. He could see one leg, clad in a bright blue sweat suit, bent at an impossible angle and protruding from the bush. The leg was soaked with blood.

Slowly, Higgins stood. He kept the barrel of the Club trained on the broken form. It was a corpse, no doubt, but it never hurt to be careful.

"You alive?" he said.

No reply. He hadn't expected one.

He moved away from his own bush and angled up the hill, moving low and crabbed, just as he'd been taught. Nor did he take his eyes from the bloody leg up ahead. Dead men had been known to rise before.

His concentration was perfect; so he didn't see Josh Tower rise, naked, from behind another wedge of scrub ten feet behind him, sight carefully, and blow his left leg off at the knee.

The first thing that Higgins noticed when he woke up was the absence of pain. He knew he'd been badly hurt; his vision quivered with a yellow, fading light that meant shock. But he couldn't figure out what had happened. The last thing he remembered was advancing on the target's position; then something had slammed his left knee with such crushing force that he'd felt himself thrown back, arms flailing for balance. Why couldn't he catch his balance? He was healthy, in superb condition, well trained in the arts of falling and rolling.

He blinked. The hazy hillside popped into sudden focus, as if zoom lenses covered his eyes. He smelled the dank, sour stench of charred wood and water and a softer, dryer odor that hinted of dust and wind. The sun seemed very bright, but he wasn't overly conscious of heat. In fact he felt happy, the same kind of loose, cool satisfaction that gripped him after a successful mission. Something told him this was no longer a success, though—there was a problem. Doggedly he began to retrace his memories. The shout of attack, him rolling and firing on the flash of bright blue cloth mostly hidden in the leafy foliage. Quite particularly he recalled the surge of triumph at the sight of the target's bloody leg and the shortly savored hope that maybe the man was still alive.

Then sliding darkness.

''You're awake.''

He blinked again, but his body didn't move. He was propped on a slight incline of rock, partially shielded by a bushy overhang, so that the sun was mostly out of his eyes, but the rest of his body was in full daytime glare. He could look out over the broad, wooded valley to the brown hills on the other side, but from his present position he was able to see little else. His body, for instance, was a mystery to him. Nor could he see the speaker. Oddly, he felt no inclination to turn his head. It was better simply to wait, to watch the valley, to smell the dusty morning, slow and hinted with salt from the sea.

Fingers—he knew they were fingers, for they had a yielding hardness different than metal or wood—poked at his shoulder. He waited. Then the man swam slowly into his field of vision.

This was the target. Higgins knew it, but he felt little emotion other than recognition. He stared at the man with mild interest. He'd obviously had a hard time of it. Higgins didn't know much of his history, but he understood the man had been badly injured in the same accident that had killed his wife. The effects of the double trauma showed on his face, which was thin and prematurely lined. Traces of sagging flesh remained beneath gray-blue eyes that were surprisingly clear in the lucid morning light. There were scars as well, but they had mostly faded to pale, thin lines. His light brown hair was in need of a cut but seemed shiny and healthy. The man—what was his name? Tower?—smiled at him.

There was one strange thing: Tower was naked. He didn't understand, nor did he comprehend his reason for returning Tower's smile. That wasn't normal either: smiling at a target.

What was wrong here?

Maybe Tower would tell him.

Tower said, "How do you feel, Higgins?"

"I feel fine."

Tower grinned again, a cheerful, infectious expression. When he smiled like that, he reminded Higgins of a friend he'd had in second grade. But that was a bad memory, too, for the friend had deserted him one day. He couldn't quite recall the reason—something to do with Missus Barstow's fat old cat—but suddenly he felt weak and uncertain. Tower was the target. He wasn't supposed to smile at him.

"Good," Tower said. He kept on smiling, but it seemed to Higgins that some strain had come into his features, as if it was hard for him to maintain the expression.

"How do you know my name?" His words were clear enough, but they echoed tinnily in his ears, distant, almost like somebody else speaking.

"This." Tower held up Higgins's wallet and let it fall open.

"That's mine." A slow curl of anger moved in his belly, then subsided. It didn't matter, did it? "You shouldn't have it."

Tower sighed. "Old buddy, I hate to be the one to tell you, but right now that's the least of your problems."

"I've got problems?"

"You bet your ass."

* * *

Tower stared at his captive. Higgins—his ID gave his full name as Henry Allen Higgins, and Tower had a sudden, incongruously funny picture of this killer playing the famous role in the classic Broadway musical—was a mess, but he didn't seem to know it. Tower had moved quickly after Higgins went down, out like a light from both the impact of the high-powered shell and from the almost instantaneous systemic shock the terrible wound engendered, but even so he'd been afraid he might lose the man. Higgins turned out to be a bull; his short, massive body had endured punishment that would have killed a lesser man. The Club had simply vaporized the knot of bone and cartilage and flesh that had been his knee, leaving a short length of white, shattered bone protruding from greasy tatters of skin and muscle. It had taken him several seconds to strip off the man's belt and rig a makeshift tourniquet. Once he was satisfied that Higgins wouldn't bleed to death, he pulled off his suit jacket and rifled the pockets until he found the leather case he was sure would be there.

The leather case was a marvel of compact construction. Fully opened it revealed a small pharmacy, and once again he found something new. Carefully contained in thin plastic packets were several lozenges about the size and thickness of a dime, in various colors: red, blue, green, black. There were also tiny crystal vials, needle pointed, as well as squat silver cylinders that were designed to fit the miniature hypospray clamped to the leaf of the case. He was familiar with the hypospray, as it had been standard issue in his day. The lozenges had only been rumored for field use back in those times, and he wasn't certain of their utility. He knew what they were supposed to be: a foam-plastic that had been impregnated with one or more drugs in a flesh-penetrating suspension, coated on one side with a skin adhesive that would hold for many hours. The idea was to apply the—he remembered then what they were called—derms to an appropriate spot, where they would leak measured doses of the drug directly into the patient's system. There were no instructions inside the case. It wasn't intended for amateur use. He puzzled over the colors for a moment and finally decided he didn't know enough. He had once known color codes for similar kinds of equipment, but they might have changed, and he didn't want to off this bastard by accident. However, the hypospray might be all that he needed. If that was still the same, and it looked to be, then his own experience should be sufficient to get him through this part.

He loaded the spray with a cylinder—marked one; there was also a two and a three—and applied it to the unconscious man's neck. He heard a short, hissing sound as compressed gas punched a precise dose of painkiller right through Higgins's skin. The DIA man made a soft whuffling exhalation, but his eyes didn't even flicker. Then Tower sat back to wait.

He was feeling better than he had in weeks.

"You fucked up," Tower told him.

Higgins stared at him calmly. "What are you talking about?"

Tower showed him the case. "Recognize this?"

"No."

"I'm going to ask you some questions."

Higgins shook his head slowly. "Sorry. I'm all out of answers."

"No, these are real easy questions. See, Higgins, they're important, too: They might save your life."

Higgins made no reply. His face was very pale underneath a dark layer of tan, and Tower wondered where they'd pulled him in from. He looked something like an aging beach boy with his thin, greasy blond hair and wide, flat face, but no beach boy would have eyes like that—the color of muddy stones dried in the sun. Flat and emotionless, they were the eyes of a man who would gaze blankly at his victims, even as he murdered them.

Tower knew the type. Once, he'd almost been one of them. Until Julia—no. Don't finish that. Don't even think about it. He shook his head. "Did they tell you I used to work for the outfit?"

"What outfit is that?"

"Defense Intelligence Agency."

Higgins closed his eyes. "Don't know it."

Josh grinned. "It's on your ID card."

"Don't know nothing about it."

Higgins was out of it, no doubt; he'd given him a big enough dose not only to kill any pain from his ruined leg but also to render him groggy. Nevertheless, the man was good. He followed the book. Keep your mouth shut, deny everything, and hang on. Wait for help.

"There's no help coming," Tower told him. "Not in time, anyway."

Higgins opened his eyes and stared at him. Tower showed him the case again. "You aren't going to tell me anything of your own free will. I know that. What I need to know is about this case. These derms here, for instance. I'm pretty sure that one of them will open you up. But I don't know which, so unless you tell me, I'm going to have to experiment. How does that sound to you?"

Silence. Tower felt the sun burning on the back of his neck, an itchy, prickling sensation. He was still naked. He would be sunburned soon, maybe badly. But his clothes were shredded and soaked with blood, and he didn't want to wear Higgins's coat. It seemed out of place, unsettling, since he might have to kill the man.

"You aren't as good as you think," he told Higgins suddenly. "You were pretty easy to take."

That seemed to penetrate the fog. Higgins's eyes narrowed slightly. "Fuck you," he said, although there was no emotion in the words.

"No, really. You're kind of a pussy, big boy. In my day they left men to do the real jobs."

Higgins's lips worked. He tried to spit, but his mouth was too dry. He stared at Tower, who leaned over and propped him up further. "There. See? A kid's trick, and you fell for it."

He aimed Higgins's face at the bush and held it until he felt the muscles in the man's shoulders slump slightly. "Cute, huh? Stuff my pants with my shirt, put a sock and shoe on one leg, and leak a little blood on it. Looked real, didn't it? And tear off one sleeve so you had something to waist ammo on while I shot you. What do you think, Higgins? Are you a pussy, or what?''

Higgins's voice was slow and mumbling. ''. . . get you, asshole.''

"You won't," Tower said, his voice turning sharp and scornful. "Take another look, sucker." He forced him all the way up, so that he could see the emptiness below his destroyed knee. "You're retired now, bad ass. No more field work for you."

Higgins moaned. Tower let him down and moved in front of him, where he could watch his face. "I've got you doped up, so there shouldn't be any pain. Now, why don't you quit fucking around and tell me which one of these pretty colors to use? You know what I want. Tell me!''

Higgins's skin had gone gray and sagging as the full import of his failure began to sink in. But he was a professional. He had reserves. Maybe this crazy asshole had ruined him, but he wasn't done completely. If he could just stall long enough—he wondered how long he'd been out—somebody would come at noon to relieve him.

"The red one?" Tower asked.

Nothing.

"How about blue? That's a nice, peaceful color."

Tower watched his eyes carefully, and was finally rewarded. "Ah," he said. "You don't like the black much, do you? Good enough. That's the one I use, unless you tell me different.''

Higgins licked his thick lips. He stared at Tower's fingers as he pried one of the tiny black derms loose from the case. He tried to flinch away as those fingers came closer to his neck.

"How about it, Higgins? Is black the one I want?"

For a moment, electricity seemed to sizzle between the two men. Then Tower smiled slowly and touched Higgins's neck with his bare fingertip.

Higgins gasped with horror. *"The blue, you son-of-a-bitch! Not the black! Get that fucker off me!"*

Tower leaned back, the derm still on his fingertip. "That's better," he said calmly. "It's nice to know the color coding hasn't changed."

Then he set to work.

After half an hour he stood up slowly. The joints in his knees popped, and he windmilled his arms to get the cricks out of his back and neck. Under the influence of the drug, Higgins was beginning to wander, his disjointed sentences taking on an eerie, hallucinatory quality. Tower shook his head. He wasn't sure about the combination, the painkiller and the truth serum. Maybe there was a synergistic effect.

A slow wind was rising, cool off the ocean, and he felt a sudden chill. He stared at Higgins, who no longer looked at anything much in particular. The man's eyes had gone even flatter, shading into the lidless stare of a dazed reptile, and his lips moved faintly as he mouthed meaningless sounds. Shock seemed to be setting in with a vengeance; there was a faint bluish tinge to the DIA man's lips.

Tower ignored the feelings of disgust that made his stomach gripe as if he'd eaten something greasy and rotten. He'd gotten soft; he understood that. Once he'd not have thought twice about something like this, but now, after ten years, those old calluses had smoothed away, and he'd become almost civilized. Or had he? He'd come back to this all right. He might have felt a moment of queasiness here and there, but he'd been able to function just fine. No problem—blow a man's leg off, then fill him full of arcane drugs and fry him under the sun until he spilled the few pitiful fragments he had.

Tower rubbed his cheek, hard, and stared thoughtfully at the wrecked man at his feet. Higgins had never heard of Condor, nor did he have any idea who Tower was, beyond a target. He took orders, he said, and when Colonel Tagg told him to do somebody, he by god did him. But there was one bit of data he'd overheard: Tagg chattering quietly into a comm unit as they pulled up to Tower's house, speaking perhaps more clearly than he should have.

Lincoln Foster.

Higgins knew no more than that, but Tower had the missing pieces. DIA was after him, and he'd been with the outfit once. So had Foster. Now Higgins's boss knew the name.

It could only mean one thing.

He bent over and, grunting at the man's surprising weight, pulled his inert body deeper into the shade of the bushes. Somebody would find him when they came to relieve him—Higgins had said noon, and he had no reason to disbelieve him. He picked up the leather case and held it as if it were an object for meditation. Since Higgins had lasted this long, he would probably make it the rest of the way. Unless he used the black derm . . .

Tower stood for almost half a minute, staring at the leather case. Finally he sighed, closed the case, and tossed it down on Higgins's chest.

He hadn't regressed quite that far. Not yet.

He added Higgins's Club to his arsenal and began to make his way down the hill. There were some things in his bedroom he would need. Julia had avoided the innocuous box kept securely on the top of his closet shelf; perhaps she'd always known its contents. The sun blared in his eyes and his skin prickled as he moved. He pictured himself, a naked man standing on the hillside, slowly turning pink. Ridiculous.

He wondered if he could get to Foster in time.

Chapter Five

In a way, he'd always envied Link Foster and at the same time feared him a little. Foster wasn't that much older—only ten years, but it was a decade of real distance, that of a brother from a different time, before the world had changed for good. From his reading of history, he understood the Vietnam era to have been a similar gulf, when older brothers kept their crew cuts while the younger ones waved farewell from an uncrossable chasm of long hair and acid rock. And yet he loved the big old bear of a man, for his masculine kindness, his tough, unyielding loyalty, and for the simple steadfastness of his example. If anybody had taught him to be a man, it was Link Foster.

The wind moaned across the dunes, chasing before it dusk and ragged hanks of gray fog. Further out the endless Pacific boiled from a great bank of pewter clouds, rolling and rolling onto the rocky beach. Soon it would be night, the slow, drifting approach familiar only to those who live on the edge of vast waters, where the moon was a stranger and the stars were few and far away. Tower bellied forward through the thin scrub of a raddled dune top and wondered if it was already too late.

It had taken him longer than expected to scrabble and climb through the charcoaled wreckage of his house, working with one eye over his shoulder, watching the road for the relief DIA team and trying to keep from breaking his neck on the chancy ruins that threatened at any moment to collapse into the basement. He'd gritted his teeth as he clambered across the soggy mass that had once been a sofa, inhaled sharply at the new gashes on his palms, and finally groaned out loud when an unseen nail ripped a long wound in his left calf. The back end of the house was hardly damaged at all. It was eerie. One part of the place he'd lived in so happily for years was only a shattered, blackened skeleton; and the next, ten feet down the hallway leading to the bathroom, his office, and the two bedrooms, was like nothing had happened. He pulled himself up on the undamaged carpet and sat for a moment, hugging his knees and breathing hard.

All at once it seemed hopeless. His breath burned in his chest and gritted through his throat with an audible, harsh, rasping sound; blood leaked from the freshly reopened wounds on the back of his left hand; his badly seared skin—now he realized how stupid that had been, prancing around naked like a kid—seemed to suck all the juice from inside him; and the line of torn flesh on his calf throbbed with the same beat that pounded in his ears. On one side of him the blackened desolation of his home—Julia's home—made small tick-tick sounds as the embers cooled. Beyond him, at his back, the smoky residue of the blaze still settled on the familiar stretch of hallway carpet. The carpet was maroon; he remembered buying it just a week after they moved in. Now his blood dripped onto it and disappeared into its darker nap, and he simply huddled there and held himself, for it was beyond his strength to rise.

He became aware of it without realizing he knew. He had no idea how long he'd crouched there, his mind full of red-shot fog, listening to the tiny pip-plap of his blood dripping to the floor, before it began to call to him. Overhead, blazing through the gaping wreckage of what had once been a roof, the sun climbed toward its zenith. Slowly, he turned. The hallway, quiet as a tomb, stretched on toward the rooms where he'd lived, it seemed like an eon ago, though it was only a day. He raised his head, following the line of carpet to the wallpaper, patterned in stylized peonies and

thick green leaves, and further up, to where *it* danced
before its window in the noonday sun.

Small and cheerful as some brightly plumed bird, a
cardinal or a hummingbird, it fluttered delicately as
the slow breeze stirred its crystal wings; and now they
chimed together and cast their prismed reflection, and
he thought of her.

Julia.

This had been their home. This had been their life,
and before some unseen force—for he could think of
it in no other way than as a vast, impersonal *thing*—
had crushed the life from her, they'd been happy here.
He'd been happy. Now only the faceted bits of glass
pirouetted to her memory and the promise of her child.
Nothing else was left . . . except him.

Me, he thought: Joshua Tower, survivor. But what
reason was there to go on, to keep on surviving?

The wind chime answered him, and its song was not
vengeance—not quite. Something more elemental, a
need to make her death count, to make it *mean* something beyond a cheap, careless accident. At the moment it was shrouded in mystery, but as long as
someone remembered, someone cared, then in a strange
way not only did she live, but so did her unborn son.
There was a memorial there, somehow, but he must
keep on living. He must not let them wipe him away,
as casually, as unthinkingly, as they had all the rest.

He had no real idea who *they* were. Only a name or
two, a bone-deep hunch. But now, as he wiped his
fingers across the blood drying on his calf, as he
pulled himself up and stood on wobbly legs, as his
eyes fixed themselves on the stumbling, fragile bit of
light upon her wall, he understood: there was no giving up, not for him, not ever.

Not *ever*.

He didn't walk well, but he walked. Down the hall,
toward the bedroom, toward tomorrow. To whatever
he *had* to do.

There were lights on in Foster's beach house. Dusk
was falling thickly, and a long curtain of mist off the

ocean blurred and twisted the remnants of the light at the rim of the world, but the rambling brown clapboard pile at the edge of the sand beckoned with its squares of glimmering gold. He'd been crouching on the dune top for some time now and had seen no one; but DIA knew Foster's name, and he was too conscious of the possibility of another Higgins spotted somewhere, waiting patiently with a sniper's Club, to simply walk across the sand and up to the broad wooden doors facing on the wide veranda. At some point in the day he'd decided to live. Now he would have to draw on every shred of his near-forgotten training, watch every step, until it all came back. There was an old saw—he could barely remember it— about the hangman's noose being a wonderful aid to concentration. His neck was well and truly in that noose; he knew it, and he considered carefully his every step.

Some cold part of him had begun to function. It was the same thing that had reached up out of his gut and moved his fingers when he'd terrified the would-be mugger, that night before—no. Better let that go, too. But he was glad of it, because it might be enough to carry him through. It made judgments for him that were not conscious: If they've gotten him, it's too late now. But if not, then wait for night and move quickly. No matter how good the light-gathering scopes are, the infrared and ultrasonic, the thick blanket of fog that bellied off the water would be hard to breach.

He had to warn Foster, and he hoped to obtain his help. He would go it alone if he had to, but once, in a darker, bloodier time, the two of them had been a mighty team. And despite the loss, the plain, numbing *shit* of what had happened, another bleaker part of him welcomed the reunion.

Julia would not have understood that. He wasn't sure he did, himself. But it was a good thing, in its horrible way. Once he'd been a killer. If he intended to survive, he'd better learn how to kill again, and—romantic literature to the contrary—the best killers, on some level, enjoyed their work.

Every one of his senses seemed to quiver with an aching perfection. He couldn't recall a seaside dusk more perfect than this. The dull, roaring boom of the surf was a primeval music, the mist a balm to his nostrils. Day ended cool and damp. He felt soothed.

It grew darker while he crouched, waiting.

Lincoln Foster crumpled another can of Coors and tossed it at the growing pile in the wastebasket next to the corner of his desk. His computer hummed faintly, a thin, beelike sound. Outside, the sun had gone at last and fog licked at the big north window of the room. The house rattled and groaned around him, its wooden bones bending to wind and salt. He had mentioned something to Tower about selling the place, made a bitter joke of it, but he would never leave. It was as much a home as he would ever have, and he knew it. Through all the deadly years, when a hundred Josh Towers had come and gone, he'd nurtured the dream of this place. And the endless procession of women through it, some married, some not, some even married to *him*, were only a confirmation of the essential stability of the sprawling hodgepodge of rooms and windows.

He lit another Winston and paused in what he was doing to stare out the window. This room where he spent much of his time was light and airy, wrapped on two sides by floor-to-ceiling glass and further illuminated by a long skylight that he had to sweat to keep unfilmed by rimes of salt. At night, it seemed to grow smaller, as the fog pressed in like a lover. He thought about lighting a fire and glanced at the big fieldstone fireplace, its maw blackened by hundreds of other blazes. A pile of gray wood rested there, held by brass teeth; he considered, then reaching for the ice-filled tub of Coors at his right hand. Such amenities were another advantage of a womanless house, though times did come when the women outweighed the amenities. But, he thought with a glimmer of sadness, those times never lasted, and he always ended alone, communing with the sand and the beer and the fog.

Someday, he decided ruefully, I'll just say the hell with it and give up the women. They never work out anyway; I'm just too stubborn to admit it.

Scritch . . . scritch.

He continued to stare at the fireplace as if he hadn't heard the soft, scratching noise. But his left hand, concealed from the windows by the bulk of the desk, moved like a large, fleshy insect, slow and certain, to one of the desk drawers. He looked at the fireplace and smiled faintly and nodded, as if communing with himself—just a big, harmless boob alone in an empty beach house, a perfect victim—while his fingers slid into the drawer. Then, in one lightning movement, he crashed out of the chair, which bounced to one side as if dynamited, slammed down behind the desk, and slapped both hands onto the desktop, the barrel of the big silver .44 magnum revolver pointed directly at the window from where the sound had come.

He knew there were more potent weapons, Clubs and wideband rippers and such, but he was something of a traditionalist, and the old .44 would put a hole in a man big enough to drive a truck through.

Josh Tower knew this, and he put both his hands in the air and smiled through the smudgy glass at his old boss. "Let me in," his lips shaped.

Slowly, Foster pushed himself up from his knees. It didn't seem apparent, but even as he smiled and motioned with his big, grizzled head toward the line of windows and doors across the back of the house, the barrel of the .44 still remained pointed more or less at Tower's chest. Tower nodded and stepped sideways out of the window. Foster watched his shadow slide past the second window, then disappear in the direction of the back. His wide forehead crinkled; he stuck the silver weapon in the waistband of his jeans, shrugged, and trudged out of the room.

"That is a very good way to get your fool head blown off."

They stood in the kitchen, one of the sliding glass doors open to admit the chill evening air, while Tower shucked out of the big canvas backpack and accepted a can of Coors. He grinned nervously. "Sorry. I would have knocked, but things came up."

"Things? What kind of things? By the way, you look like shit. Been punching out windows? I thought I told you to call me." Foster's voice was gruff, but there was an undertone of worry and concern in it.

"They burned my house, Link. Fuckers burned it right to the ground."

Foster stared at him. He took in the fresh wounds on Tower's hands, the livid flare of his sunburned face, and the way he favored his left leg when he limped across the linoleum to accept the can of beer.

"Let me close that door and pull some drapes. Go on into my office and wait. I'll just be a minute. Then we can talk."

Tower popped the rim seal and raised the can. His voice quivered slightly as he said, "Thanks, Link. I knew I could count on you."

Foster shrugged. "What are friends for?"

Thick burlap curtains masked the windows of the office, making the room seem much smaller, more cozy, safer. Foster squatted by the fireplace, muttering softly to himself as he coaxed the weathered logs into a flame. Finally he stood up, his big features shadowed and flickering in the warm, luminous glow. Tower sprawled on a huge, rump-sprung sofa against the far wall; he looked as if he'd just finished a marathon race. Foster grunted softly as he restored the chair he'd knocked aside earlier. The chair squeaked sharply as he sat down, and Tower blinked at the noise.

Tower fished in the melting ice for another Coors, popped it open, and swallowed half of it in a single gulp.

"Okay. I think you'd better tell me," Foster said, finally.

Tower did. When he finished, he drained his Coors, belched, and said, "Now, would you take that hogleg out of your pants? I really didn't come here to shoot you."

* * *

The fire had burned down to a crown of shimmering embers; the room was full of the sweet odor of pine. There were only two cans of Coors left in the tub, floating forlornly with a few chunks of ice. The .44 gleamed flatly on the desktop next to the computer where Foster had placed it. Neither man said anything, but both realized it was within easy reach of Foster's big hand.

Tower was grateful: Foster had reacted as he'd hoped. There had been no disbelief, no questioning stares. Foster had nodded carefully at each revelation, filed each startling fact with no more than a soft click of tongue against teeth, and when Tower had finished his story, leaned back against his chair and said, "Defense Agency guys, huh? That is going to be one Jesus-jumped-up bitch, buddy."

"They have your name. That Tagg guy—"

Foster moved his hand slightly, a dismissive gesture. "I know Tagg. Used to be a punk. Must have come up in the world. You say he's a colonel now?"

"That's what Higgins said."

"Christ! What's the army coming to these days?"

Tower's voice was worried. "Coming *for* me, Link. And maybe you, too."

Foster was silent a moment, his features distant. "I haven't seen anything."

"Nothing? No worries? You hauled that blaster out pretty fast for a man with a clean conscience."

"Mm," he said absently. "My conscience is okay. I always have something handy. Don't you?"

Tower started to answer, then realized the difference between his old boss and himself. Foster might be technically retired, but he would never have allowed himself to become as slack as Tower. He had been out of the trade longer, but Tower suddenly understood that if a DIA fire team had come to burn *his* house, the outcome might have—most probably *would* have—been different.

"You got this place buttoned up pretty tight, Link?"

"Tight enough. I hadn't switched on the night

alarms, or you'd have never gotten that close to the window.''

"How good is your stuff?"

"Good enough. Good enough to keep them away for a while, tonight at least, till we decide what to do. I turned everything on while you were waiting for me.''

Tower almost felt as if he were floating on the big, soft cushions of the sofa, but it wasn't just the furniture; he felt safe here. Foster wasn't letting him down. He was as tough, as sharp and ready as ever. Tower felt himself slipping back into the old routines, deferring to the older man's greater experience, his unbelievable competence. You couldn't understand that competence unless you'd seen it, but Tower had, many times.

Then he shook his head. It wasn't Foster's fight, not really, and to think he could return to the safe past was only another mistake. He'd made enough mistakes already.

"This isn't your problem, old buddy. I just came here to warn you, maybe get out of the rain for the night. I'll be out of your hair in the morning.''

"Like hell," Foster said, his voice a low, throaty rasp. "I don't understand what the hell's going on here, but it looks like I'm tied in to it whether I want to be or not. A fish goes rotten from the head down, Josh. I taught you that. If the outfit's sending out their wet-team psychos after you, the orders came from somewhere high up. I can't just call somebody and tell them, hey, listen, there must be some mistake here. Please take Link Foster's name off your wet list.''

Tower glanced at him with interest. "You still got people you can call?''

"Sure I do. And some of those people would have to know about a thing like this. Which really worries me.''

"Why?"

Foster snorted. "Because it's still going down. They knew, and they didn't stop it, or warn me. I wonder if I've got any credit left at all.''

Tower shook his head. The fire popped once, sharply, and spat a tiny coal onto the hearth. Foster leaned forward and crushed it out with one huge shoe. "What do you think I should do?" Tower said at last.

"You? Nothing. Not yet. Let me play with it for a while. Besides, if I looked like you, I'd check into a hospital for a few days. Since that doesn't seem like a good idea right now, you know where the bedrooms are."

"Link," Tower said seriously, "I don't want to drag you into this."

"You're missing the point, my friend. I already am. So why don't you help me finish these last two beers, and then you hit the sack. Let Papa Link do what he does best."

"Yeah? What's that?"

"Keep my fat ass in one piece. And maybe yours, too."

Josh woke up at nine o'clock in the morning. He could see the reassuring digital clock across the room with its squarish red numbers. It was one of those perfect California beach mornings that are so much more rare than tourists realize. The bedroom he'd taken—the big house had six bedrooms, most never used—looked out through a glass wall at the ocean. The house was situated on a low, sweeping rise, so that it looked down to the surf line, where dark green water boiled across toothlike black rocks in sudden, frothy white explosions. The Pacific stretched out to a distant horizon smeared with haze, seeming to rise in a slow green surge to the sky. The sun was still to the east, beyond his vision, touching faint curly whitecaps with glints of diamond. The endless sky was perfectly blue and perfectly empty, and the beach itself, running from the house to the water, shone silent, pristine, and white.

It made him feel better to look at it. He lay on his bed between clean sheets, covered by a woolly-smelling thick red blanket, and blinked fuzzily, content simply to awaken slowly, without thought, without memory.

His condition lasted about half a minute; then his left calf began to throb, a hot, pounding sensation, as if his heart had somehow moved to his leg—infection there, maybe. He closed his eyes and clenched his fists, and that movement caused him to suck air between his teeth. His hands, palms, and knuckles felt as if they'd been dipped in acid. Then, when he began to push the covers away, dreading what he might see, his sunburn chimed in, prickly, itchy, hot. Every muscle in his body ached.

"Oh, *shit*!" It was agony to shift himself into a sitting position and put his feet on the floor. He sat naked for several moments and listened to the silence.

"God, you look awful."

Foster rumbled into the room carrying a tall glass filled with some thin, orange liquid. "Drink this," he said.

"Go away."

Foster's rumbling basso was horribly cheerful. "Aside from your obvious injuries—how'd you get sunburned down there?—you have a hangover. You just feel too rotten to realize it. So drink this—it'll cure what ails you."

"No . . . booze."

"Sure thing, just a little vodka with orange juice. Medicine. All that vitamin C. Drink it."

He was inexorable, a natural force. Tower took the glass, tasted, swallowed, and coughed suddenly. "A *little* vodka?"

"Well, enough. Come on, drink up. Coffee's in the kitchen and fresh towels are in the guest shower. Get moving, Captain Tower. We've got work to do."

He bustled out of the bedroom singing an off-key ditty about three women and a whale. Tower shook his head. But the first taste of the screwdriver was making a nice warm ball in his gut, and maybe a little more vodka would spread the fire a bit. He finished the drink in two gulps; a moment or so later the edge went off his various pains and aches and agonies, and a moment after that, a shower sounded like an excellent idea.

"Old fart knows his business," he mumbled grudgingly. He scratched his head, watched the beach a few more seconds—one white sea gull dived, skimmed the wave tops, flew away—and headed for the bathroom.

It was the other day for which he'd lived to fight.

The proposition seemed about fifty-fifty.

There was a breakfast room off the kitchen, a smaller area raised off the main floor about six inches and furnished with an ancient round oak table whose three clawed feet Josh found oddly reassuring. Foster had opened the drapes so that their view of the beach was unimpeded, and two of the windows were also slightly ajar, admitting the faint taste of salt and a welcome whiff of ocean breeze.

The rich smell of Colombian coffee filled the room. Foster poured another cup for himself and said, "How about you? You ready?"

"I'm fine." The remnants of a huge, country-style breakfast—scrambled eggs, homemade biscuits, sausage gravy, ham, toast, and home-fried potatoes—occupied a pair of large platters in the center of the table. "You'd make somebody a hell of a wife, buddy."

Foster's big, craggy features twisted into a reminiscent grin. "That's what my second mistake said. She didn't like to cook. But she didn't like my cooking enough to stick around, either."

Tower added a bit of honey to his coffee. He like it sweet enough to gag the normal palate. Julia had said it was the kid in him. "You keep on keeping on," he said absently.

"How do you feel?"

"Better. Not a hundred percent, but better."

"Take care of that sunburn. It looks nasty. I've got some stuff—"

"I may not live long enough to worry about it."

Foster's gunmetal eyebrows lowered. "Yeah. There's that." His huge, sloping shoulders raised and lowered. "I did some work while you were snoring away."

"I don't snore."

"You do. Sounds like somebody strangling a pig. Anyway, you're right. It does look like there's a problem."

A faint chill ran up Tower's spine. The room, the morning, seemed so peaceful. In the kitchen, Foster had fired up a new pot of coffee, and the dripolator was gargling happily away. The beach remained deserted, a travel agent's wet dream. And the vodka, food, and coffee had done their work. He felt better than he had since he'd seen the arsonists come in the night. That had become almost dreamlike, as if it had happened to someone else.

But it hadn't. He'd heard that tone in Foster's voice before. Once, Foster had led a hit team against a nest of terrorists in Lebanon. Tower had been second in command, and three others—what were their names? He couldn't recall, except Jenkins, of course—had completed the squad. Just before they jumped off from Haifa, riding microlite gliders down to the ruins of Beirut, Link had said, "This one may be a problem."

He'd been right. The other two guys had simply disappeared in a huge explosion; Jenkins had been captured. Foster had performed a miracle of stealth and violence to get him out, but they'd carried Jenkins back to Israel minus his hands and his sanity. Foster's original prediction had been spoken in exactly the same timbre he used now. Tower felt a shadow settle on the bright, peaceful morning.

"That bad, uh?"

"Afraid so, Josh. But it's not hopeless."

"Nothing's ever hopeless." It was an old credo, one that had gotten him through many terrifying nights. But he wondered if Jenkins still believed it. He wondered if *he* still believed it.

"I've got a few ideas . . ."

Tower sighed. "Let's hear them."

As Foster spoke, his voice took on a dry, measured rhythm, almost as if he were lecturing. Which, Tower reflected, he was. Foster had an enormous capacity for violence—Tower had seen it over and over, feats of death and destruction almost beyond human imagination, but that bubbling cauldron was overlaid with the calm, thoughtful patina of an intellectual man. Foster *planned* his efforts, as thoroughly as any grandmaster planned a chess game; he knew his own strengths, and considered his ability to explode in a frenzy of annihilation nothing more than another asset to be used and exploited in the accomplishment of his goals. In a way, the contrast between this big, beer-gutted, soft-voiced man talking quietly in the calm of his own kitchen and the horrors Tower had seen him perform with his bare hands made him seem all the more terrifying. Suddenly, Tower was very glad that Link Foster was not his enemy.

". . . used the Deep."

"What?" Tower asked, stirring from his fog of reminiscence.

"I used the Denver Deep. I was worried about my credit, remember. So I had to find out whether my linkages were still any good."

Tower nodded. It was hard to sink back into the old lingo, the jargon of tradecraft. But he remembered the Deep, and was mildly surprised to hear it still existed. In his day, the Denver Deep had been an illicit—a *black*—datanet, operated by six or seven unknown systems operators. These operators—sysops—rotated on the net so they would be harder to trace, but no matter who maintained the Deep on any given day, it was always open for business. Perhaps the powers that might have done something about it turned a blind eye, and that helped too; the authorities found uses for the Deep—as a well of undercover information, and a place to make their own deals, the kind of necessary agreements that no government, no police force, ever wants to see the light of day. You could unload stolen data modules in the Deep; hire anything from a garden-variety mercenary to the most exotic of data thieves; find a new identity or bury an old one; arrange a murder, a ransom, a betrayal, an election—anything. Anything at all. The dark world came together in the

Denver Deep. If it still existed, Link Foster was one of its natural denizens, a lord of twisted rule.

"The Deep still around, huh? What did you find out?"

Foster's thick lips curved. He looked like a degenerate Santa after a fresh shave. "I tried to hire myself."

Tower grinned. It was a good ploy. Rather than checking out his contacts on his own, he'd tested the lines of communication. Sometimes more could be learned from the existence of channels than the terminus of the channels themselves. "And?" Tower said.

"I'm still open for business. Somebody wants me, they can go through . . . certain people, people still in DIA, and reach me. If they know the codes and the cut-outs. Nothing's different."

"So why did this Tagg guy have your name?"

Foster shrugged. "I can think of a hundred reasons, but the easiest is that you are on somebody's shit list, and my connection to you is well known, particularly with our old mutual employers. Maybe it was just a cover check. Maybe a warning. I don't know for sure, and I'll follow up, but if I were on a wet list I'd be too hot for my buddies to keep advertising my shingle. Which brings me to the not so good part."

Tower nodded. He knew what was coming.

"My scalp isn't hanging on the bulletin board, but yours is. A full term on sight, and an ongoing project assigned exclusively to little old you. This Tagg bozo is in charge of the team." He shook his head. "Like I told you, the man's a creep, but he *has* come up in the world. A shame. From what I can find out, he's still an asshole—but don't misunderstand: He's a dangerous asshole, and for you he has *carte blanche.*"

Tower eyed Foster gloomily. "It's about Condor, isn't it?"

Foster blinked. "Condor? Oh, that stuff you were worried about. No, I didn't hear a word about Condor, whatever it is. It's worse than that, anyway. The orders didn't originate in DIA. They came from outside."

"Huh? From where outside?"

"The executive branch, down through the Joint Chiefs. The executive—the president of the United States."

Tower stared out the window, trying to make sense of that incredible revelation, when the flat blue cigar of an attack sub surfaced a few hundred yards offshore and began to disgorge men in shiny orange rubber boats.

As his belly tried to cram itself into his throat, he realized that, whatever it was, it was bigger than he'd even *begun* to imagine.

Chapter Six

Dorothea Lynn Kelly couldn't get him out of her mind.

It had been several weeks now, and the memory of him should have faded, as it did with most of her patients; he hadn't died, he'd been one they'd saved. He'd walked out of the hospital. The ones who rotted away, smiling bravely or shaking with fear, the cancer patients, the AIDS babies who still cropped up—of course she remembered them and prayed for those horrible images to blur, to become indistinct, to leave her in peace. But she remembered Joshua Tower, also, and she was afraid she knew why.

Nurses were human, too. That was the problem.

She left her cozy one-bedroom apartment on States Street, halfway up the hill overlooking the Castro District, at six that morning and paused to glance at the thick ruff of silver-blue fog still piled on Twin Peaks behind her like frosting. There was a nip in the air, and she pulled her coat more tightly around her shoulders. Down below, she could see the beginnings of the early morning crowd pushing into the entrance of the underground Metro station. There was a slight breeze coming from the west, the direction of the Bay. It ruffled her short-cut blond hair and cooled her cheeks, which were mildly flushed from three cups of strong coffee. Coffee was usually her only breakfast; she knew it was unhealthy to begin her day like that, but she'd always hated breakfast. In fact, she didn't much like mornings at all and often wondered how she'd ended up a nurse, with such erratic hours and so little time to settle into a routine.

If she had her way, she'd never rise much before noon. It wasn't that she was lazy, but her body clock seemed attuned to night. Unlike the title of the ancient Greek play on which she often punned, morning did not make her electric. She smiled a little at the ridiculous thought and began to walk briskly down the hill toward the station.

She still couldn't get him out of her mind.

San Francisco General was the usual hodgepodge of buildings that seemed an inevitable consequence of big-city hospital construction. She worked in North Tower, one of two thirty-five-story spires constructed in the last ten years. There were other towers, lower buildings as well, even a few of the original wards, now given over to cramped labs constructed of time-stained red brick. General was a small city, bustling in the surge of early morning business. Nurse Kelly was in her ward by seven, gingerly balancing yet another coffee, this one in a paper cup, and a fresh croissant she'd picked up at the tiny bakery across the street from North. Since croissants didn't remind her of eggs, she didn't consider the flaky, buttery horns as breakfast.

Sylvia Parthrod, graying, fiftyish, cheerful, greeted her.

"Quiet night," Syl said.

Kelly set the croissant down on the corner of her desk, shrugged out of her coat, and hung it on the ancient pine rack at the back of the small office, where it dangled next to the ward collection of battered umbrellas. In San Francisco, it was good to keep a supply of rain gear handy.

"Mr. Ingels?" Kelly asked, sipping at her coffee and making a face. The stuff from the machine was nasty, but it was caffeine.

"Just fine. On staff rounds they reduced his meds. I think they'll be releasing him tomorrow."

Kelly smiled sadly. Mr. Ingels had been in the ward almost two weeks now. He was seventy-three and he had lung cancer. Kelly thought he was one of the

sweetest men she'd ever met. He was a retired cable-
car operator—the cars were but a memory now—and
as soon as he'd been able to get out of bed, he'd badg-
ered them into letting him into the children's ward,
where he spent most of his days making brightly colored paper constructions and intricate wooden constructions out of tongue depressors and rubber bands
and bits of wrapping. Some of those kids hadn't
laughed in weeks before Mr. Ingles came along. She
would miss his birdlike features, the cloud of white
hair like cotton candy, his slow, ready chuckle. When
he came back—and he would—he might not be able to
keep it up.

Life and death. The hospital was full of both.

"I'll miss him," Kelly said.

"Yeah. We all will," Syl acknowledged. She cen-
tered a funny-looking flowered hat on her gray curls
and asked, "Cold outside?"

"There's still fog. Don't forget your coat."

Syl nodded and slipped a somewhat dilapidated rab-
bit cape around her substantial shoulders. She spent
most of her clothing money in second-hand shops.
Somehow, on her roly-poly figure, the cape looked
good.

"Oh," Syl said, "you had a message earlier."

"A message?"

"Some man, wouldn't leave his name. I told him
you'd be in at seven. He wanted your home number,
but I didn't give it to him. That was right, wasn't it?"

"Of course. Thanks, Syl."

The shorter woman was at the door now. "Have a
good one."

"You bet."

The phone made its irritating wheep-wheep sound.
Kelly glanced at the big, round, old-fashioned clock
on the wall. Seven on the dot. She picked up the
phone.

"Nurse Kelly?"

"Yes, it is. . . ." She recognized the voice.

"This is Josh Tower. I need your help."

* * *

Once upon a time, she thought. It was a silly line—
like other silly lines the voice inside her head tossed
to the surface. Like many who lived alone, she carried
on a running conversation with herself, often not even
realizing that she did so.

Once upon a time . . .

That terrible beginning to all fairy tales; sometimes,
she thought, the beginning to all of life. She stared at
the hands on the big round clock—five after seven,
only five minutes—and now, in the breathless quiet of
her tiny office, once upon a time had become now.
She smoothed the front of her starched uniform and
felt the firmness of her breasts, her belly. It was a good
body; she took pains to keep it that way, and why not?
She could afford the thousand-dollar membership in
the health club; there was no one else to spend the
money on, and she enjoyed the thrice-weekly visits.
She felt a certain calm satisfaction in measuring her
body against younger, prettier women. Yes, *prettier,*
she thought defiantly—her features would never launch
ships or even ferries across the Bay to Sausalito. She'd
been born with wide-set eyes, a too-snubbed nose, and
a dusting of freckles that didn't seem dark but defied
every layer of makeup.

Her mother had told her she was plain: "Live with
it, Dotty, you have other things."

And so she had, she reflected. She liked to think of
herself as a strong person, calm and unshakable, an
unbending support for those who needed her. Nursing
suited her that way, if not in the matter of hours. Nursing had always suited her, except for . . .

If only he didn't remind her so much of Carl!

There, the other voice piped up. *Now you've said
it—so you might as well think about it. You'll have to
anyway, you know.*

It had not been a marriage made in heaven. His parents had told her so. She remembered her mother-in-
law's gimlet eye on her as she'd said, "Actually, dear,
we'd hoped better for our boy, but . . ."

The implication had not needed further explanation.
Carl Kelly, golden youth, surgeon to be, was stepping

far down to take the hand of snub-nosed Dotty Arznaky, who came from out in the Avenues of San Francisco and whose parents were, respectively, a secretary
and a plumber. Nothing wrong with that—no, good,
honest occupations—but what did Frank and Kitty
Arznaky know of the world of Lyman and Patricia
Kelly, up on the view ridges of Pacific Heights?

They'd married anyway. She was two years older
and working already, which she continued to do while
he progressed through his residency. He'd been lithe
and blonde, almost pretty, with liquid dark eyes that
gave rise, in San Francisco, to nasty jokes. She knew,
first hand, that the jokes weren't true—Carl Kelly had
been a demon in bed. Nor was he weak in other ways;
his appetite for the unbelievable hours of medical
training, the time spent half groggy in emergency
rooms, in wards, grabbing a few short hours of sleep
in tiny cubby holes, was insatiable. He was a working
fool. Sometimes, of course, he cut corners. Everybody did. In a hospital as busy as General, overburn-
dened residents did whatever it took to get the job
done.

The regs called for blood tests in certain cases, but
when Carl Kelly had opened up Theo Linabarger on
an emergency appendectomy, he hadn't bothered. Linabarger was twenty-two, married, with one child and
another on the way. He seemed healthy enough, except
for the hard belly and fever. But Linabarger had been
just delirious enough that the diagnosis questionnaire
had been only perfunctorily completed with the aid of
his pretty young wife. Then Carl had opened him up.
The job was a piece of cake, except for one thing. Carl
was just a bit fogged—he was on his second round in
forty-eight hours—and he slipped once and inflicted a
tiny gash on his left thumb. Nothing much.

Theo Linabarger's mother had been a heroin addict.
He was proud that he'd been able to save himself from
the morass of her awful life, and though she'd died of
some dismal disease before his twelfth birthday, he'd
survived to make a life for himself.

Because of her addiction, no one had paid much

attention to the cause of death. In those times in San Francisco, the cause might simply have been listed as extended suicide. But there had been a cause: HIV infection leading to eventual destruction of her immune system. AIDS. She'd had it for fifteen years before it killed her, and so, of course, her son, Charles, carried the virus as well.

AIDS was curable. In almost every case, the arsenal of antivirals knocked it down quite nicely. Those treatments would, eventually, save Theo Linabarger's life as well.

There were, it was true, a few instances when the virus, a ferocious mutator, met a host it really enjoyed. Those were the exceptions. Carl Kelly was an exception.

Even so, he fought it. He fought it for almost three years before the great killer of the late twentieth century claimed him as one of its few victims of the following hundred years.

Dorothea Kelly fought it as well. One day, however, was lodged in her memory like a small, sharp rock. It was toward the end, far enough toward it that both of them knew. Carl had never been a big man, but now the disease had shrunk him to under eighty pounds, the average weight of a nine-year-old boy. His bones inhabited his skin like crooked sticks in a paper bag; he was too weak to use the bathroom on his own, so she carried him when it was necessary. That morning he'd asked in a whispery voice—Kaposi's Sarcoma had nearly ruined his vocal cords—and she'd lifted him up, marveling in dull terror at how birdlike he'd become. His head lolled on her shoulder. She herself functioned in a state of near exhaustion, for she'd continued to work. Carl's insurance was good, but it didn't extend to the hiring of nurses to carry him to the bathroom, nor would it compensate for her loss of income. Carl's parents could have helped, but his mother—darkly gleeful, it seemed to Kelly—had suggested she make do on her own. "You're a nurse, aren't you?" As if daring her to prove her wrong.

She set him on the commode and waited while he

strained weakly to shit out a couple of hard, blood-stained turds. Then she wiped his ass and lifted him again, and she realized he was crying. ''Ah, God, I hate this,'' he husked softly.

''No, baby, don't,'' she soothed.

''I wish I was dead.''

She didn't say anything, because, in her bleakest moments, she wished the same thing.

''Would you—oh, Jesus, Dotty, would you?''

No, she wouldn't. Not then.

But maybe later . . .

Carl was gone, buried on a cold day in Colma, the cemetery town south of San Francisco, beneath the tight-lipped, blameful gaze of his mother—''I told him you weren't good enough''—and the scars she bore were mostly hidden now. There was no way the old harpy could have known, beyond a gut-deep intuition that stoned all the crows—but Kelly knew. She knew who had gently helped Carl Kelly to his final rest. And those scars remained hidden until she came across another Carl, another soft on the outside, hard on the inside man who needed her. Whom she could help. With whom she could atone.

Joshua Tower. She wondered what the beautiful little wife had been like, the one whose death obsessed him so much he'd blocked the very memory of it from his mind, the wife who'd blinded him to the woman who had nursed him through his recovery and walked him out of her life. But he remembered well enough to call when he needed help.

You're a fool, Nurse Kelly, the inward voice decided.

She stared blankly at the clock and murmured aloud, ''I know. But nurses are human, too.''

The little orange boats bobbed on the green water like cheerful corks—not so little, those boats, he realized: Each one held four men. The men wore dark green wetsuits and helmets and carried deadly looking assault rifles. He didn't recognize their weapons. Something new, he supposed.

"Link. Look out the window. The beach."

"What the hell?" But again, Foster didn't let him down. He barely missed a beat, although his face went red, almost bruise colored. "Okay. Come on." He was out of his chair, coffee forgotten, and moving through the kitchen. He scooped up Tower's backpack from where he'd dropped it the night before in one smooth motion, hoisting the heavy load—Tower knew it was heavy, as he'd loaded it himself—as if it were a sack of feathers. "I said come *on*!"

Tower rose and followed him across the kitchen, watching his big hams pump like muscular pistons; Foster was really moving now. "You wearing everything you brought with you? No, it doesn't matter, if they ask—everybody knows we're friends, I can explain it—"

"Link, *who are they?*

"Don't know. DIA kill team. The fucking navy, for all I know. But they'll have the place surrounded. A goddamned submarine, for Christ's sake!" His deep voice was curdled with disgust.

Foster had opened the door in the hallway and flipped a light switch. Stairs stretched down into gloom. The big man was already halfway down the steps. His voice echoed flatly. "Move it, buddy. There's not much time."

Time for what? Tower wanted to ask. He felt totally disoriented. The tiny men in their brilliant tiny boats didn't seem real. And a submarine? Surely not for him. It was insane. His mind began to ratchet wildly, barely catching on a random gear here, a broken tooth there, but Foster had that old command tone in his voice. Tower's body followed him numbly, even as his brain said over and over again, *What? What what what* . . .

He'd never been in Foster's cellar before, didn't even know it was there. The temperature was quite cool, and it was quiet as a tomb. That's it, he thought, a tomb; the small room—much smaller than the house as a whole—seemed to be carved out of solid rock.

"Come on, give me a hand with this." Ropes of muscle stood out on Foster's back as he bellied up against a huge tool cabinet against one wall and began to push it away. Tower stepped in beside him and lent his own shoulder, and after a moment the thing began to move.

They pushed sideways, well away from the wall. Tower stared at the space revealed, but it was blank, empty.

"Not the wall," Foster said. "Below."

And there it was, barely visible, the faint outline of a square. It looked as if a slab of concrete had once been lifted, then cemented back down. Foster went to a workbench on the other side of the room, opened one of the drawers, and took out a small black transmitter. He thumbed a red button on its front, and the square of concrete sank smoothly away.

"It's designed to look like a buried sump pump. Here." The big man handed Tower the transmitter. "You'll need it to get out the other end. But wait. Don't use it till dark. You know."

Through all the confusion, Tower felt a few lucid thoughts bubble to the surface. What the hell did Foster really do, to need a bolt hole like this? Or was he just naturally paranoid? Did it matter? A part of his mind had been keeping count, without his conscious knowledge—the same part he'd once thought entirely dead. The men from the sub would be on the beach by now, perhaps moving more slowly than necessary, restrained from their usual all-out charge because they wouldn't know what Foster might have waiting for them. Obviously they thought it might be a tough nut to crack: Why else send an entire sub full of men? Not to mention the small army that must be spread out around the rest of the house, probably closing in even as he vacillated on the edge of the escape hatch.

It was insane. He took the transmitter. Link heaved his backpack down into the dark, square hole revealed in the floor. "Go on, get your ass down," he rumbled. "It's shielded. They won't find it, I don't think. Hurry up. I want to get back upstairs. Be drinking my innocent cup of coffee when those bozos come trespassing on my property."

Tower jumped down into the passage. He looked up. "Link—"

"Flip the switch. Shut the door," Foster said crisply. "Hurry up."

He pushed the button and saw the slab of concrete begin to rise, narrowing the rectangle of light. Foster's big face watched impassively. Finally, just before the light became a wedge, a line, and winked out, Foster said, "Good luck, buddy."

Darkness.

"Good luck to you, buddy," Tower whispered. Very faintly, he heard a heavy, scraping noise as Foster shoved the cabinet back in place. Then, silence.

He wished he'd had time to take a leak.

But you never did. Another axiom of the spy business: You almost always got left with your dick in your hand.

He crouched in the hole like a rat. No, that wasn't right; weren't rat holes supposed to be dank, full of the plink-plink of water dripping? This was dry. Foster had done good work. He wrapped his arms around his knees and sat and listened to the dark. What was going on upstairs?

There was a faint, thin smell he couldn't quite make out, almost like vinegar; then he realized: It was his own sweat. And that thumpa-thumpa-*thump* was the sound of his own heart beating. Fascinated, he listened to the rushing thrum of his blood through his veins. Then, like a little kid, although it was so pitchy he couldn't see his fingers in front of his face, he squeezed his eyes shut. Almost forgotten, he waited for the game to come back, and it did: slow, curling red flashes, like a fire beyond a black horizon. The sight of his own blood tripping chemical events in his brain.

Something shook his hideaway ever so slightly, not really a sharp movement, more like somebody had dropped something big—a bale of hay, a sack of flour— far away. His heartbeat fluttered, and the stink of his perspiration increased in intensity. Foster was up there alone, facing—what?

A submarine full of trained killers, that's what. Foster hadn't seemed unduly worried about this Colonel Tagg having his name, and Tower had to trust that. Foster certainly knew his own connections better than Tower ever could. But a submarine! He knew it was in the power of the Joint Chiefs, certainly within the authority of the president, to order such a thing, but for one man?

They wanted him. Somebody wanted him bad enough to call in heavier artillery than he'd ever heard of. It didn't make any sense.

Two quick, flat noises, muffled by layers of concrete, barely at the edge of hearing. He bit his lip and tasted sudden blood, cooper, and salt. Foster's .44. But he'd not been expecting real trouble. He couldn't have, or he'd be right down here in his bolt hole, waiting for his own chance to escape.

Foster could be wrong, though. He hadn't expected a full-scale commando attack, complete with ocean-going support vessels. Wild pictures began to chase themselves across the landscape of his imagination. Foster lying bloody across his oaken kitchen table, his brains leaking out in crimson gray pudding. And Tagg, the mysterious Tagg, standing over his corpse, a thin, carnivorous smile on his face.

Thin? Carnivorous? A dry chuckle rasped through his lips. Tagg could weigh three hundred pounds, look like the last porker, look like Jesus Christ, look like *anything*. . . .

Was Foster dead?

He brought his wrist up to his face and stared at the bright red numerals on his watch face. It was a little past ten; Foster had told him to stay hidden—don't even poke your snout out—until after dark. Eight hours at least.

Would they find the opening? The thought made him nervous. He stretched out his feet until one Adidas running shoe connected with his backpack; the movement elicited a soft clink. There were two Clubs in there—the one he'd taken off Higgins, and the smaller model he'd retrieved from the other sentry. A lot of firepower—the magazines held a thousand rounds of the tiny shells. If somebody came down here they were in for a surprise.

Yeah, surprise. What a joke! If they discovered his hiding place, a few doses of almost any kind of gas would do the trick. The passageway was small, perhaps three feet on a side. He doubled over to his hands and knees and began to crawl, pushing the backpack in front of him. One, two, through the dark like a spider; he stopped and inhaled three times, slowly. Got to get a grip. Get those funky weird ideas, those bizarre thoughts, out of his skull.

He wouldn't be any good to Foster or himself this way. After a while his heartbeat finally began to slow, and the acid burning in his stomach subsided a bit. The wound on his calf throbbed with heat. He waited another five minutes by his watch before pushing on. After a time he came to the end—a blank space of rough concrete that wouldn't respond to his tentative shove at all. Whatever the door was made of, it was heavy and thick. A good job all the way, but then, that was the only kind of job Foster knew how to do.

Was he dead?

He leaned up against the end of the tunnel and breathed softly and wondered how he could bear the weight of another death.

Dead?

Tagg. Colonel Tagg. And Condor.

Those were the places to start. Those were the beginnings. If this wasn't the end.

Colonel Aloysus Tagg—"Loy" to his few friends, "Colonel" to everybody else—paused at the door of the hospital room and glanced back over his shoulder. He'd told Kinger and Johnson to stay put, and keep their big asses down by the nurse's station. He wanted to check this out by himself.

If there was any truth to the wheeze that men came to resemble their jobs, Loy Tagg was a living refuta-

tion of the idea. If he resembled anything, it was a
schoolteacher. An English teacher, perhaps, high
school or college, stuck forever trying to pound dusty
classics into skulls thickened impenetrably against any
kind of learning.

He knew what he looked like. Sometimes he made
a game of it, picking out single words that described
himself. Tentative. Bumbling. Vague.

He wore thick glasses, the round kind with thin gold
rims, although his vision could have been easily cor-
rected either with surgery or contacts, but he preferred
the distant, distracted look that glasses gave to his face.
His eyes were watery and greenish brown, a shade that
would be called hazel in a more forthright gaze. He
tended to look away from whomever he spoke to, although he missed nothing.

He was big and shambling and sloppy. He favored
nubby tweed jackets that didn't match the baggy pants
he also favored. He did not appear to be in shape; his
chest joggled when he walked, presenting the embar-
rassing impression of tits. His ties always seemed to
be partly unknotted, and there was always a stain—
brown gravy, raspberry jam, pizza sauce. He sometimes wondered what he would have done, if he'd been
regular army and had been forced to wear a uniform.
He looked even worse in uniforms.

His hair was still black and shiny, what there was
of it, but mostly his scalp was bare as an elbow. Except for a port-wine birthmark an inch over his right
eyebrow, shaped like a butterfly. He kept his nails very
clean. The palms of his hands were soft, uncallused.
When he spoke, his voice was clear but quite high
pitched, the voice of a young boy, and people always
looked at him twice, surprised, upon hearing him
speak.

Of course, most people never looked at him twice.
In a crowd of three, the other two would never notice
his presence. He was a cipher, a zero, a big, sloppy
man who wasn't there.

He nodded thoughtfully. The two gorillas were

where he'd left them. That was good. He wanted no problems.

But there shouldn't be. It wasn't much of a job. Killing Henry Higgins should be no problem at all.

Higgins dreamed he was running. He was running across a barren hillside, seared stone and brown dust beneath a screaming sun. It was very quiet. He wasn't sure whether he was running from something, or toward something, but it was very bad. Very *wrong*—as he loped steadily on, across that endless shit-colored hill, his right shoulder seemed out of balance. The rhythm was there, just fine; he'd been a cross-country runner in high school, stocky even then and not very fast, but his endurance had been phenomenal. He could run all day. So he knew what it was supposed to be like, and this wasn't it.

Now, suddenly, the sun began to set. How could that be? Only a moment ago it had been high noon, a flat glaring nova in the top of the sky, and now there was nothing but a smudgy red film, like the closing of a bloodshot eye.

Shadows leaped up all around him, moving, flickering phantoms, turning the hillside into a forest of vague teeth, barely glimpsed claws. He still couldn't get his shoulder right, and now his stride had gone off. Have to watch that, be careful; a single misstep and he'd fall right off the side of the mountain, down that bottomless pit.

What?

He looked down then and saw the horrible thing in the wan crimson light of the dead sun. His left leg. Nothing below the knee, nothing at all, but a few ragged shreds of flesh, a hank of bone like something protruding from a half-carved roast, and now the flies were coming, swarming in. . . .

He screamed.

Colonel Tagg stood at Higgins's bedside and stared down at the sedated man. Higgins was completely out of it, buried beneath a rainbow of soporific drugs, but he still quivered and thrashed and moaned. His legs twitched.

Tagg wondered what Higgins's dreams were like. He recognized the movements.

Higgins slept like a dog.

He didn't know it, but it saved his life.

At three o'clock in the afternoon Dot Kelly put on her coat and said hello to crusty old Maggie Meade, a woman built like a bowling ball and just as hard, even though she had to be pushing seventy. Maggie kept on working because her mother was creeping up on the big one hundred and showed every sign of going on for another twenty, thirty years, but she needed special meds from Maggie that weren't covered by the MediCal Comp plan. Maybe Maggie would have worked even if it hadn't been for mom at home; she had the face of a drill sergeant, wore her hair in a crew cut, and positively enjoyed terrorizing the ward orderlies and candy stripers. At home, Kelly knew, Maggie's mother wouldn't put up with it for a minute, nor would the five cats the two women shared their apartment with.

"Slow day," Kelly said.

Maggie Meade was in a foul mood. She scowled and muttered something that took Kelly a moment to translate. She thought it was "Life's a bitch, then you die."

"Well, have a nice evening, anyway."

Nurse Meade, with a nasty gleam coming into her ball-bearing eyes at the sight of Twinkie Nichols, a recently hired black orderly, flapped one hamlike paw in dismissal as she dove to the attack.

"Right," Kelly said, and she walked out of the office.

She took a freight elevator down. It was shift change and the public elevators were jammed. On the ground floor she crossed the lobby, ignoring the faces that turned toward her like pale sunflowers. They didn't see her, she knew. They only reacted to the white uniform, the official status. Those faces were full of questions, the kind that demanded only dreadful answers. When

she'd first started nursing, such things had depressed
her terribly. Now she barely noticed.

She walked up to Market Street, stepped into the
mall, and headed toward Van Ness. At the United
Nations Plaza she stopped and sat on one of the stone
benches next to the FrisBowl.

As usual, the bowl and the area around it were
jammed with kids. A fat woman with blue hair and
sunglasses carrying a shopping bag that read "Hoosiers are Human Too," turned to her husband, who
wore baggy shorts and a sweated-out black T-shirt,
and said, "Herman, would you look at *that?*" Her
voice was thick with fascinated horror, and Kelly
turned to see what had shocked the woman so. She
couldn't find anything out of the ordinary.

The kids looked the same as always. She enjoyed
watching them. The Frisbee Bowl was great round circle, like a shallow pan, that rose about five feet from
its center to the rim. The bowlers swooped and glided
and pirouetted like fantastic birds or insects. They
wore black; thin, skintight outfits that accentuated narrow, bony frames and set off the gold, silver, rhine-
stone, neon masks that covered their faces, the
towering feathered headdresses that dipped and bowed
above the masks like lunatic flags.

Kids. It was San Francisco. A girl swooped by, fourteen, maybe fifteen, in a ruby mask with matching
ruby nipple guards on her bare breasts. Perky, Kelly
thought, and then she realized what had shocked the
woman from Indiana. They probably didn't see a whole
lot of that back in the Hoosier state.

She stifled a grin.

It was almost four o'clock. She had another hour to
wait; her stomach made a plaintive sound. A strange,
chilly-happy feeling had been growing in her all day.
She didn't examine it closely. Instead, she left her seat
and walked over to a pizza stand and ordered a slice
with pepperoni and calamari. Juggling the hot slice
carefully on its plastic wrapper, she returned to her
bench and chewed the tip off the slice, being careful

not to spill any of the rich red sauce on her white uniform.

The sun was still well up in the blue sky, shepherded by a flock of böuffänt clouds. She felt adventurous. It had been a while.

You're a fool, Dot Kelly.

Shut up, she told the inner voice. I'm busy.

The woman from Indiana shrieked and covered her eyes.

"You shut up too," Dot Kelly told her softly.

Colonel Tagg watched Higgins with utter satisfaction. His curiosity was getting the best of him. He had almost decided not to kill the man.

It was certainly Higgins's lucky day.

Chapter Seven

Josh Tower spent eight hours in utter silence and darkness, trapped with no company other than his own body. In that constricted limbo it began to seem like some other thing; his flesh, with all its rips and tears and burns and scars, was apart from him. About half an hour before he knew he would chance opening the door—he couldn't wait any longer, as he was beginning to get seriously crazy—he fumbled open his backpack and, working by touch alone, fingered out the darksuit.

It was an interesting piece of clothing, one of several items he'd salvaged earlier from the plain cardboard box in the bedroom of his ruined house. Like most old soldiers, he kept his souvenirs. He supposed there were new and better versions of the same thing now. Probably, the men who'd come for him out of the sea, or the others, creeping invisibly across the land, had worn such things. He worked himself around in the cramped confines of the end of the tunnel until he could slide off his Levi's and T-shirt. He barked one elbow on the rough concrete facing the exit hatch but barely noticed it; his sunburn was a solid skin of pain. His breath came in short gasps; sweat rolled down his face, his chest, and gathered on his palms. He was slick with it. It made pulling on the one-piece darksuit that much harder, but finally he was finished. He rested a few moments, hearing the harsh, roaring sound of silence in his ears.

He loaded everything else back into the pack and pulled out the smaller Club. Adrenalin was making his teeth click together, and he'd started to stink again. He'd had to crawl back to the beginning of the tunnel twice to piss, and the stench of that rode the air as well—thick, stinging, musky.

He took the controller in his left hand and grasped the Club with his right. His knuckles stung slightly as the tension cracked fresh scabs open. He shook his head, inhaled sharply, and checked his watch a final time.

Seven o'clock.

He pressed the button on the controller and fell forward from darkness into night as the exit opened soundlessly before him. Fog rolled around him, thick as dirty cotton. He could taste it, smell it; but it was as dark outside as it had been in the tunnel.

"Thank God," he whispered. "Thank God."

He spent five full minutes doing nothing but breathing the cool salt air.

Sound filtered into his fuzzy awareness. The surf pounded nearby, a deep, continuous, rolling thunder, and above it the long moan of wind off the water. As his eyes adjusted, the fog took on a swirling luminescence, not enough to see by, but enough to make its presence visible. Shapes began to form around him, vague and sticklike. He hitched himself forward. He was on dry, hard-packed sand. Pain prickled his left palm; he hissed softly and pulled his hand away. Sticker bushes. He was in a dense thicket of scrub. It was too dark to make out where the exit of the tunnel was. Not that it mattered; that other route was blocked, for there was no way to move the heavy tool cabinet that rested on top of the inside entrance.

He began to relax. There was a storm in the air. The fog and wind, the roar of the surf, all were harbingers; something massive was striding and gliding across the ocean, moving closer. The sentries who'd been left behind would be almost useless, their effectiveness reduced by the weather. Nobody could maintain a picket line in this stuff, no matter how good their equipment, how vigilant their watch. He'd made it. He was home free. Slowly, he slipped the straps of the backpack over his shoulders, wincing at the pressure on his sunburn. The pack remained silent; he'd muffled its contents as well as he could with his jeans and shirt.

The air was damp and full of claws, but he felt pleasantly warm. The darksuit was doing its job. It was an almost perfect insulator, trapping his body heat but allowing his skin to breathe. It could keep him comfortable in subzero temperatures, if necessary, and it would shed water like a duck. It had one other attribute, and this gave him the most confidence of all.

The darksuit was near-perfect black. It absorbed visible light and certain other wavelengths as well. While he wore it, he would be, at night, almost invisible to both the naked eye and several kinds of machines.

God damn, I'm going to make it!

The sudden surge of glee made him lightheaded. He waited until his emotions calmed. He would have to do this by the book. A single mistake would probably kill him. So breathe in, breathe out, and go slow.

He raised the Club to his chest and began to move back toward Foster's house. The first thing was to find the guard.

The second, to kill him.

Colonel Tagg tapped his vaguely yellow teeth—he didn't smoke, brushed regularly, and still there was a faint, lemon stain—with one manicured thumbnail. He was dimly aware of the hospital hustle behind him, doctors and nurses passing by the door of Higgins's room on squeaky rubber-soled shoes, the mechanical nattering of the PA system; none of it disturbed him. The full weight of his formidable concentration rested on the short, stocky man who thrashed fitfully on the bed.

He'd come here with the general idea of killing him, and he'd brought several implements that would do the job simply and cleanly. One of them, in fact, was in his hand now, a tiny hypospray loaded with a chemical that caused instant cardiac arrest. It was untraceable, wouldn't show on any autopsy, and would take him all of a second to administer. But he tap-tapped away and considered. Another idea was beginning to form.

There was no particularly pressing reason to terminate Higgins. It was more or less standard operating procedure—not DIA but Loy Tagg's SOP—because Higgins had not only failed in his duty, but had been possibly contaminated as well. Better agents than he had been turned through the skilled use of chemicals, and by Higgins's own admission, he'd been under at least an hour. The target—briefly, Josh Tower's name flashed up, then faded away; Tagg didn't like to think of targets as humans with names—had once been a member of the outfit himself. His skills might have gotten rusty, but he'd handled himself awfully well for a man out of the field ten years. So, while it was unlikely he'd managed to rearrange Higgins's loyalties, it was better to stay on the safe side. A simple push with the hypospray and it would be over.

He moved forward, and something stayed his hand. He stepped back, puzzled. Finally he put the hypospray back in his pocket. He went to the door and stuck his head out. Kinger saw him and raised his black eyebrows. Tagg nodded, and the big man walked down the hall to him.

"I'm going to close the door. You stay here. Nobody in, understand? Nobody at all. *Especially* doctors."

"Yes, sir." Kinger was huge. It was an all-purpose description. His face looked carved, his shoulders like sacks of concrete. He could close his fingers completely around a normal man's skull. Only a few of his friends knew he was an excellent chess player and that he raised prize Siamese cats.

"Good," Tagg said. He stepped back in and shut the door.

Higgins moaned. Gibberish bubbled on his lips. Tagg was quite familiar with his psych profile. It wouldn't take much.

He reached into the inner pocket of his coat and took out a neat leather case.

No, it wouldn't take much at all.

* * *

Tower discovered that the thicket of scrub was only about fifteen yards from Foster's house, down in the wash, but the exit point was probably invisible even in broad daylight. The house sat on a rise, which dipped both front and back—toward the beach in one direction and in the other, down into a wash protected from the wind and covered with shrubs, small trees, and thick stands of tough grass. He'd noticed the wash before but had never walked in it. Even in bright sunlight, it wasn't an inviting place. Tower doubted that DIA had placed a sentry within the wash area; the location commanded only a view of the back of the house itself. If there were an outside man, he'd most likely be placed higher up, probably just off the road, where his sight lines could cover the whole beach.

Even that was a dubious proposition, however. He had no idea what Foster might have told the small army that had invaded his house; or for that matter, if he'd had a chance to tell them anything.

But if Tower had been doing the spotting, he wouldn't have left an outside man at all. They already knew he might find the watcher; he'd done so before and given them a crippled Higgins for their trouble. The safe thing was to leave a man inside the house. After all, they would reason that the house was his objective. Make him come to them.

He was quite certain that that's what they'd done. It felt right. And at that moment, he had little to go on but his feelings. Branches pulled gently at his darksuit, but the slickly surfaced fabric offered them little purchase. Step by step, he worked his way closer, grateful for the continuous churning of the surf and the rising wind.

He reached the back wall of the house, which abutted the upper lip of the wash, without incident and crouched there, leaning against the rough wooden shingles that protected the walls. The roar of the wind was quieter here, although errant clouds of sand spit and rattled around the corner with a gritty, scratching sound.

Okay, now what?

His first instinct was to somehow lure the inside guard out of the house, as he'd done with the sentry in the car at his own place, but he quickly shelved the idea. The man would be alert, his head full of tales about the fates of his earlier colleagues. He would be determined that the same thing wouldn't befall him. Further, the sentry would no doubt have communications capability; he might, in fact, be on some sort of dead-man system, where if he fell out of touch at all, an alarm would bring a full team to the site. In fact, the more Tower thought about that, the more likely it seemed. It complicated his task even further.

So what's the answer, buddy? Pretend you're Link; what would he do? How would the old bear crack this particular nut?

The wind from the shore rose to a sudden, howling shriek. It reminded him of another wind in another place, and he smiled. They said you couldn't teach an old dog new tricks, but sometimes, if the tricks were old enough, they became new again. He shucked out of the backpack, let if fall softly to the sand, and opened it. It took a moment to find what he needed, and once again, he blessed whatever nostalgic impulse had kept that box hidden away in his bedroom closet.

Or maybe I knew. Maybe I always knew.

Dot Kelly's feet ached. Nothing new; after years of nursing, she felt lucky the intermittent pains weren't worse than they were. Even so, it was nice to laze in the sun, relax on the concrete bench like some kind of lizard, and drift in the soft hum of the afternoon. She was glad the weather was back to normal; the storm the night before had been wild and frightening, weather very unlike the usual San Francisco pattern. She remembered standing in the window of her living room, looking down on the lights of the Castro; fog had rolled swiftly over Twin Peaks by dusk, turning the streetlamps below into fuzzy yellow globes. Then the wind had begun to rise, tearing the fog to shreds, and as the last light went out of the world, the huge, rolling thunderheads had come, roaring and spitting lightning. The storm had gone on for several hours; when it had finally passed overhead, tearing its way across the Bay to Oakland and the outer towns beyond, she had been saddened to see that the big pine just beyond the corner of her building had lost several branches. She clicked her tongue against her teeth at the memory; the pine had been huge and old and beautiful. It was a shame. . . .

"Miss? Excuse me, miss?"

"Hum? I'm sorry, what?"

She looked up into the earnest face of the lady from Indiana who was so proud of her Hoosier origins.

"I didn't mean to bother—well, do you live in San Francisco? Are you a *native?*"

Kelly couldn't help smiling. The way the Hoosier lady said it, the word sounded like something exotic, almost bizarre. "Yes, I live in the city. Is something wrong?"

"Oh, no. We're just visiting . . ."

Oh, really?

"And, well, Frank here, he was wondering about those kids."

Kelly looked over her shoulder again, just to make sure the Frisboarder hadn't done something particularly outrageous, but things seemed calm enough.

"What about them?" Kelly asked equably.

"What are they doing? How do they glide around like that? Our son Jack has a skateboard at home—you know how kids are—but those little round things, they don't even have wheels."

"Frisboards," Kelly said. "Of course they don't."

"By the way"—the woman stuck out her hand—"my name's Janice. Janice Pelkington, and this here's Frank. We're from Indiana. That's what my shirt means: Hoosiers. People from Indiana are Hoosiers."

"Dot Kelly. I'm pleased to meet you, Janice, Frank. Welcome to San Francisco. Are you having fun?"

"Oh, yes, this is our first time. We've always wanted to—haven't we, Frank?—but we didn't think we could afford—oh, you don't want to hear that, do you? No, we love San Francisco.''

Frank had said not one word, not even when he'd touched Kelly's hand lightly with dry fingertips, then stepped away to let Janice do the talking.

''I'm glad to hear it. What was it you wanted to know? About the kids?''

Janice glanced at one boy, no older than thirteen, who had swooped completely across the diameter of the bowl, moving so fast his long blond hair streamed out behind him like a banner. He rode up the lip and continued on into a double backflip that brought applause from a few spectators. The Hoosier lady said, ''How do they do it?''

Kelly had to rummage her memories for a moment. She'd read some articles in the *Chron* about this latest fad and tried to recall what little she could of the details.

''Superconductors,''she said at last. ''Those round, Frisbee-shaped disks they stand on have superconductors in them. And the bowl, there, is one huge magnet. I think they repel each other somehow, like when you push two magnets together.''

''Oh,'' Janice Pelkington said, two fingers across her lips. ''It looks so dangerous.''

Kelly laughed. ''They know what they're doing. You know kids.''

Both women chuckled softly. Janice's eyes widened once again as a truly bizarre costume flashed by: flat black body suit decorated with bright chrome chains, a heavily padded codpiece that made the young man who wore it seem deformed, and a headdress in which his pure white hair was interwoven with a fantastic crown of rhinestones, sequins, and peacock feathers. His face was covered with a blank silver mask, but his gray-blue eyes seemed full of laughter.

''Well,'' Janice said. ''It was nice talking to you.''

Kelly nodded. ''You have a good time, now.''

The Pelkingtons wandered away, seeking other San Francisco oddities with which to regale their unbelieving friends back home in Indiana, and Kelly settled back on her bench. Her feet felt somewhat better.

It was almost four o'clock. He's said between four and five.

A fool, Dot Kelly.

We'll see.

It wasn't quite a hurricane—would that be *typhoon,* since it was coming out of the Pacific?—but it seemed close enough that Tower wondered if his plan were moot, if he'd gain entrance only to find Foster's house collapsing around his ears. Two houses destroyed in less than a week; that would be something, wouldn't it? The wind had become a continuous banshee choir; it reminded him of an earlier time, in Manila, when the wind shrieked a similar hysteria, and he and Foster had barely accomplished their mission and made it out before the whole damned island shut down.

He glanced at the icepick in his hand; it was the electronic equivalent of an old-fashioned lock pick, but it was designed to open different doors. Buffeted and distracted by the storm, it had taken him quite a while to find the comm-power pipe, which extended in a short curve from the wall of the house into the ground, where it joined the buried cable that served this whole area. It seemed that Foster had armored the pipe somehow, so that Tower had further torn his already ragged palms breaking into it. Luckily, despite the heavier than usual insulation, one of the joints near the wall had corroded halfway through, from the salt in the air, he supposed.

The tiny display screen on the icepick tossed up a cheerful cloud of random static; the light from the screen wasn't enough to see by, but he didn't need vision. It took him about ten seconds to attach the leads from the pick to the cable he'd exposed. Then, working from touch and memory, he began to insulate himself into the low-level data stream generated by the house computer. After a minute or so he grinned: What had Foster said? He wouldn't have gotten past beer.

The old skills were coming back. He still remembered how to virus a chain of seeker commands. And the house machine wasn't as well protected as that Philippine Army computer they'd turned into schizophrenic mush that long ago night in another typhoon.

The icepick uttered a soft beep, almost inaudible in the howling of the storm. The screen glowed green. Tower repacked the little machine and pushed his backpack as close to the house as he could. He touched the commando knife that rested on his forearm in a quick-drop sheath; another souvenir. Then he began to work his way to the wall of glass that dominated the back of the house, out into the full force of the gale.

Calvin Teeters sat at the oak kitchen table inside Lincoln Foster's house and watched the storm build toward complete insanity. It made him nervous. He was a California boy and counted himself lucky to have gotten the San Francisco station, but he didn't think much of this duty. Colonel Tagg, for instance: A big, bumbling slob if he'd ever seen one, but he came in a flurry of Code High Blue bulletins with his phalanx of psycho killers—Cal knew what Henry Higgins was the moment he laid eyes on him—and just . . . took over. Cal didn't quite know what had gone on here—nobody had seen fit to tell him, and when he asked, one of Tagg's goons had told him he didn't have a need to know—and this stake-out made him uneasy.

He was, in the parlance of the trade, a street man. Usually he spent his time "putting people in the box," another bit of jargon that meant covering a target so thoroughly he couldn't break wind without it being recorded, weighed, and measured by at least two of Cal's regular team. He sure as hell hadn't volunteered for this, but since he was the only stake-out expert handy when Tagg had blown into the office earlier in the day, he'd gotten himself drafted.

"You just keep your ass inside that house, and if the target so much as shows the tip of his little finger, you hit the panic button. You got that?" Tagg had been quite emphatic, even though he refused to look Cal in the face.

The panic button. He didn't like that setup, either. The briefcase was only a couple of feet away, resting on the table beyond his empty mug of coffee. He thought about going into the kitchen and putting another pot on to brew but decided to wait. He'd been here all day, not doing much but sitting right at this table and slurping down cup after cup, and if he wasn't careful, the acid would eat a hole right through his stomach lining. Usually he took a canister of fruit juice with him on assignments like this, but Tagg hadn't given him enough time, and he felt a certain ghoulish distaste about raiding the refrigerator.

Which was another thing. He hadn't missed the long swipe of blood, almost like some Chinese ideograph, which disfigured the smoothwhite tile of the kitchen floor. What kind of shit had gone down here, anyway? It had been all over when they brought him in, and Tagg—the bastard—hadn't been in a talkative mood. "Just sit your ass down and stay buttoned."

Usually he had some idea of the point of the mission, but not this time. *And that was bullshit too, wasn't it?* He'd been around the block a couple of times; he was a player, and this whole setup smelled like dead fish rotting on a beach. They hadn't told him anything, but he had a feeling. When you want to trap a tiger, you bait with a goat. And that's exactly what he felt like—a goat.

The briefcase held a transmitter-receiver relay, which picked up signals from a biomonitor strapped around his left wrist. If he got himself killed somehow, the monitor would know, and the relay would send the information somewhere else. Likewise, if he and the briefcase got separated by a more than twenty yards or so, a similar alarm would be transmitted. It was an old gag but effective. He wondered if the target knew anything about it. He sure as hell didn't know anything about the target, beyond the head-and-shoulders holo cube he'd been given earlier.

In the cube, the man looked sick. His eyes were closed, and there were deep red scars on his face. He'd seen things like that before, and they'd always turned

his stomach. The Russkies called it reorientation, and
the Americans preferred deep debriefing, but whatever
slick gloss you put on it, it was still torture. This man
looked like he'd been tortured, long and strenuously,
and Cal wondered how anybody who'd gone through
that could still be a threat.

Maybe it was a long time ago, he decided. The guy
had gotten all recovered and decided to take a little
revenge. But that didn't sound right, either; men who
went through deep debriefing didn't usually recover.

He jumped slightly as a particularly vicious gust of
wind took hold of the whole back of the house and
rattled the glass like a drum. Eight o'clock.

He hoped he wouldn't have to spend the night.

The thought had barely subsided when the kitchen,
where only a single dim glowstrip illuminated the part
of the counter where the coffee maker sat, exploded in
a hard yellow glare.

The band started playing an instant later.

Higgins's eyes bulged. His flesh had turned a doughy
gray color, like putty; the muscles beneath the skin
and along his neck stood out like thin ropes, yanking
his lips into an extended rictus that exposed his teeth
in a death grin. He made small grunting noises—huh
uh! huh *uh!*—which Tagg ignored.

The colonel carefully applied another derm to the
area next to Higgins's carotid artery. This derm was
pink; there were others, many others, of all different
colors, so that Higgins looked as if he were suffering
from some fantasy skin disease; clown cancer, perhaps, or polychromatic psoriasis. The air in the room
was rank with the sour smell of Higgins's sweat. Tagg,
plagued with a surprisingly fastidious olfactory sense,
managed to ignore that, as well.

A moment after he applied the pink derm, a host of
muscular ticks began to jump on Higgins's face. It
looked as if he were being assaulted by hundreds of
tiny, invisible fish hooks. The harsh sounds he'd been
uttering ceased. His eyelids snapped shut, then opened

again; the surface of his corneas seemed dry, like polished glass. A doll's eyeballs.

Tagg leaned close and whispered a few words in Higgins's ear: *"Find the power, burn the tower."*

Higgins moaned; it began low and rose swiftly into a whine, then a thin, screaming squeal, like fingers dragged across a chalkboard. Tagg smiled benignly. It was going well.

He wondered if he would have to return for a second session, but decided that, as nicely as Higgins was responding, it probably wouldn't be necessary. That was one of the advantages of full familiarity with the psych profiles: If you decided to tip a man the rest of the way into the darkest abyss of madness, you knew all the switches to flip, all the neural plugs to pull. And it helped that Higgins was pretty well gone to start with; Tagg had uses for a man who really *enjoyed* deep debriefing, but Higgins was nearing the outer limits of even that necessary skill. He would have been sacrificed soon anyway; retired on a good pension and, sooner or later, put quietly to sleep, like a mad dog.

Yet even mad dogs have their uses, Tagg reflected. Higgins would recover physically, but he would have to retire. The DIA wasn't a charitable organization and had no place for agents missing large parts of their bodies. No doubt the people here would rig up an excellent prosthesis; after all, the Agency would pay, and in such cases the pockets were very deep. Within a week or so—if the electrical stimulation designed to speed healing worked, and the doctors seemed to think it would—Higgins would be up and about, and a week beyond that, he'd most likely walk out of the hospital, to consider his options in retirement.

Except that Tagg had decided to spare him all that. The colonel had promises to keep and interests that were separate from those of the DIA and, he assumed, the government of the United States. It just so happened that those interests coincided at the moment, so he was happy to carry out his orders. But such might not always be the case, and a careful man made plans for such a contingency.

His orders were to take Tower alive.

Many people wished to know what Tower knew. But the man was so slippery; they'd missed him at his own place and again at Lincoln Foster's house, which was itself a whole other, touchy mess. Nevertheless, his orders remained, and he certainly would like to put his hands on the target.

As to the part of taking him alive or, perhaps, keeping him in that condition, well . . .

A prudent man planned ahead, and used whatever tools came to hand.

He added another derm and Higgins screamed without sound. It was an interesting effect. As he stood there, one finger resting lightly on his right cheek, Colonel Tagg smiled. In an odd way—for he was not usually a prideful man—he wished he could invite Kinger in to observe. The man might learn something, watching a true artist at work.

Cal Teeters stood there with his mouth hanging open. He felt like a pure, hundred-proof idiot. At first, he'd leaped off his chair like a cat with its tail on the stove, one hand clawing for the Club under his coat. Jumpy as a bat in a bandbox he'd been, and then the kitchen had gone crazy.

Now he grinned. Something to do with the storm, he supposed. He hadn't thought to find one of these sophisticated setups out here in the boonies, in the deserted house on the beach, but whoever lived here had spared no expense. He'd only had his own version installed three years ago, although Agnes—Aggie, his wife—had bitched about getting one ever since she'd heard about it. Aggie wasn't much for doing the groceries; she was always griping about having to load up the car and lug all that stuff around. Now she just loved her new holographic system—everything automated including delivery, right in the comfort of your own home, just like the ads said.

Maybe the storm had caused a power surge or a short; something like that. As he watched, an enormous pig tap danced across the kitchen floor, right up to him, grunt-snorting something about hams; and here came a fizzing beer bottle, big as a chimpanzee.

Feeling faintly silly, he stepped into the kitchen, trying to find the power shutoff. The house computer terminal should be somewhere around here.

But five minutes later he still hadn't found it. Now his half-foolish, half-amused mood was fading; sure, anything to break the monotony, but this was ridiculous. The kitchen was full of singing, shouting, capering shapes, pop bottles and loads of laundry and quartets of harmonizing chickens, their flesh naked and bony.

"*God damn it.*" The noise had overridden the storm, and the cavorting shapes were beginning to confuse him. Every time he thought he'd found the computer terminal it would turn out to be an oven door or the controls of the stovetop. The air was thick with electronic specters, and his ears rang with their wild whoops.

"*Damn.*"

Something that looked like a gigantic parade float, something from the Rose Bowl, maybe, was growling out of the wall, and from it, men dressed in black threw wads of lettuce, piles of green beans, and carrots. Insanity! Cal spun slowly around, nauseated with the riotous noise, and disoriented by the bounding, cackling shadows. He didn't hear the faint tinkle of glass breaking, and when one of the black men stepped right up to him and popped him hard under the jaw, he was absolutely, totally, *completely* surprised.

Tower blew on his knuckles. It felt like he'd broken the middle one. There was a purplish patch of swelling there, and the flesh was tender to the touch. Stupid. He knew better than to slug a guy on the jawbone with his unprotected hand. But it had worked.

He looked down at Cal Teeters, who sprawled limply on the kitchen floor next to a long swoop of dried blood.

Whose blood? Dead?

He stared at Teeters for several seconds, his eyes

narrow and hard. He knew what he should do next; that was SOP, too. But something in him kept him from simply murdering the unconscious man; finally he sighed and turned away.

He opened the briefcase carefully; it didn't appear to be trapped, but you never could tell. The receiver-transmitter inside was nothing unexpected—standard, off-the-shelf issue. He was pleased to see that it looked like a rush job—just slammed in there as if somebody had been in a hurry; he decided there were probably no surprises. He was familiar enough with the setup. He returned to the kitchen and got a good hold under Cal's armpits and dragged him into the dining area, cursing at what that did to his wrecked hands, and got him more or less upright. Inside his coat, he found the neat leather case and fingered out a derm. Then he checked the man's wallet. Another DIA agent; the card read San Francisco station. Local boy, probably pulled in on an emergency basis.

Well, Mr. Calvin Teeters, he thought, *you struck out tonight. Sorry about that.*

As the derm took effect, Cal seemed to melt inside his skin. He'd be out for a while, but he would wake up eventually, which hadn't been Josh's first intention. He wondered if Cal had even seen him and decided probably not. The man's eyes had rolled once, totally shocked, just after the punch and before his brain decided to take a rest, although his body was already falling.

"Sweet dreams," Tower said softly, and he patted the man on his cheek. He moved the briefcase over close to him, checked to make sure the relay appeared to be functioning properly, and saw the holo cube.

He pulled it out and looked at it. He didn't remember anybody taking his picture, but that didn't mean anything. Half the time of his recovery he'd been in a drug-fogged haze; the days had slid by without notice and visitors had been only shadows on darker shadows.

The man in the cube looked like a stranger: those terrible scars, the yellowed flesh. But it was him all right; judging from his condition in the holo, it had been taken not long after the accident.

"Here you go, Cal," he said, and he tossed the cube onto his lap. He paused, then retrieved the drug kit and put it into a Velcro-sealed pocket on the thigh of his darksuit. Things like that had a way of coming in handy, and you never knew . . .

He left Cal sleeping soundly on his chair and the house rocking and rolling around him in the grip of the meteorological slam dance outside. He headed toward Foster's office, looking for his computer, looking for answers.

Chapter Eight

Are they after me?

The thought struck Tower so suddenly, and with such force, that he paused in the long hallway leading to Foster's office and simply nodded out on a hideous painting of George Washington throwing the eternal dollar across the Delaware. Link had very pronounced and very awful taste in art, but Tower wasn't seeing the picture before his nose. Instead, he saw the medium-sized assault force that had come out of the sea with such terrible abruptness.

Why send an army after me?

Maybe he had it all ass backward. They knew his condition; that bozo Tagg had no doubt pored all over his hospital records. It wasn't necessary to send a full-scale tac company after a man barely recovered from total invalidism.

Maybe it was Link, after all.

That made more sense, a hell of a lot more. Tagg had access to old DIA files on Foster and perhaps even more current appraisals, if Foster still had contacts with DIA, and he said he did. They would have known to bring guns, lots of them, if it were Foster they wanted.

But did they know Tower was here when they came swooping down? Or had they come for Foster? And if so, why? *Why come for Link?*

His head began to throb softly. There was so much he didn't know. Even his slowly returning instincts were no good without some facts to chew on. At the moment, all he knew for *certain* was that a high-level coverup was going on about the weird accident that had claimed his wife and unborn son and that somehow a shadowy company in Denver called Condor looked to be involved. But how would DIA know about it? And why would they be a party to anything so brazen as openly attacking civilians?

He rubbed his forehead over the spot where the ache was the worst; he kept going round and round and had no idea where things might eventually stop. There were connections and linkages he hadn't even thought about yet—if only he could *remember*. But the wild night when he'd destroyed his own computers and nearly wrecked his home was still a blank. Thank God Foster had come along when he did. He'd obviously been out of his mind, no telling what he might have done later. Maybe gotten up, drunk a case of Budweiser, and turned the house into his own funeral pyre.

But wasn't that exactly what Higgins and the rest of the hit team had in mind?

Round and round, round and round . . .

He shook himself like a dog coming up out of a lake. No use torturing himself when maybe he could find some answers right down the hallway.

"Ugly picture," he remarked softly. "*Very* ugly picture."

The headache wouldn't go away.

Rather than mess around with whatever ungodly protections Foster had programmed into his computer operating system, Tower decided on a different approach. He went back into the storm—now a frenzy of solid, sheeting water—and retrieved his pack. He set it on the seat of Foster's desk chair and took out the icepick. It took him a few moments to separate the tangled connector cords with which the various machines had been crosswired. The machines themselves, the central processing units, were quite small, perhaps half the size of a brick. Foster had seven of them, each about equal in power to an old-style supercomputer from half a century earlier. It was an enormous amount of data-processing capability, much larger than Tower's own setup had been. Uneasily, he wondered just what sort of business Foster had been conducting on the side.

But there was a way into even a behemoth like this. The high-temperature superconducting cables that joined the individual machines could be breached with the icepick, if you knew what you were doing. Instead of firing up the whole network, you attacked the problem a machine at a time; the first computer in the linkage usually controlled the security system for all of them. The trick was to bypass that machine.

Carefully, Tower attached his icepick, sent an infinitesimal current down the wire—and froze. Sweat popped out on his forehead; his heart slammed three times—bip bip *bip!*—in his rib cage; and the headache screeched right into overdrive.

Something was wired into the system that shouldn't have been. That drew an inordinate amount of power, that was in the wrong place, that was *bad*. He could taste the *badness*—a sour, brassy flavor in his mouth—and his stomach slowly, lazily, went into a double backflip.

Had he triggered it?

Unless it was on some kind of timer, he hadn't. The proof was simple: He was still here.

He'd seen setups like this before. He had, in fact, wired up a few of them. Somewhere, in one of the monitor cases, or underneath a touchpad, or even in the shielded boxes of the computers themselves, was a tiny fist of explosive—hyperplastique, maybe, or one of the newly tailored coal-tar derivatives.

The simple act of naming the device in his own mind freed his muscles from the spasm that had locked them tighter than a streetwalker's heart. Slowly, he forced his fingers to move; the tiny muscles there wanted to shake, but he bit his lip and tried to think of those hands as belonging to somebody else. Slow and easy, hell yes: One little mistake and old Josh becomes hamburger pizza on the wall of Link Foster's nice computer room.

He'd stopped breathing entirely; sweat rolled into

his eyes, making the thin cable and the icepick shift and blur, but he couldn't spare enough movement to wipe it away. He was working mostly by touch anyway; it was just a matter of gently pulling the connector wires away from the main cable and doing it so that the *thing* lurking somewhere in the system didn't get grumpy and decide to special delivery his head to Borneo.

There.

His chest expanded in one single, mighty gulp. Stars flickered for a moment behind his eyes. He breathed out, long and slow, and breathed in again, savoring the cool glow. Finally he wiped his face on his sleeve; sweat glazed the fabric from wrist to elbow.

The headache was gone—and he was relieved to find that he didn't need to change his underwear. *Tougher than you thought, old bird.*

But that was a lie, wasn't it?

Not tough. Just lucky, this time. Just lucky.

He didn't waste time trying to locate the bomb. He wasn't even sure there *was* a bomb; but that signal had been hard to dispute. Something that *shouldn't* be in there sure as hell was; and he wasn't about to mess with it. Maybe if he'd had a lot of time and a lot more equipment, he might have thought about playing grab the brass ring; but he had an unconscious DIA agent sprawled in the kitchen, a pisser of storm raging outside, and a whole lot of disconnected bullshit that didn't seem to add up to anything except trouble. It was time to bail out.

He tiptoed backwards out of the room, feeling both bone-scared and sheepish, and gently shut the door. One more mystery for the pot: Who had wired a bomb into Foster's computer system? Foster? The DIA? Somebody else?

Who or whatever, he wouldn't be able to get a look at his friend's files. That was for sure; Foster's machine was as far out of his reach as his own ruined system.

And wasn't that a coincidence?

How about it, pard? How do you like them *apples?*
It was enough to make a man downright paranoid.

He went out into the night as carefully as he could;
Cal Teeters didn't note his passing, even though he
paused by the unconscious man and patted him lightly
on the cheek. "I was lucky tonight," he told him
softly. "And so were you."

Then he stepped off the back veranda and made his
way around the house and down into the wash. He
followed the wash north until the ground began to rise
and flatten out. Here he felt the full fury of the storm—
the shrubs and low trees that had given him some protection earlier petered away. He crept on slowly
through the springy beach grass, which was bent almost horizontal from the force of the wind.

The rain was driving nearly sideways; drifts of water
pounded into him, and the wind and darkness made
him feel as if he'd fallen into some wild, screaming
world of fantasy and horror. Surprisingly, he was able
to see some distance down the beach when lightning
illuminated the line of surf in fitful, strobing flashes.
There was no fog; the ceaseless wind wouldn't permit
it. He licked his lips and tasted salt; this close to the
ocean, the blasts ripped off the top of the boiling surf
and flung it at him like a circus knife thrower.

He was soaked through—his darksuit had remained
waterproof, but spray had leaked in at the neck—when
he finally reached the road about a mile and a half
upcountry from Foster's place. The region here was
rocky and barren, from the road itself up into a low,
rounded range of hills; there was no sign of human
habitation. His recollections of the area were hazy, but
he thought that if he stuck with the highway, he would
eventually come to the small crossroads of Los Pinos.
Shivering, he stepped off the crest of the road and began to parallel it, clumping through sliding mud and
torn brush, and after two hours, he found his memory
was correct.

The village was dark and deserted except for a small

diner with a light showing dimly behind partly drawn blinds. He walked up to the door and banged on it.

Something rattled the door; then he heard the metallic rasp of a key being pushed into the ancient round lock. The door opened. The man behind the door was drunk as a busted pisspot; his ragged gray beard was stiff with dried food, and his nose looked like a tomato that had done hard time on a bad piece of road. He was nearly bald. He wore bibbed overalls without a shirt, and he said, "Git you ass inside, you fool. You want to get us both drownded?"

"Name's Fogarty," the old codger grunted as he slammed the door in the teeth of the gale. He turned around; his bright blue eyes flashed disconcertingly. Drunk he might be, Tower warned himself, but he wasn't blathering yet. "You got a name, mister? Or you just out for a little evening stroll?"

"Smith," Tower said. "John Smith." There was no reason to give his real name; it couldn't help, and it might even be harmful for this creaky geezer.

Fogarty cackled, revealing a toothy vista that reminded Tower of Lebanon after a particularly vicious raid. Some of the teeth were gone; others were black and rotted almost to Fogarty's gum line. In a time when medical care was available to all, this told Tower something about the man: He was one of the hermits, the twenty-first-century dropouts. There was a lot of that on the North Coast.

"John Smith, huh? Not a real common name, is it?" Fogarty lurched away from the door; he had a huge steel ring full of keys, which he carefully placed in a pocket of his overalls. He cackled again as he stomped up to the round table where Tower was shrugging of his backpack and shaking his head, sending water droplets flying.

The diner was about fifteen by thirty feet; opposite the door ran a counter with a cracked Formica top, fronted by a line of seven round, chrome pedestal stools. The red plastic cushions of the stools were patched with peeling duct tape, beneath which peeped straggled hanks of gray stuffing.

The front of the diner was glass windows overlooking booths in no better shape than the stools at the counter; the windows were covered with thick blinds, of a kind Tower hadn't seen since he was a little boy. Some of the slats were missing; others were chipped and yellowed by age—like Fogarty's teeth. Two large circular tables occupied the space between the booths and the counter; ancient plastic Tiffany lampshades dangled on tarnished chains from the ceiling over each table. One of these was lit, casting a malign, brassy glow on the full bottle of Dewars White Label that rested next to a cheap restaurant water glass and a black rubber dishpan full of ice. Next to the full bottle was an empty one. Fogarty had prepared well for the storm.

The old man wore lace-up hunting boots that came to his knees; he'd stuffed the bottoms of his pants legs into the boots, which gave him a slightly rakish, almost martial air. He seated himself, belched a long sigh that sent Tower back a step, and grabbed the bottle.

"You want a taste, glasses is in back of the counter. I ain't no waitress."

Tower turned away, trying to hide the grin that threatened to break out on his face. Any port in the storm, and he'd been in worse; Fogarty might need a bath, but his preference in booze was just fine. Tower found a tray of glasses and held one up to the light.

"Ain't nothing on there gonna kill you, boy. If there is, the scotch will kill *it.*" Fogarty seemed to find this hilarious; he cackled for almost a minute and finished up wheezing and spluttering. Tower had sense enough to whack the old fart on his back; after a moment, Fogarty recovered.

He poured Tower's glass half full and topped off his own. "No ice?"

Tower shook his head.

"I thank you, boy."

"What for?"

"I'm an old man. I get to coughing like that, people just naturally think they got to do something for me. But I don't need anything *done* for me, you understand?" His blue eyes glittered suddenly.

Tower shrugged. "Didn't think so," he said.

"Good. So's we understand each other. You running from the police, boy?"

Tower had settled on the chair opposite the old man. Every bone in his body ached, and the warmth of the diner had yet to penetrate much into his chilled skin. But the first taste of scotch had been like a dream, and Fogarty's question snapped his head up. "What?"

"You deaf? I said, are the police after you?"

"No."

Fogarty glared at him. "Wouldn't make no difference to me. Can't turn a man away in a storm. Wouldn't be human, a man do a thing like that. But you don't look like the robbing kind. Not that there's much here to steal—you can see that."

"Thanks for letting me in. And for the scotch."

"No matter," Fogarty said vaguely. He waved one hand. "Don't like to drink alone, anyhow."

Tower nodded. "You got a comm unit here?"

Two sharp lines appeared in the mass of wrinkles on Fogarty's forehead. *"Comm unit?* You mean, *telephone?"*

"Uh, yes."

"Got one of those. Don't hold with that fancy comm unit bullshit. Old phone works just fine for me. It's back in the back, there." He waved again, not in any particular direction, but Tower nodded.

"Can I use it?"

"You go right ahead. Takes a ten-dollar piece."

That was right. Once you'd had to put money in phones. Where had Fogarty gotten an antique like that? Then he understood: Fogarty and the phone had grown old together, just like this diner.

"I don't have a dollar. Just a credit chip."

"Good God, Smith, you some kind of panhandler?"

"I'm sorry."

Fogarty unleashed another of his glares, but this time Tower didn't believe it. He was starting to like the old geezer—which was about right: Fogarty here might be the only person he knew in the whole world who was both still alive and not trying to kill him. Except . . .

"Here." Fogarty fished in the overalls pocket on his chest and came up with a small silvery coin. "I'll just pull it out later. I own that phone anyway."

"I'll pay you back."

Fogarty swallowed a healthy slug of his drink and smacked his lips. "With your credit chip? I suppose. You don't have to, though."

"Sure I do."

The old man nodded. "Take your time. This here scotch ain't going no place at all. And if it does, I got more."

This time Tower couldn't hide his grin.

"Back there" was behind the counter and beyond a pair of grease-stained swinging doors that groaned evilly when he shoved them aside. The glass inserts in the doors were so smudged by smoke and the ghosts of prehistoric French fries that he could barely see through them; but they admitted enough light for him to find the old-fashioned Pacific-Toshiba wall phone hung just inside the kitchen.

Insert coins and wait for dial tone.

He hadn't read anything like that in years—decades. He looked down at the small shiny coin he held between thumb and finger.

Now what? Just who are you going to call, slick?

Nobody. There was nobody left. Nobody at all.

It was a horrible, empty, vacant feeling, and all of a sudden he stood on the edge of the pit and looked down, and he realized he was falling, falling.

The kitchen was a dark, humping, monstrous collection of looming shadows; even the sound of the storm seemed muffled. He stood there with his ten-dollar connection and riffled through a mental address book. Can't call Julia, no, she's (dead) not around anymore.

Nothing left of Foster but a bloody swipe (dead?) next to the refrigerator. And, to be real honest, there wasn't anybody else, was there? Hadn't been for a long time. Hadn't *ever* been. Certainly nothing from the bleak years, growing up in a succession of hell holes, trying to keep his bones safe from the maniac who called himself a father.

The time in the army, well, you didn't make a lot of close friends when your mutual interests were mostly murder and sabotage and death.

Can't even call home; sorry, that line is out of service, too. We cannot complete your call, sir, because that home has been burned to the ground. The number has been changed for eternity, please make a note. Besides, they don't want to talk to you anyway. Certainly not about your unborn son; we'll just keep *that* a secret until it's *too late*.

He inserted the silver coin into the round slot and listened to the bing-bong-*clink* down into the innards, and the receiver at his ear suddenly emitted a harsh, mechanical humming. The dial tone of childhood.

He inserted one shaky finger into the dial and wheeled it around. Whirr-click-click-click-click-click . . .

"Hello," he said at last. "May I speak to Nurse Kelly, please?"

It was almost five o'clock. The plaza was filled with the office rush, thousands of blank-faced commuters crowding down into the Metro underground, clutching briefcases and shopping bags, their eyes distant from their fellows, encased in that transparent membrane that insulated them from the sheer weight and mass of the city.

Maybe he isn't going to come, she thought suddenly.

She had purposely tried to keep her mind empty; after Carl's death, she had tried to lead what a philosopher called "the unexamined life," although the same philosopher had warned it wasn't a life worth living. Well . . . maybe. But all the examination and soul-searching and rummaging hadn't added worth after Carl's death. He had died a tiny, shrunken, pus-

filled caricature of a human being, and she saw the
same shadow hanging just behind the face of anybody
who still walked and breathed. Which was a consequence of her own daily routine: There might be fresh,
unsullied infants over in the maternity wards, but
mostly the hospital catered to death, and eventually,
even those little babies would have to return, to wards
named cancer and cardiovascular and . . .

Those weren't scabs she wanted to look under; she
already knew what was there. Better to take what
came, to accept; life was short and then you died. Try
to have a little fun along the way.

But there was something about Josh Tower that
warmed her. She saw people at their worst, sick and
frightened and dying. She had few illusions. Yet Tower
had strummed some chord deep inside; and though she
wasn't quite sure of the melody, his unexpected reap-
pearance in her life was welcome.

He'd said he was in trouble.

Nurse Kelly knew all about trouble.

But now he was almost late, and maybe it was time
to pack up and join the crowds heading home, although it had been nice sitting here, with the air fresh
and clean after the storm, watching the kids at play.

They'd killed his son. Maybe he saw it that way,
maybe not. It wasn't the hospital's fault—no, his wife
hadn't been far advanced, but if they'd known . . .

She had a sneaking idea why Julia Tower had not
registered the fetus. She'd listened to his nightmares;
she'd wanted to wake him up and tell him he couldn't
shoulder all the guilt, not *all* of it, but he wasn't ready
for that wisdom. She understood. It had taken her a
long time, too.

Was he ready now? Was *she?*

She glanced at the big antique clock planted on the
plaza atop an ornate wrought-iron base. Five on the
button.

Time to go. She folded up her thoughts and put them
away and stood up, vaguely wondering whether to walk
or take the Metro. It wasn't that far, and—

"Hello."

The black-clad Frisboarder with the silver mask stood next to her elbow like some incredible emissary from a dream.

"Yes?" He probably wanted spare credit. She fumbled in her purse.

"Nurse Kelly."

Startled, she paused. "That's my name, but I don't—"

"Yes you do," the Frisboarder said; one of his slate-blue eyes closed in a slow wink.

"Oh," she said. "I do, don't I?"

Colonel Tagg was monstrously angry, murderously so, ready to bite the heads off chickens or even small children, but nobody knew. He stared vaguely over Cal Teeters's left shoulder and tapped his yellow teeth with his thumbnail and made soft, mild humming noises; in general, he presented the impression that he was thinking about something else—and he was: He was thinking how good Cal Teeters would look with a red-hot butcher's knife jammed right up his ass and twisted around a couple of times.

"No," Cal was saying in a slow, fuzzed-out voice, still groggy from having been dermed into unconsciousness with his own drug case—*his own fucking drug case!*—"no, I don't remember the guy. I didn't even see him, for chrissakes!"

He seemed upset. That was good. Not near as upset as he would be when he found himself transferred to Nome or some malaria-infested post halfway up the Amazon, like those two fuckups posted on the road who hadn't seen anything either. But that was minor, that was only taking care of business, a little pop to keep the troops on their toes, and right now, *it wasn't the fucking point*.

The point was the Tower had waltzed in here clean as you please and made it back out again, after doing—what? That was the question, wasn't it? What had he been doing here?

Tagg wondered why Tower had come here. Tower's records said he and Foster were old army buddies. Maybe Foster was mixed up in this somehow, but he'd gotten clean away. He'd escaped the house in the first wave and left the blood of one of Tagg's agents on his kitchen floor to underline the point. Still, Foster wasn't on his list, and he didn't relish taking on the old wolf if he didn't have to. One of them was bad enough. He didn't need two former DIA killers to complicate his life.

It was all extremely unfortunate. His decision to let Higgins live was looking better all the time.

". . . all those grocery things, you had to be here, had to *see* that shit!"

Cal's voice was rising into an irritating whine. "Yes," Tagg said. "I understand all that, Sergeant Teeters."

Teeters stopped. He didn't look relieved by Tagg's acknowledgment. Good. Let the incompetent bastard sweat, before he got his *head handed to him on a plate*.

God, he *hated* this!

But all he said was, very mildly, "Be sure to get all this into your report, Teeters. It might be important."

"Yes, sir."

Well, it was done. Tower was still on the loose. He closed his eyes and envied Higgins. Higgins would get to do what *he* wanted to do but couldn't; although he planned to get some vicarious enjoyment from it. A *lot* of vicarious enjoyment.

Tagg turned to Kinger, who hovered over him like some worried mother gorilla. "Wrap it up," Tagg said tiredly. "Just wrap it up."

He lumbered out the back door onto the veranda, turned right, and was gone. Cal looked up at Kinger.

"Does he know what he's doing?"

Kinger's eyes were cold. They were both sergeants, but Kinger recognized dead meat when he saw it. "You can't begin to imagine," he said.

Tagg had pretty much called it right. It was two weeks to the day when Henry Higgins limped out of the hospital, his newly minted retirement papers in his back pocket and a hefty shot on his credit chip to ease the skid into a new life.

He'd shaken hands with the guy who'd taught him to use the new leg and had smiled loosely at the nurses when they'd wished him well. Then he'd gone out and rented an apartment. He moved in the same day, after a stop at a sporting-goods store, where he bought a sleeping bag, and at a corner convenience place, where he'd picked up paper plates, plastic forks and spoons, and some stuff for sandwiches.

He didn't need a knife. He already had one.

That night, the moon went full, and Henry Higgins went out.

He had no choice. The bright yellow worms were sucking on his brains.

Stevie Worthington had decided that tonight he was getting into Doris Glesser's pants. And why not? Everybody said she was a pure roll-over; all you had to do was apply the right stimulus.

So he'd gone to Silky Tarner and said, "I need some shit, boy. Some good shit."

Silky was sixteen going on a hundred; his pinched white face was already raddled with arcane knowledge. "Doris Glesser?" he said and exhaled a cloud of blue Marlboro smoke. Silky knew he'd get cancer, but it was mostly curable—the lung kind, anyway.

"I got a date, yeah," Stevie said. He was nervous. He didn't like Silky much—nobody liked Silky much, except for maybe Silky—but he brewed the best shit around. A regular Doctor Frankenstein of the chemical crowd.

"Doris Glesser likes seritonin analogs," Silky told him.

"That so? How do you know? You ever been there?"

Even a wide-legged piece of road like Doris Glesser wouldn't have anything to do with Silky. Silky grinned, a thin little slice of nasty.

"In a manner of speaking," he said. "Just take it from me—sero will do the trick."

"Okay. How much?"

Silky named a price that was probably too high, but he knew rut frenzy when it slobbered right in front of him. He was mildly surprised when Stevie didn't even try to haggle—but then his daddy owned Tarkington Hyundai-Chevrolet, so maybe he wouldn't have haggled anyway.

When the deal was done, and Stevie had carefully secreted three home-brewed capsules in his wallet, Silky said, "Good luck—but you won't need it."

"I hope so," Stevie said, and he left without saying another word, a worried look on his adolescent features.

"Up yours, asshole," Silky said; but he waited till Stevie was gone.

Twin Peaks was about the highest point in San Francisco, except for Mount Baldy, but you couldn't get up there because there were no roads. Besides, the Peaks were centrally located; during the day, tourists crowded the overlook beneath the forest of communications towers, taking pictures and munching candy bars and oohing and aahing over the incredible view.

It wasn't a bad view at night, either, with the city spread out below like a blanket of fireflies and diamonds. And it had one other advantage: The only people who came after dark, especially after midnight, were kids who had exactly the same things on their minds as Stevie Tarkington and Doris Glesser.

He thought that Doris had just about decided to let him. Silky hadn't steered him wrong. Old Doris wolfed down those sero caps like she hadn't eaten in a week, and now she was comfortably spooned up next to him, her black leather skirt hiked up on her fleshy white thighs, and she wasn't making any protests about what he was doing with his right hand.

He didn't know, but she would probably have let him even without the sero. Stevie was a catch, what with all the money his dad had, and he always drove a nice little sports model or convertible. She thought about riding down the street in Stevie's electro—not at night, like now, but maybe in the afternoon; cruise down

Lombard toward the bridge where everybody could see and know she was Stevie's girl.

Something told her it wasn't likely to happen, but fogged up in a dreamy embrace of the drugs, many things seemed possible. Yes, she decided, she would let him.

After all, there had been worse. At least he *acted* nice.

He saw the tiny electrocar parked over against the edge of the lookout, its front nuzzled up to the low stone wall, and he paused. He was hidden within the angular shadows of the biggest tower, a monster nearly five hundred yards tall, topped with a cluster of white dishes like huge metal flowers.

The tower (the power).

Glowing worms twisted behind his eyes like a nest of neon vipers. He could hear their hissing; the sound never stopped, though sometimes he thought the sound was something else. Sometimes he thought it was the sound of his brain frying.

Two figures in the 'tro. Kids. Kids making out, it looked like. Slowly, he scanned the rest of the big parking lot. It was deserted, a wide expanse gone smooth and gray in the light of the huge moon overhead.

It was very quiet.

The towers—tower, the *power* . . .

Henry Higgins took the commando knife out of its sheath and held the blade up. Moonlight dribbled across the flat of it, dripped and glinted from the razor line of its edge. He stared at the play of radiance on steel for almost a minute. His mouth hung open; it seemed that the whole world—great answers, the answers to everything—was in the knife.

The power.

He licked his lips. Then he closed his mouth.

Somewhere down below, the mournful whoop of a fire engine rose up into the darkness.

Higgins held the knife low, alongside the top of his pants leg, and began to walk across the lot. He clicked his tongue against the roof of his mouth—tic, tic—and it made a flat, insectlike sound—dry wings rasping against barbed joints, perhaps—on the night. But they were very busy, so Stevie Tarkington and Doris Glesser never saw him coming.

The tower!

They hardly screamed at all.

Chapter Nine

I am not a nice man, Josh thought, as he sipped his coffee on the tiny balcony perched on the back of Dot Kelly's apartment; he could hear her inside, clanking dishes and rattling silverware as she loaded the ancient Whirlpool dishwasher. He glanced at his watch; in another half hour she would be on her way to work, after a perfunctory peck on his cheek—he would smell her perfume and it would be, as always, a light dusting of rose—and he could get on with trying to figure out what to do next.

Down the hillside San Francisco was coming alive for the day; the Market Street Mall, stretching all the way from Castro to the Embarcadero, glittered in the dawn. He could feel the hump of Twin Peaks rising behind him, the sides of the big hill draped with condos packed as close as sardine crystals in a rocky can. He turned and stared; the towers looked sinister to him, a cluster of metal claws tearing at the sky. There had been a double murder up there recently, two kids ripped to pieces. The girl's head had been carefully placed on the rock wall next to their 'tro, her blank eyes frozen on the city below.

Ugly thoughts. He turned back.

Carl Kelly's blue terrycloth bathrobe fit him well; according to Kelly, they'd been of a size. He had a feeling he understood, on some level of feeling rather than knowledge, the shadowy underpinnings of her relationship with him. In how many other ways were he and Carl Kelly of a kind? He suspected quite a few.

That first night, after he'd kept his appointment with

her at the FrisBowl, he'd slept on her sofa, but somehow, on the second night, after quite a few stiff Dewars on the rocks, he'd ended up in her bed—and had
remained there since.

Not a nice man—no, not really. Julia had been dead
for only a few months, and already he'd been unfaithful. But unfaithful to what, a flat, nagging voice mumbled in his skull. She's (dead) not here anymore. How
can you be unfaithful to a (corpse) memory?

He hated the flat voice, but he couldn't silence it.
There was rent of a kind being paid here and many
ghosts to be laid to rest—hers and his both. He only
wished he felt more guilt. Then he wondered why he
wished that. He shook his head and drained the last
of his coffee.

"Josh? I'm going now."

"You have a good day, Dot. You want me to cook
tonight?"

She came out on the balcony, already in her coat,
her purse half open and hanging from her shoulder.
"There's stuff for spaghetti in the fridge, but if you
want to call down to Mei Wah's, I wouldn't mind Chinese."

He grinned. "Mu Shu pork? Spring rolls? Lemon
chicken?"

"Sounds fine to me," she said and bent over his
shoulder. He offered his cheek and felt her lips brush
his skin lightly. The dusty scent of roses—roses and
dust—filled his nostrils.

"I'll be home by five," she said, and then she was
gone.

His bare feet looked thin and white against the
weather-darkened planks of the balcony floor. There
was a rickety wrought-iron railing around the edge,
spotted with rust. An ancient black hibachi, equally
rusted, squatted in the opposite corner like some kind
of squared metallic pet; four green plastic planters,
filled with poppies and marigolds, hung from the top
of the railing.

Remember to water those today, he reminded himself.

The furniture was also redwood, worn but comfortable: two chairs, a side table, and a hassock. He placed his empty cup on the table, closed his eyes, and leaned his face up to catch the sun. The sky was blue and the air was clean; he could go on like this a long time.

But of course he couldn't.

Tagg would find him.

He knew he was exploiting her own tangled feelings about her dead husband; it was the only coin he had. But Tagg would find her, too.

He couldn't let that happen.

He was not a nice man—but he was not yet evil, either.

Kinger paused on the flat concrete stoop in front of the Coffee King Diner in Las Pinos. The glass door of the dilapidated building was so streaked and scratched it was no longer transparent, and it was further obscured by thirty years' worth of credit-card signs, Winston advertisements, and Lion's Club membership stickers. He noted that the most recent sticker was ten years old. The sun was a white-hot hole in the sky; he wished he hadn't worn the heavy wool shirt, but he wanted to fit in, and the uniform in Las Pinos seemed to be faded jeans, plaid shirts, and boots of every description. He wore a pair of Acme rough-outs—his own—that were at least comfortable.

Las Pinos was a miserable shithole, as far as he was concerned; nothing but a single two-lane blacktop road, rutted like an elephant's rib cage, connected it to the nearest civilization, which was Novato, twenty miles west cross-country. He'd had to drive in with a Shimatsu all-terrain vehicle; it used wheels, for God's sake, and his kidneys didn't feel like they'd ever be the same. But Tagg said everything had to be checked. He was armed with a sheriff's fake ID card. He'd spent the morning slogging door to door up the road from Foster's place, checking each house as he went. He showed the holo of Tower—and didn't he look like a corpse; oh yes, *that* got him a few strange glances—but no luck. The locals were an aberrant enough bunch: burnt-out cases from the late twentieth century, a geriatric hippie subculture, complete with long hair, body odor, bad plumbing, and an open distaste for anything that looked like law enforcement. He guessed they probably farmed marijuana as a cash crop; it was still illegal, mostly because the big drug companies didn't like home-brew competition for their own lines of mood adjusters.

At any rate, he had zilch to show for his efforts, his feet hurt, and all he wanted was a Bud and a double cheese with fries. He doubted Tower had come anywhere near this dipshit burg, not that night, not through that storm. But Tagg would wrap his balls around his neck if he didn't check it out, and Kinger liked the family jewels right where they were.

He pushed the door open. The air inside was thick with grease and a faint undercurrent of primordial, moldy wood. No doubt an ideal breeding spot for ptomaine, he thought sourly, and he trudged over to the counter. When he got his rear settled on the seat—too small, but they always were—his mood lightened. It felt good to get the load off his feet, and there was a plastic Budweiser sign—a genuine heirloom from the look of it, two huge Clydesdales trotting and trotting—on the wall next to the order slot that opened into the kitchen.

"Howdy, stranger."

He looked up at the waitress in surprise. Did people really talk that way, or was it some kind of local joke to let outsiders know what was what? But the woman didn't seem to have anything on her mind beyond taking his order. She was maybe sixty—young for this crowd—with stringy, washed-out gray hair pulled straight back from a broad forehead and held in place with a tortoise-shell barrette; he hadn't seen one like it since his grandma died thirty years before. Her blue eyes had been washed nearly transparent by age and sun; he suspected she wore glasses at home but not often. He got the feeling she'd already seen enough and didn't much care if she saw more. She was squeezed into a uniform that had once been white but now had a faint yellowish sheen. Pinned over one big floppy tit was a plastic tag with her name imprinted on a strip of red plastic that curled up at the end. He could still make out her name.

"Hello, Sandy," he said. "How you doing today?"

Her wide, flat features spread slightly; it might have been a grin. "Name's not Sandy. Borrowed her tag cause mine's busted. I'm Ethel, and as for the rest, I'm doing pretty good, mister. Oughtta be. I been at it thirty years." A grizzled trucker type with bulging tanned biceps shouted from the end of the counter, "Hey, Ethel, I'm starving down here," and she smiled faintly. "Nice talking, you know, but I'm in a kinda hurry, so if you made up your mind?" She licked the tip of a stubby pencil and looked at him.

"Sure. Burger and a cold Bud. Medium rare and cheese."

She nodded and turned away. Kinger watched her flabby cheeks rub together beneath the uniform and noticed for the first time she wore jeans underneath. And hiking boots with thick, dirty white socks. He sighed. There wasn't much they could do to beer. At least he hoped not.

"Hey, is that real strawberry pie, or you buy it from a factory somwhere?"

Ethel took his empty plate. The burger had been surprisingly good, the beer ice cold, and Kinger was feeling better than he had all day.

"Old man Fogarty bakes them himself," she told him. "Gets up in the middle of the night."

"I'll try a piece, then."

Ethel nodded and moved away. While she was cutting the pie, Kinger got the holo cube out of his pocket. When she returned, he showed it to her.

"You ever see this guy?"

She took the holo and held it up to the light, turning it this way and that, as if she were examining a possibly phony diamond for flaws.

"Looks sick," she said.

"My little brother," he told her. "He was in an

accident. Seemed to be doing okay, but then he wandered off from the hospital. Everybody's worried. He used to camp in this area; we thought he might have come up here. You know, if he's got amnesia or something, he might still go to a familiar place without knowing it.''

Ethel shook her head. ''That's a real shame, mister, but''—she handed back the cube—''I don't recall seeing him. Course, I see a lot of folks, but I'd remember him, I guess. All those scars—it must have been a real bad accident.''

Kinger nodded. ''Yeah, bad enough. You sure now? It would have been a couple of days ago, maybe at night, during the big storm.''

She smoothed her arthritic fingers across the front of her uniform. ''Oh, then I wouldn't have seen him. Place wasn't even open. Fogarty closed up the doors around four in the afternoon when it started to blow real bad. Sent me home, and I wasn't sorry to go. Hardly had half a dozen folks in all day, and none of them strangers.'' She leaned over the counter, her face confidential. ''To tell you the truth, I think the old fart just wanted a chance to get drunk.''

''Fogarty? Who is he? Own the place or something?''

''Yeah, last fifty years, I guess. Still does all the cooking. Lives in back; got a couple of rooms fixed up behind the kitchen.''

Kinger tried his pie. It was delicious—the berries sweet and juicy, and the baker hadn't messed it up with a lot of gummy filling. ''This is real good,'' he said, and she smiled. It made her look twenty years younger. She must have been a heller, he thought, surprised. He pushed the holo back across the counter.

''Do me a favor, kiddo. Just show that to him, would you? Maybe my brother stopped in or something. I mean, Fogarty would still have been here, even if he was closed, right?''

She nodded. ''There behind you at the round table, most likely with a bottle of scotch, be my guess.''

"Well, then, baby brother might have seen a light or something. Just check for me, would you?"

Kinger watched her bump the swinging doors aside with her flank as she disappeared into the kitchen. He sighed. A heller? What was he thinking of? This damned job was getting to him. Next thing he'd start to think this burg was picturesque. Sixty-year-old woman, for God's sake. He forked up another big chunk of pie. It sure was good. You couldn't find food like this in the city anymore. If you ever could. Methodically, chewing slowly, he finished the pie and thought about ordering another slice. He was a big man who knew he had to guard against getting even bigger, but what the hell. Probably already walked it off, and the afternoon still to go.

An old man clumped out of the kitchen and eyed the counter carefully, his gaze finally settling on Kinger with no evidence of pleasure. Fogarty, Kinger decided. He wore overalls and a ragged white T-shirt spotted with food stains. There were dried bits of something stuck in his scraggly beard, too. Kinger decided against a second piece of pie. The old man walked over to him, moving carefully, as if his joints gave him pain. He placed the holo cube on the counter in front of Kinger, who could smell his acrid aroma; it reminded him of an animal's den—a fox, or maybe a weasel.

"Now, what's this all about?"

Kinger gave him the spiel about his missing brother. Fogarty listened without interruption, his jaws moving slowly as he chewed on something. Kinger hoped it wasn't a wad of tobacco. Then he reconsidered. Perhaps it was something worse. Suddenly he regretted the first wedge of pie.

"So," he finished, "I'm just checking places he might have stumbled into."

Fogarty stopped chewing and stared at him silently. His blue eyes were flat, almost empty, like a country pond in winter, and Kinger realized the old man knew he was lying.

"Nope. Never saw him in my life. Sorry."

He began to shuffle away. Kinger felt sad. It was too bad, what would have to happen now.

Kinger walked across the hot, dusty pavement to where he'd parked the big four-wheel drive in front of Las Pinos's only gas and charging station, a GE-Shell that had seen better days. He climbed in, rolled up all the windows, clicked on the air conditioning, and fired up the comm unit. It was shielded, but no sense in taking chances. After two tries, he got through to Colonel Tagg. Tagg's voice sounded tinny and harried, and his last words were blurred by a static whine.

". . . be careful, but squeeze the old fart dry. You got that, Kinger? Dry as a bone."

"Yes, sir," Kinger said. "I'll take care of it." He switched off the comm unit and stared out the window, not really seeing anything. After a few minutes he started the ATV and drove slowly out of town. He looked for a good place to hide the vehicle—off the road, not too far away. He'd have to hike back in but after dark, when it would be cooler.

Dry as a bone, he thought. The old man was eighty if he was a day. There would be bones, all right. Probably more than one.

What a fuck of a job.

Tower didn't get dressed until almost ten o'clock. It seemed easier that way. At first, he hadn't bothered to get dressed at all. When Kelly had seen what kind of condition he was in—he'd tried to hide it, but on the second morning, after the night together, she'd awakened before him and gotten a *good* look—she'd tried to talk him into going back to the hospital. He hadn't been able to explain why that wouldn't work; but he had convinced her that he just needed a little rest.

"You're crazy, Josh."

"I can't explain, Dot—really, I can't. Maybe later."

"No."

He sighed. "Then I'll have to leave."

Something had warred in her then; he saw it in her eyes, the way they sought him, shifted away, then slid back again, as if he reminded her of something desired but terrible. "No. Don't do that. But you have to promise me some answers. When you feel ready."

He nodded. "I can—I do promise that, Dot."

"Then get back into bed."

"Why?"

"I'm the nurse. I say so, that's why."

Wordlessly, he'd crawled beneath the covers. He'd intended to do so anyway, after she'd gone to work.

"You're dehydrated, that sunburn, those cuts on your hands, the gash . . ." She shook her head. "You're a mess, Joshua." She left the bedroom. He heard her rummaging in the bathroom; after a moment she reappeared. "Here. Take these." She stretched out her hand. There were three capsules and two derms there.

"What is that stuff?"

"Antibiotics, a painkiller, an anti-inflammatory. You need more than rest, but if you won't see a doctor, these will help."

He felt absurdly grateful. She had no idea of the mess he was in, but he did, and he resolved to get away from her as soon as he could.

Now, he thought as he tossed the bathrobe at the hook on the back of the bathroom door, two weeks later I'm no closer than I was then.

He stepped into the shower.

I'll bet Tagg is, he thought suddenly. I'll bet he's closer."

Colonel Tagg composed himself before he made the call. It was an important call and he didn't want to screw it up. Those people must be made to understand what a good job he was doing. He knew they didn't like him—not as a person—but that didn't matter; not as long as they respected him for his talents, for the job he did for them.

The job he did for them. And what, exactly, was that?

He pushed his heavy buttocks deeper into the soft, plush-cushioned chair where he sat, his hands folded neatly in his lap on top of a brown, polished leather briefcase. The lobby of the San Francisco Marriott was very busy: A convention of heavy-equipment salesmen had roared into town, bent on bliss. The men all seemed to be bulky, red faced, and loud; the women mostly looked like the men. Quite a few were obviously drunk, though it was not yet midafternoon. Both lobby bars were doing a thriving business. Hookers fluttered in coveys like ungainly, bejeweled storks; the businesswomen regarded them with distaste. Clots of salesmen formed, dissolved, and formed again. Nobody appeared to notice the somewhat disheveled man who sat near the edge of the lobby, close to a bank of public comm units, observing them all with vague, muddy-green eyes.

Yes, indeed: What did he do for the mysterious *them*? What had he done? And what would he hope to do in the future?

Loy Tagg didn't often sink into introspection. Despite his appearance, he much preferred action to reflection, although he understood that thought had a role to play in things. Within limits, of course; everything must have limits. It was a cardinal point on the compass of his life that the common ruck of humanity needed—no, *demanded*—control. Without somebody to make sure the trains ran on time, the streets got cleaned, and the hideous drives concealed deep within every man's soul were ruthlessly crushed—without that, humanity was doomed. It was his cross. He would bear it. Control meant power, of course, for without power there was no means of control. He understood that equation perfectly well, which was why he'd begun to serve them in the first place, so long ago. Their money meant nothing, not in the long run. But they had promised him power, and to some extent, they had made good. Tagg felt himself to be a competent man in his own way, but he had no illusions about his rise within the DIA. He had friends in high places, without doubt. And if he had no more idea of their names or goals than the man in the moon, what of it? In the real world, results counted. His red lips flickered in a soft, secret smile. He gave them results. Had he ever failed them? *Failed* Condor? No, he had not. Nor would he this time.

Higgins would see to that.

At precisely four in the afternoon, Tagg rose from his chair and walked to the end of the line of phones—three were open, but he wanted the end—and activated the privacy shield. An umbrella of electronic impulses sprang up around him; in theory he was immune to any kind of eavesdropping. In practice, he knew at least five ways to crack the shield, but it didn't matter. This was the first in a line of cut-outs. He had twenty numbers for that many public phones. He selected three at random. All the phones were within walking distance. He punched in the number for *them*. A voice, scrambled and metallic, eventually replied.

"Yes?"

"Three one eight . . ." Tagg spoke clearly nine digits. The man at the other end would alter them according to a standard daily code. The end result would be Tagg's next location.

The line went dead. Tagg stepped away from the booth and lumbered out of the hotel, absently fending off a pair of sequined prostitutes. It was good to be smart; but it was better to be careful.

He ended up outside a Greek corner market, a few hundred yards from the stupendous sprawl of the Hunter's Point New Town. He was a man of his times and found no incongruity in the ironic juxtaposition of the tiny ethnic market and the brassy pyramids that rose, shining in the sun that burned on his back, like monuments to great dead kings. He only wrinkled his nose at the odors drifting from the shop; he thought Greeks smelled funny, probably because of their food. It took him a moment to attach the relay microphone bead to the mouthpiece of the telephone. The mike was wired into a small infinity scrambler, about the size of an old-fashioned pocket watch, and thence to a tiny speaker embedded beneath his left ear. The scrambler broke his subvocalized words into binary impulses, changing the breakdown two hundred times a minute.

Only he, and whoever took his call, could possibly make any sense of this electronic hash—and he knew of no way to crack it without a full-scale omnicomputer.

"Tagg," he said.

"Yes."

"I have located the target."

"Good."

"He's staying with a nurse who treated him after his accident."

A moment of buzzing silence. "Is there a connection?"

Tagg shrugged. "I don't know. Possibly."

"Take him alive. We must know what he knows. Can you debrief him privately?"

Tagg mulled it over. *Privately:* That meant without the knowledge of his governmental superiors.

"It would be difficult," he said at last.

"But possible." The voice was flat and full of certainty.

"Yes . . . possible."

"Report as soon as you have anything."

The connection went dead. Tagg frowned. This was mildly unsettling. It appeared they were beginning to take him for granted. He certainly couldn't allow that.

Luckily, his position was such that he didn't have to.

Robert Hilkind turned to Mitsu Fujiwara and said, "Tagg's found Josh Tower."

Fujiwara nodded. His black, button eyes glittered in the harsh glare of the overhead lights. His facial muscles remained impassive, so that he resembled a primeval Japanese war god summoned back to life. "Tower is a problem. But Tagg could become a problem. Is that so?"

Hilkind's features were feral and mean, his blue eyes like a pair of gunshots above a lean body made of wires buried in skin. People feared him simply because he looked treacherous; he was, but only in the line of duty. He closed his eyes. It was like extinguishing a pair of blowtorches. The ridged tendons beneath his sharp cheekbones smoothed out. Fujiwara had the feeling that Hilkind had gone away. In fact, that was precisely what he had done. He was one of the very first face dancers, whose skull was full of the implants that let him exist on the man-computer interface. The name itself was old, but it had new meanings now, and Hilkind was one of Luna's greatest hidden weapons. Within ten seconds, he returned.

"There is that possibility."

"Too much hangs in the balance for possibilities."

"What do you suggest?"

They both knew the answer. Hilkind grinned; he didn't smile at infants. They burst into tears. Fujiwara didn't smile at all, but then, he never did. The third member of their trio was absent. Compared to these, that man seemed entirely human. He could have mingled with the salesman in Tagg's hotel lobby as easily as a fish swims through water. He was perhaps the most frightening of them all, but he was gone. His name was Lawrence Schollander.

"Lawrence would agree," Fujiwara said softly.

They nodded at each other, in perfect concurrence.

"I will inform *him* immediately."

Fujiwara turned away. He knew what they were unleashing.

Tower slammed his fist down in frustration next to Kelly's pitiful little Tandy Ten. It was a perfectly fine machine for remembering to make the coffee, placing routine grocery orders, and keeping track of her accounts, but for his purposes it was worse than useless. He'd been trying for a week to re-create his files on Condor, but the machine simply didn't have the sophistication to support the AI programs he'd brought from the old place; and without those programs, he had no hope of approaching Condor's fortified electronic walls without triggering off another round of search and destroy. It was useless. He'd gotten nowhere at all.

He sighed and leaned back. Condor. It was the key

to everything. He didn't know how he knew, but he
knew it. Everything led to that tiny, obscure stock-
trading house in Denver. When he'd somehow goofed,
and given them a line on him, killers had come to burn
his house. He'd kept that in mind while he tried to do
what he could with Kelly's Tinkertoy setup, but there
was no way to break through.

So, fine. What next?

The current situation was obviously no good. Not
only was he making no progress on his own private
war, but each day he spent in this apartment placed
Kelly in greater danger. They had taken, or killed, his
oldest buddy, as easily as he might swat a fly. Was
there any reason to think Kelly would last longer in
the withering glare of their attention?

He picked up his coffee mug—it had a picture of a
duck wearing spikes and neon tattoos, and sporting a
condom over an enormous erection—and drained it.
He felt better physically, at least. The sunburn had
faded to a light, skin-peeled brown, and the cuts and
gouges on his body were well scabbed over. Kelly's
antibiotics had knocked down the infection on his calf
and, though it should have had stitches, it was healing
cleanly. He was beginning to experience a need for
action. He was surprised to discover that his muscles
craved the routine of night running and protested its
absence with spectral aches and sudden itchy pains.

The answer was obvious: Hit the bricks. No further
good could come of this situation, except for those
who hunted him even as he sat here. Two weeks was
a long time. Despite his precautions, they were probably getting closer. He'd been careful. He never left
the apartment, never tried to reach Foster, never ap-
proached the tracks and trails of his previous life. But
nobody could hide forever.

Surely the connection with Kelly was so tenuous they
wouldn't check it. But of course they would. They
would check everything. Not right away, perhaps, but
eventually. And eventually was just about now.

He stood up and headed for the tiny kitchenette with

his obscene duck mug. He would tell her that tonight.
It was the best thing.

So why didn't he feel better about it?

She worked that day with half her mind elsewhere.
Mr. Ingels had returned, and she didn't think he would
make it out this time. His frail, jaundiced body made
her sad. At least his passing would be cleaner than
Carl's. Not much, but a little.

She wondered if Tower would be gone when she got
home. He hadn't said anything, but she could sense
his frustration growing as his wounds healed. He'd
been very good, very close-mouthed. She had no real
idea what had brought him to her. She wouldn't have
endured that ignorance for a moment, except she
sensed he meant well. He thought he was protecting
her. But from what?

What might a datahunter know that could be dangerous to her? She recalled the obsession with the
death of his wife that had begun in the hospital. He
must have stumbled onto something that had made a
further shambles of his life. And that worried her,
too. She perceived a fragility in him that he probably
didn't know himself; the possibility of breakage, and
the creation of something unforeseen. Something
dangerous, perhaps. Dangerous even to her. It wasn't
a happy thought. She looked up and peered through
the window of her tiny office; Mendoza, one of the
orderlies Maggie Meade enjoyed terrorizing, saw her
looking and tossed her a jaunty wave. She waved back
and wondered how her life had become so *complicated*.

She might never know. He was nerving himself to
leave. She felt the tension in him as he slept and listened to the broken chatter of his nightmares.

Maybe tonight.

She hoped he would still be there, so she could tell
him it was okay. That she understood. Perhaps she was
lying about that, but she doubted it. The details might
be cloudy, but she understood the larger issues.

* * *

Later, Tower would decide that it had all been simple coincidence, that his karma was just bad enough
to destroy everything around him but leave him un-
harmed, isolated in the rubble. That would be later,
however, and he wasn't thinking about it when he
checked the fridge for spaghetti makings.

Should he try to make the pasta instead of calling
down for Chinese food? She had a machine, an old,
hand-cranked beast, but it was oiled and in good condition. There was flour and water, and the noodles
would taste far better than anything he could buy. He
decided to give it a try. It would be their last meal
together. He wanted the memories of it to be good.

As he puttered, kneading the dough, putting out tomatoes for the sauce, chopping onions, he wondered
what way would be best. Tell her during dinner? Or
wait till bed? A dinner announcement seemed more
honest; that way, it wouldn't seem as if he'd held off
merely so he could sleep with her one final time. He
didn't want her to see it that way. He'd used her but
not her body. That part of it had been real. He wondered how it had become that way, but the thought
tapped wells of guilt he was afraid to plumb. Julia.
Dot. Link. How *complicated* his life had become.

It took him several minutes to figure out the proper
operation of the pasta maker. He pulled a big lump of
dough into several smaller pieces and fed one into the
stainless maw of the machine, then turned the hand
crank slowly.

It felt good to do something mindless but productive
in the slow afternoon. Just to the left, in the corner of
his vision, was the balcony door, open to the breeze
and, beyond it, the postcard hills of the city. San Francisco, he had heard, had changed less than any other
North American city. He had no idea what that meant,
but he loved the place, with its hills and ever-blooming
flowers and time-worn, fog-shrouded vistas of the Bay.
He wondered if these might not be his last hours of
such pleasure.

The pasta seemed to be turning out. The noodles
looked even. Cheered by this unexpected success, he

fed in another doughy lump. When he finished, he started on the sauce. Olive oil, onion, garlic. The rich smell filled the tiny kitchen while he chopped tomatoes and scooped out three cans of tomato paste. It should simmer all afternoon, he thought, and he opened the door to the spice cabinet.

The only thing that looked promising was a small glass jar filled with crumbled leaves, labeled "Italian seasonings." He opened the lid and sniffed but couldn't smell anything. Old spices. He frowned. It seemed a shame, to ruin the whole production with cheap herbs that probably had no flavor left at all.

He walked out onto the balcony and peered down. He couldn't quite make out the sign, went back inside, and found her binoculars: a nice pair of Zeiss-Asakos with polarized lenses. Now he could read the letters above the door of the shop on Castro, a block away at the base of the hill. Canellaro's Italian Deli. He considered. Fresh basil, oregano, maybe some fat mushrooms. Yes. The sauce deserved it. He turned down the heat under the sauce, covered the pasta with a paper towel, and went to the bedroom.

The room seemed very silent. Almost foreboding. He paused, looked around, but saw nothing out of the ordinary. Finally he shrugged. Nerves and guilt. The shop was only a block away. Not much chance of being spotted. If Tagg had somehow discovered him, his teams would already be here, crashing down the door.

He locked the door behind him, but a prickle of unease remained. Almost as if he knew what would happen. Perhaps welcomed it.

He was at the corner of Castro and Market, jouncing his way through the midday crowds streaming from the underground, before he saw them. Rather, he recognized the pattern before he saw the men and women who made it. He had once been trained to recognize patterns. Every crowd has its own dynamics, its own chemistry of movement. Here, for instance, the entrance to the subway was the focus, currents entering and leaving, to dissipate in all directions. But, almost unnoticed, the hunters held their positions in the crowd, moving slowly against the grain. His nerves jerked all at once. Then training took over. He let himself go with a knot of chattering boys who were heading for one of the local gay bars. He attached himself to their group without seeming to do so. There was a trick of walking, of glancing and nodding, that signified membership, even to those strands of the human net that was slowly extending itself throughout the neighborhood.

Finally, at Nineteenth Street, he reached the boundaries of the massive infiltration. From outside, if you understood the signs, you could discern the focus. Without haste, the teams moved toward a point somewhere beyond the Castro Market intersection. Toward States Street.

He knew what he should do. There was no time left for anything but flight. But he had used her. Could he throw her to the wolves? He stepped around the corner and stopped, his insides churning. Maybe they've already got her. Walk away.

Do it now!

He had turned to face the wall of a Chinese restaurant. The peeling paint there fascinated him. He leaned his forehead on it, trying to cudgel his aching brain into some kind of decision.

"You're supposed to know all the moves," a man's deep voice said behind him. "So don't make any moves at all."

Chapter Ten

The small brass sign on the plain gray door read
DREYER CRANDALL TECHNOLOGY, INC. Tower noted
it, and he noticed the way the big man who held his
left arm had to push hard to swing it open. It was
painted to look like wood, but there was steel under
the veneer, and the hinges were silent. The door was
out of place in this long, decrepit hallway on the fifteenth floor of the decaying Transamerica Tower. The
distinctive pyramid-shaped building was still a local
landmark, but it had been half empty for years. The
big man who had captured him shoved the door
closed. It made a thick, solid sound as it thunked
shut. Tower thought it sounded like a bank vault—or
a coffin lid.

"Sit," the big man said. He pointed at a bare metal
chair in front of a gray steel desk.

"What's your name? Or is that classified?" Tower
asked.

"You don't need to know." He raised his bushy eyebrows. "But it's Kinger."

"Well. What happens next, Kinger?"

Kinger stared at him a long moment, then turned
away. "According to your file, you used to be with the
outfit."

Tower nodded. "That's right."

"Why ask, then? You already know the answer."

Tower sighed. "It hasn't changed?"

"No. It hasn't changed. Not the end. Only the way
you get there."

* * *

Kinger said, "Put your hands down. You know the drill."

Tower nodded. He put his wrists next to the side rails of the back of the steel chair and waited while Kinger cuffed each wrist to the metal. When his was done, Kinger stepped back and stared at him.

"Something funny?" Tower asked.

Kinger grinned faintly. "You don't look like much for all the trouble you've caused."

Tower shrugged. The movement made the chains of his handcuffs jingle. "Sorry. I didn't mean to put you out."

"Not me," Kinger replied, his craggy face pensive. "Other people, though."

Tower looked away. An old man named Fogarty was the farthest thing from his mind. "The woman doesn't know anything," he said at last. He knew it was useless, but he had to try.

Kinger's voice was a soft, deep rumble. "That's not my business, either."

So they did know about Kelly. But of course they did. They'd tracked him to her apartment. He thought longingly of the backpack hidden in her bedroom closet. If he'd only carried one of the Clubs with him when he'd gone on his errand—but that would have been futile, as well. Kinger was a pro. He'd had him cold when he'd taken him. Even a Club wouldn't have made any difference.

He tried to find a comfortable position on the hard chair seat. Kinger moved over and perched on the corner of the desk. He lit a Winston and ignored Tower, who closed his eyes.

It was a little late for it, but he still tried to put things together, to figure the edge, to ferret out the slightest hint of opportunity. They would take Kelly. No doubt they already had. She might not know anything, but they would have to learn that for themselves. He'd lived with her two weeks. They'd want to know anything he might have let slip.

But how did the Defense Intelligence Agency come

into this at all? He still couldn't understand it. The Agency's brief was to gather intelligence and wage covert war on behalf of the United States Armed Services. The CIA occasionally became involved with domestic business situations, despite their avowed limitations, but he'd never heard of DIA doing so. Could Condor have been some secret military front? Or was it Condor at all?

That was the greatest frustration. Somehow his life had been torn apart, and as far as he could tell, it was all an accident. Positing the idea that he and his wife had been singled out made no sense whatsoever, unless he allowed himself an even greater paranoia than he already felt.

Moreover, it was unlikely now that he would ever know. They would pick him clean—use the whole bag of tricks: drugs, hypnotherapy, subconscious suggestion—but unless he could somehow remain conscious, he would remain forever ignorant. Which was the point of it all, anyway. He had done it himself, in times past. Information was for the Agency, never for the target. Somebody wanted to know what he knew, and he might not even know what it was. And when they were done—what?

There was a standard procedure for that, too. He shivered at the thought. He believed that his own life after Julia's terrible death had no meaning, had become only a burden. But faced with the imminent reality of mortality, he found that he cared very much. He didn't want to die.

Kinger ground out his cigarette on the bare concrete floor and lit another. The room was very silent. The air-conditioning system seemed not to be functioning, because the smoke hung in the air, a thin blue cloud rising toward the ceiling.

He suddenly understood that this was all very wrong.

Great resources had been committed toward his capture. Entire teams of street sweepers, actions squads, even a heavyweight named Tagg had been thrown into the fray. Yet his destination was a barren, deserted room in a tattered office building.

Why not the local DIA office? Or a fast plane ride to Washington, or the guarded privacy of a military base? Why here?

He worried at the thought. Somehow, if he could figure out the implications, perhaps there would be an opening. If he could understand the game these people played, then he could plan his own move. And for the first time in a long while, he was grateful for his dilapidated appearance. Trained men—and Kinger was certainly that—were instructed from the very beginning never to let down their guard, never to give the enemy any opportunity. But even trained professionals were human. Kinger outweighed him by a good eighty pounds. Tower knew what he must look like, with his emaciated frame, his still-livid scars, the bags under his eyes. And he was handcuffed to a chair.

If he was careful, if he timed things exactly right, then he might have a chance.

Only one, though. No more.

Such a slim note on which to hang two lives.

Kinger continued to smoke and to ignore him. That is, Kinger's professional awareness was engaged—if Josh were to try to come out of the chair or otherwise move suddenly, the bigger man would react immediately—but beyond that necessary caution, as far as Kinger was concerned, his prisoner might well have been just one more item of furniture in the stuffy, barren room.

As he contemplated the situation, Tower kept coming back to his original question: Why here? Was this merely a transfer point, a safe-house way station?

But that didn't seem to fit either. There was a stolidity to his captor, a sense of waiting. Kinger seemed familiar with the room, as if he'd been here before. He had not, for instance, looked at the desk as he sat on its top, nor had he wiggled around to make himself comfortable. And when Tower looked down, he saw the faint remains of black scar marks—evidence of other, older cigarettes ground out. Smoking was a rare enough habit that it strained coincidence for two men to sit in the same spot and crush spent butts in identical patterns.

Good, then. Play it from there. This was a destination, not a temporary holding pen. What next?

Obviously, what was euphemistically referred to as a debriefing. Most likely with all the bells and whistles. This nearly empty room in a nearly empty building was a good choice for that. Tower had no doubt the heavy steel door would muffle any noise he might make. He had himself torn men's brains apart in similar rooms. But only in the field, in far-away places where the safety and convenience of more established facilities was unavailable. Such was not the case here.

So why would Tagg use such an unorthodox location? Tower could only think of one reason: Whatever Tagg had in mind was not officially sanctioned. Or at least this part of it wasn't. And that fit in with the general weirdness of the whole thing. If, somehow, Condor or whoever Condor represented had coopted Tagg, either through bribery, blackmail, or some other means, then this whole situation made perfect sense. Use the DIA apparatus to capture the target—it was easy enough to fake an acceptable reason—but when the goal was accomplished, the results had to be kept hidden from superiors. An official debriefing was monitored, the results checked. Perhaps whatever Tagg was after was as big a secret to his own superiors as it was to Tower himself.

The more he thought about it, the more sense it made. And if that were the case, then he understood with sickening finality just what they were waiting for.

All the eggs were to be gathered in a single basket. They were waiting for Kelly. That made sense. They wouldn't try to grab her from the hospital. Not when it was much easier to wait, to take her in the crowded subway or later, when she returned to the privacy of her apartment.

He couldn't read his watch. But it had been early afternoon when they'd snatched him. There was time. If he could think of something. Anything.

Anything at all.

Finally, while Kinger lit yet another cigarette, Tower closed his eyes and let himself drift. It was an old habit. Sometimes cudgeling away at a problem produced a mental blockage, an inability to consider new paths. When that occurred, if time was available, it was better to let the unconscious chew on the situation. He reckoned he had time—and the past minutes of deep, frantic thought had not provided him with any new answers.

With his eyes shut tight, he became aware of the smell of the room. Idly, he began to catalogue the different odors. There was the sharp, vegetal char of cigarette smoke and beneath it, the faint, bitter aroma of Kinger's body. A higher, thinner smell, closer at hand—what was that? Then he realized it was the sweaty smell of his own fear. And beneath all this human medley, a deeper, more fundamental stench, dank and rotting: the swampy stench of the crumbling building, as it settled deeper into the fill upon which it was built. It reminded him of other days and other places, hidden sewers in ancient European cities, times of sharp danger, when he was younger and the world was an easier, if not safer, place.

Oh, Link. Was I happier then?

Goaded by the scent of the past, he saw a tiny cellar room in Vienna. He and Foster and a thin, pasty-faced specialist checking each other's kit before setting out on a raid. He could barely remember the target—some Fourth World diplomat who had stepped beyond doubling into the confusing treachery of the triple agent and who had finally attracted the attention of the big players. What he did remember, as clearly as he could remember anything, was Foster, who had sensed his tightly wound state of mind, and who had soothed it.

"You're gonna be fine, Josh," Foster had said then,

his flat green eyes glowing faintly. "Everybody gets butterflies before a mission."

"Do you?"

"Well, hell yes, boy. What do you think I am? Superman?"

The pallid specialist, an old hand at this sort of thing, had gone on checking his arcane tools with a sort of reptilian certainty. He had made Tower's skin crawl.

"What if we blow it?"

An unholy glee had suffused Foster's big face. "Then we blow it. And maybe we die. It happens, you know. Any little thing. I can remember once . . ."

And Link told him a story of such a time, punctuating the narrative with sudden, rasping chuckles, patting his belly once, bulging his eyes out in mock surprise at what had happened and what he'd done.

"So if I hadn't moved my fat old ass faster than I ever did before," he had finished, "that little sucker would have had me for lunch."

It had been a puzzling anecdote, but Tower had seen the point. Even the best—and he still thought there had never been any better than Foster—could make a mistake. Could be caught by chance, or coincidence, or simple human courage. But you couldn't worry about those things. You could only do your job and hope that nobody had put a check mark against your name.

"Brave little son-of-a-bitch," Foster had mused. "I don't know if I'd have had the guts. Keep it in mind, Josh. The little guys are the ones to watch out for. They don't screw around. They'll kill you."

And as he recalled what this particular little guy had done to Foster, a ghostly grin began to play across his lips. He looked toward Kinger, who was certainly a big guy.

Which makes me a little guy.

Kinger stared dully out the window at the city below, his back toward Tower. Now was as good a time as any.

"Don't know if I'd have had the guts," Foster had said.

Tower didn't know if he did, either. But as his stomach knotted into a hard, cold ball, he knew he was about to find out.

He closed his eyes and let the minute sounds of the room sink into his ears. Kinger's breathing was a long, soft rasp, accompanied by an occasional tight hiss as the bigger man inhaled his cigarette. The slide of fabric across flesh, as Kinger rocked softly from one foot to the other, unconsciously adjusting his balance. Distant city sounds, bleats and honks and the sudden firecracker resonations of laser taxis taking off and landing at the pads farther north along the Bay.

He would have to fit his own actions into this mosaic. It would have helped if the room itself hadn't been so quietly insulated, but it would be nice if hell had air conditioning, too.

Slowly, willing his mind away from the agony of the physical monstrosity he was about to attempt, Tower extended the tip of his tongue out half an inch between his teeth. He was careful to keep his lips shut tight over the bit of muscular flesh. Then, eyelids still squeezed into a thin line, he began to grind his teeth across the meat between them. A single sharp crunch would have been easier, but he feared the clicking of his teeth together would alert his captor.

The sharp edges of his incisors bit into the fleshy outer layer of skin; a wave of agony bulleted through the back of his eyes and filled his skull. Slowly, he clenched his fists and concentrated on keeping his respiration steady. Kinger would pick up on any sudden change immediately.

He felt the muscles beneath his ears and down his neck contract. Every nerve in his body cried out for respite. But he kept on, slowly grinding, chewing away as if his tongue were only a bit of gristly steak. Blinding white circles of stars exploded in the darkness of his concentration, then waves of red anguish washed through the white like a tide of blood. Throat reflexes tried to jerk the tongue tip back into his mouth, tear it away from the terrible damage his teeth inflicted.

Slowly, the red inside his brain began to fade, to go to black, and he realized he had only a few moments left before pain—the final warning—knocked him out.

He inhaled very slowly and spasmed his locked jaws one more time. Felt a tearing, a giving way, and then the sinewy shape of the gobbet of flesh that had once been a part of him was now caught between the front of his teeth and his lips.

A tide of dizziness threatened to pull him under, and he forced his eyes open. The light seemed blinding, but it diminished the effect of incipient shock. And Kinger was still gazing out the widow, a cigarette clasped between two yellowed fingers, his breathing steady and unconcerned.

Thick, warm, coppery liquid began to fill his mouth. He wanted to gag, to spit out the blood, expel the ruined bit of gristle, but not yet. He breathed in slowly, deeply, through his nose, trying to hyperoxygenate his muscles for the supreme effort yet to come.

At last his cheeks began to bulge slightly.

In a surge of agony and ecstatic release, he permitted his body to move.

He drummed his feet on the floor. Arched his back against the chair. Yanked frantically against his handcuffs until flesh tore at his wrists.

"What . . ." Kinger stared at him, his gaze wide.

Tower bulged his eyes, rolled them back in his head, and opened his mouth. A huge gout of blood spewed forth, covered his chin, dripped down in a wide fan on his chest.

"Oh, Jesus Christ!" Kinger gasped.

Tower let himself go limp. The throb of pain from his devastated mouth beat in his ears like a maddened drum. His head dropped forward, spilling ever more blood.

Kinger was at his side now, fumbling with the handcuffs on his right.

Tower waited until he heard the faint click of the lock snapping open. Then he moved.

He lurched sideways out of the chair, grabbed Kinger's lapel, and pulled him down hard.

He used the bigger man's unbalanced weight to jerk Kinger across his lap. He grabbed his thick hair and yanked his throat across the chain of the other handcuff.

He pulled the chair up, and over, and down.

Kinger bucked beneath him like a great sea animal, his massive fists pounding, clubbing, and Tower held on to the chair with all his strength. Kinger grabbed one foot and twisted, and Tower felt a toe crack. His breath rushed out of him, and he dripped blood on Kinger's head like an emptying pitcher.

He heard a low, gasping moan and suddenly realized that he was himself making the awful noise. Kinger flopped back and forth, trying to scrape Tower off against the desk, the wall. He sank his teeth into Tower's ankle, eerily silent, because his windpipe was choked shut. The metal chair pinioned the chain around his neck, and as long as Tower could keep hold of it, Kinger's every movement only pulled the chain tighter. Unless the big man could break the steel chair, snap the chain, or pull Tower's arm from its socket, he would die.

He knew it.

In one final, titanic convulsion, Kinger managed to rise halfway to his feet. His face was blue, his lips almost black. He launched himself backward with all his remaining strength, using the great leverage of his own weight to crash Tower with terrible force into the wall.

Tower's lungs flattened. He felt a rib snap. The edge of the chair sliced across his cheek and, in that final spasm, his left shoulder separated from its socket.

Everything went slow and blurry.

Hold on! he told himself, as darkness crept up, threatened to overwhelm him. Then, without warning, all the pains—shoulder, tongue, chest, ribs, foot—rose up in a medley of outrage and rolled him down, into a thunderously final surf.

He awoke to the sound of something dripping.

Plat. Plat, plat. Plat.

What?

His entire skull seemed wrapped in cold fire. His left shoulder was another flare of agony, and his chest felt as if he'd been kicked by a horse. The minor throb of his broken toe and savaged ankle was a trivial counterpoint to the rest.

After a moment his vision cleared. Something dark, greasy looking. Kinger's hair. His face was resting across the back of Kinger's skull. A few inches away, Kinger's left eye blared redly.

He jerked himself up, but the eye didn't move.

Blood trailed in thin lines from Kinger's open mouth, down his massive chin. Plat, plat. His tongue protruded between his bloody lips like some ruined, blackened slug.

"Jesus," Tower whispered. The sound of the word was loud in the silence of the room.

He lay there and stared at the big dead face, which stared blankly back at him. After a time, when he couldn't bear that gaze any longer, he pushed himself up.

Kinger's head lolled forward. The handcuff chain was buried an inch into the folds of his neck. Another necklace of blood—Kinger's, this time—dripped from the shiny steel links.

Groaning, Tower shoved the big man's body forward, until he could unwind the chair and the chain. When he finished, Kinger was on his back, sightless eyes aimed at the ceiling.

Tower leaned back against the wall. Then he turned his head to the side and vomited.

His left arm dangled uselessly. He could move his fingers but only barely. It took him a minute to find the chip that released the lock on the other set of cuffs. After he was free, he returned to Kinger's body.

The weight of the man's Club, taken from the snap-release holster beneath his left armpit, was immeasurably comforting. He continued his search and finally came up with the DIA man's wallet. Surprisingly, Kinger was not equipped with the standard drug kit. Grunting with effort, he dragged Kinger's corpse behind the desk, where it would not be immediately visible from the door. When he had finished, he set the steel chair upright and collapsed on it. Time to take stock.

What he found was not encouraging. He had been more badly injured in the past—the laser-cab wreck, to name the most recent incident—but he understood that he would need help soon. It had taken a supreme expenditure of will and energy to survive this battle. His body had been in no great shape before, and now he realized that he teetered on the edge of complete collapse.

He hefted the Club.

He got up, dragged the chair behind the desk, sat down, put his feet on Kinger's back, and put the weapon in his lap. Then, his face a red mask, he began to wait.

Somebody would come. Not many, because this was not a legitimate operation. He was gambling everything on that, but he was certain he was right.

Somebody would come, and with them would be help. If not, then he would die. And why not? He wasn't far from it anyway. A part of him almost welcomed it. But another, bleaker part looked for something else.

That part had enjoyed killing Kinger.

It looked forward to killing again.

Colonel Tagg had not wanted to use Cal Teeters again, not after the disaster at Lincoln Foster's place. Indeed, he had already begun the transfer process that would eventually send Cal to an obscure posting in Nome, Alaska, at the huge base there. But, given the delicacy of this particular mission, it had seemed better to use men already involved, so as not to spread covert knowledge any further than necessary. So, when Kinger sent him word of the capture, Tagg had personally led a very small squad to the doors of San Francisco

General Hospital, where they easily picked up Dot Kelly as she hurried toward the subway entrance. A simple flash of phony SFPD badges had done the trick.

"What *is* this?" Kelly had seemed irritated but relatively unsurprised—almost, Tagg considered, as if she'd been expecting something like this to happen.

He'd sent Cal's partner, a small, thin man named Axelrod, back to the local office, leaving himself and Cal as the only witnesses to what would happen next. Since Kinger was alone with Tower, and Cal would soon be headed for the frozen north, Tagg felt secure in his ability to keep the upcoming debriefing a secret from his superiors. He'd already fogged the issue with falsified reports that hinted Tower had cracked certain army databanks for purposes unknown, and while he didn't have perfect *carte blanche* on the case, as long as it remained a field operation he had wide enough latitude for his purposes.

As he stepped out of the rickety elevator on the fifteenth floor of the Transamerica pyramid, he felt a certain satisfaction in the way things were going. Everything was finally falling into place. The small, unofficial safe room down the hall would do nicely for a private debriefing session, and when that was done, he could always engineer a convenient escape attempt. The sort of escape that often left no survivors. In fact, as he thought about it, it might be best if no one but himself walked away. Kinger was solid, but perhaps Cal wasn't. Why take chances? It wasn't in his nature to leave such loose ends unresolved. He decided to test the possibilities further as he went along.

The small party halted in front of the door displaying the legend DREYER CRANDALL TECHNOLOGY, INC. Tagg pulled a chipcase from his pocket, handed it to Cal, and muttered, "Number three."

The two men had sandwiched Kelly between them. After her initial question, she had remained silent. Tagg thought he sensed a tension in her, a readiness, and he kept her left elbow firmly in his grip. He knew very little about the woman, beyond the fact that she had nursed Tower through his recovery from the accident and then, for some reason, had taken him in later. Perhaps there was some romantic relationship. Perhaps Tower had spilled his guts to her. Either way, he would soon know all he needed to know.

And so would his invisible employers. Or would they? His last conversation with them had hinted at a lessening of respect on their part, a condescension. Maybe they needed to learn his worth again. Possibly, he thought with growing satisfaction, they should bargain a bit for his information. And be reminded just how good an employee they possessed.

Yes. He felt almost expansive as Cal, his shoulders hunched, fitted the chip into the door lock and swung the door wide.

Ka-phoomp!

The sound was low and penetrating. Cal's body seemed to implode around an invisible fist as he was physically lifted off his feet and blown backwards into the hall.

Kelly screamed.

Tagg had one glimpse of the dark silhouette rising from behind the desk. Backlit from the window, it was hard to make out features. But in that instant he saw the figure was much smaller than Kinger, and he realized what had happened.

Loy Tagg didn't stop to think. Just that one terrifying glimpse, and then he lumbered down the hall, lungs laboring, heart pounding. It took him ten seconds to reach a corner, and lurch around it to safety. With each frantic, pounding step, he'd felt unseen crosshairs focused on his back.

He kept on going, sparks flashing in his vision, until he reached a staircase exit door and flung himself inside. He paused to catch his breath. Then, moving as quickly as he could, he began to descend.

Somehow, Tower had done it again.

As he reached the tenth floor, let himself out, and found an elevator, he understood his mistake.

He wouldn't make that error again.

It was time for Higgins.

And with the clear vision of hindsight, he realized that it had been time for Higgins all along.

No matter what Condor said.

Kelly shook her head. There was a low buzzing in her ears, and something heavy and slippery rested across her upper body. She tried to think. First the strange, sharp, coughing sound, and then the man in front of her had flung himself backwards. That was it: She'd fallen; must have hit her head and stunned herself momentarily. Okay so far.

Things still seemed dim, but crazy, flashing shapes burned in her eyes. She shoved weakly at the mass that pinned her down. Her hands slithered, as if the bulky thing were covered with thin grease. She grunted. Then her vision cleared and she stared at her hands.

Red.

Her hands were covered with red. The distinctive odor smote her in the face. Foggily, she put it together. Red. Copper smell. Her hands were covered with *blood!*

Gallons of blood!

She screamed. Or she tried, but something soft covered her lips. She bit at the softness, but it squeezed her jaws, forced her teeth away.

"No, Dot, no. It's all right. Don't. You're okay."

The words penetrated slowly, not as individual sounds with meanings, but as a low, soothing hum. After a moment she recognized the voice. She quit thrashing.

"Dot?"

She pushed again at the corpse—yes, that's what it was; there was a body crushing her down—and the hand over her mouth went away.

"Josh?" she said.

"It's okay," he repeated, and then she felt the body move slowly off her chest. She blinked. His hands took her shoulders, moved her to a sitting position. Then he came around in front and stared into her face.

She gasped. He was terribly wounded. Blood
dripped from his mouth, washed down his face from
a wide gash in his upper cheekbone. Above the crimson mask his skin was completely leached of color.

Shock, she thought absently. He's in shock.

Oh, my God, what's happening?

Tower kept on tugging gently at her arms, pulling
her up, forcing her to stand.

"I need help," he said softly. "You have to help
me."

She looked down. The dead man's chest was nothing
but a charred hole lined with bits of white muscle tis-
sue and gray chunks of lung. He rested in a spreading
pool of blood. So much blood.

She jerked in a shuddering breath. The world steadied. Tower clutched her arms—whether to hold her or
himself upright she couldn't tell.

She nodded.

He waited a moment, looked into her eyes, then
bobbed his head in return.

"Help me get him inside," he said at last.

She remembered that she was a nurse. Blood was
part of her job. So why did she have to swallow, to
lick her dry, hot lips, exert every ounce of control to
keep from vomiting?

While she waited inside, he'd taken off the man's
coat and used it to sop up as much of the bloody pool
as he could. It wasn't a perfect job, but it was no
longer as obvious as it had been. Now he was back
inside, speaking rapidly. She felt distant, and his words
were hard to follow.

"Have to go; we can't stay here. They'll be looking
for you now, Dot, not just me anymore. If you can
keep me together, we have to run. . . ."

An endless outpouring of words. She wanted to interrupt. Say in a calm voice, "Josh? There's another
body here. Behind the desk. A man who appears to
have been strangled. Josh? There's another . . ."

But she didn't.

I'm in shock too, she realized with an exhausted kind of wonder. That hasn't happened in . . .

Words, so many words, chasing themselves around and around . . .

He slapped her.

As soon as he'd pulled Cal's corpse off her, she'd become zombielike. She'd spoken his name only once, but she seemed able to move okay. He'd been terrified at first, when he'd blasted Cal as he'd stepped through the door and then seen her face behind the DIA man's shoulder. He knew the capabilities of the Club. Its .35-caliber ramjet projectile developed more than enough velocity to slam through not only the DIA man but Kelly and two or three more people.

He'd thrown himself at the door, cursing inwardly, and caught a faint glimpse of a fat, lumbering man as he turned a corner at the end of the hallway. There had been no chance for a shot, and besides, his entire concentration was on Kelly, on her small body almost hidden beneath the welter of blood and shattered bone that had been her guard.

His relief had been immense when he'd discovered that none of the blood was hers, but now, as the red imprints of his fingers faded on her cheek, he wondered if she hadn't been damaged in some more fundamental way.

Her washed-out blue eyes had faded nearly transparent. They were round as marbles. Her pupils had distended. Her only reaction to his slap had been a slow, waxy silence.

He hissed air past his teeth, into his lungs sharply. He knew that he was shocked almost to his physical limits, but he couldn't allow himself the luxury of collapse. Yet, if she, suffering from her own emotional shock, was unable to help him then they were both doomed. He'd escaped them three times. Didn't things come in threes? Or was that only bad things?

He couldn't remember. Why was it important? He shook his head and tried to reel in his jumbled thoughts.

His brain kept wandering off down these useless pathways, no longer able to distinguish between the important and the trivial. It all melded into a confused lump, and he couldn't allow it.

Wouldn't allow it. He shoved the ragged tip of his tongue across the lower edge of his teeth. A grenade of pure pain erupted in his skull, wiping the pall of confusion away.

She stood behind the desk, spraddle-legged over Kinger's slowly blackening corpse.

"Come on, Dot," he pleaded.

It was as sudden as a light clicking on. He could almost *see* the shutters behind her eyes flip open. He raised his hand, ready to cover her mouth if she tried to scream, and winced as she flinched away.

"No," she said. "Don't hit me again."

"Are you back? Are you with me now?"

She licked her lips. She swallowed hard. Her hands, unbidden, rose to swipe with futility at the great red swatch across her chest. "Yes," she said slowly. Her voice was flat, without emotion, but at least she made sense now.

He realized he'd been holding his breath, and he let it out.

"We have to leave," he said gently. "We have to get out of here."

Her eyes flickered down, then up again. "Josh?"

"No, baby," he said. "There's no time for explanations now. You'll have to trust me."

"Trust you." Again the flat voice, leached of all feelings.

"Please. You're in danger, too."

After what seemed an endless moment, she nodded slightly. "Okay. Tell me what to do."

He took her hand and tugged her away from the desk, led her around Cal's shattered body. He opened the door and peered out. Nothing. He guessed he had a few minutes yet, if his reading of the scenario was correct. But a third man had escaped. He wondered if it had been Tagg himself.

In any event, the safety margin for escape numbered minutes, perhaps only seconds. "Come on," he said, and he led her from the room. The patch on the floor had already gone dark and sticky. She stepped over it without seeming to see it at all.

He shut the door. The heavy steel met the jamb with solid finality. The sound seemed to galvanize her, as if something terrible had just been made to disappear.

Out of sight, he told himself. Out of mind. Even he felt a little better, knowing the results of his handiwork were hidden from view.

"This way," he said and pulled her down the hall. Faster and faster; at first they walked, then jogged, their hands clasped like children.

They were running when they reached the second exit door. They didn't know it, but they wouldn't stop running for almost three months.

Tagg had regained control of his breathing by the time he reached the street. He tramped north on Columbus, and with his usual skill he disappeared into the rushing business-hour crowds. Several minutes later, he turned into a small tavern, found an empty booth in the rear, and ordered an Anchor Steam beer. The rich, dark-red local brew flowed down his throat like a blessing. He was suddenly aware of sharp hunger, and he knew it was an aftereffect of the burst of adrenalin that had carried him this far.

He motioned the waitress over and ordered a large pizza with all the trimmings. While he waited for it to arrive, he took stock.

First, this whole Tower business was completely out of control. Three of his men were casualties—one crippled, two more dead. His superiors would want to know why.

Second, Josh Tower had proved a far more dangerous adversary than anybody could have guessed. Had his mysterious Condor masters known this and failed to properly warn him?

Third, his own neck was on the line. If the powers at DIA began an investigation into his handling of this mess, he might well find himself court-martialed. He owed the Condor people many things but not his own career, or his own freedom. No, the time had come to resolve the matter in the most final way possible.

Capturing Josh Tower, or the woman he had probably rescued, was no longer a priority.

But killing them was; and, fortunately, he was still equipped to accomplish that.

and . . . will find intimate coo-marriage . . .
. . . who people sometimes . . . but not his
. . . . past freedom. No, the time has co . . .

Chapter Eleven

As Loy Tagg wheezed his way north on Columbus
Avenue, Josh Tower and Dot Kelly staggered from the
shabby freight-loading docks of the Transamerica
Tower and headed south on the same street. Tower led
the way. Soon they had lost themselves in the warren
of narrow roads that made up the old business center
of the city. Further south, across Market, the gigantic
towers of the New Center gleamed in the last sun of
the day. People stared at them, astonished, as they
lurched past, but San Francisco was a big city. Injured
pedestrians, unless they actively solicited help, were
gawked at but otherwise ignored.

Nevertheless, Tower didn't want to leave an obvious
visual trail. Kelly wore a dark, knee-length coat. Although it was streaked with blood, the drying liquid
blended into the fabric and might have been some ordinary stain.

"Button your coat," he told her.

She nodded. Two red patches of color had returned
to her cheeks. Her eyes glittered harshly. He pulled
her to the edge of the sidewalk, out of the traffic
stream, and put his lips close to her ear.

"Are you going to make it?"

"I don't know. Josh, this is crazy. Did you kill that
other man? Who *were* those men? They said they were
police. Are you—"

"They weren't police."

"Why are they after you?"

"I can't tell you now. It's too long a story. Dot, we
don't have much time. If they catch us, I think they'll

177

kill us. If not immediately, then eventually. Do you understand? We're both running for our lives. You are running for your life. That's my fault, too, but it doesn't matter. We have to get away first. Now, are you going to be able to function?''

In the dim light, her eyes had darkened somewhat and looked almost sapphire. She straightened her shoulders, took a deep breath, and rubbed her chin hard. ''Yes.''

''Good.'' He straightened up and stepped back on the sidewalk. ''I have to get fixed up. I need some clothes and something to cover my face.''

She nodded. ''There's a clothing store up the street.'' She reached into her purse. Somehow, through the entire insanity, she'd kept her purse. ''I'll buy something.''

''Yes. But don't use your credit chip. Use this.'' He rummaged in his jeans pocket and withdrew a scuffed wallet. He took a chip from it and gave it to her.

''Calvin Teeters?''

''Just use it. They may have your name on the net by now. I know they have mine.''

Two doors before the store loomed an alley mouth, half choked with rusty dumpsters. Tower paused. ''You go ahead. I'll wait here.''

''Josh, I—''

''Later,'' he said.

She seemed about to say something else, but the expression on his face stopped her. ''Okay. Don't go anywhere.'' She tried a shaky smile. *''Please* don't go anywhere.''

Wordlessly, he patted her on her shoulder, then moved back into the darkness. Above the city to the west the sun finally sank behind Twin Peaks and painted the sky with red.

The room in which the three men customarily gathered was small and plain and white, not at all what their peers would have considered an appropriate setting for so much power. It had several advantages, however. It was virtually immune to all forms of electronic eavesdropping. It provided certain connections necessary to the proper functioning of one of them. And it provided the other two sufficient communications input to allow administration of their far-flung business ventures.

Its location was one of their most closely guarded secrets.

Robert Hilkind returned from his electronic netherworld. An iridescent spray of superconducting optical cables extended from the sockets inset into his skull to the machines on one wall, which created the peculiar interface upon which he danced. The cables coruscated in a shower of multicolored light as he moved his head.

"Tagg lost him. There's a woman involved. Two men dead. And Tagg is off the leash."

It was crushingly bad news, but neither Mitsu Fujiwara nor Lawrence Schollander altered their expressions in the slightest. As always, the Japanese seemed to be contemplating some serene piece of sculpture. And Schollander, his car salesman's grin utterly fixed, merely nodded.

Hilkind retreated once again. His eyes went blank. He danced upon the face. He returned. "The odds have dropped. We now stand only a sixty percent chance of success."

Fujiwara glanced at Schollander. The bigger man shrugged. "Kill them," he said simply. "Kill them all."

The face dancer nodded. His eyes went blank as his machines began to comb the nets. He was confident. Nobody could hide forever.

Unfortunately, their timing didn't allow for forever.

"Denver," Tower said quietly.

"Lean back," Kelly said. "There."

"Ouch."

She finished gluing a flap of artificial skin down over the gash on his cheek and settled back on the small banquette seat in their private compartment. Outside the polarized window the long, hot flatland of the Sac-

ramento Valley rushed by at a hundred and sixty miles
per hour. Despite the speed of the bullet train, the
interior of the room was nearly silent. "Let that skin
set a minute. Then I'll put some makeup on it. I don't
think it will be very noticeable."

"Did you hear what I said?"

"Yes. Denver. What about it?"

"That's where we're going."

Her eyes widened. "But you bought tickets for New
York."

He nodded. "Nobody says we have to stay on all
the way."

There was a kind of resigned, numb air to her now,
as if so much had happened that her facilities were
mildly shut down, accepting everything new as only
another, absorbable shock. He was beginning to worry
about her.

"Dot, I'm going to tell you the whole story."

"Do I need to know?"

Now he looked surprised. "Don't you want to?"

"You said, trust you. Well, I'm here. I'm not with—
with those men, or at a police station. I'm with you.
So I guess I trust you. Or if not, then I don't have a
lot of options left, do I?"

His ankle throbbed. His tongue was a constant ache.
She'd taped his ribs and bandaged his ankle and fixed
his face, and there was nothing they could do about
his tongue. Luckily it had stopped bleeding. He was
weak from loss of blood and more tired than he'd ever
thought he could be. "They won't be looking for Calvin Teeters's name yet," he'd told her when he'd purchased their tickets. And when they did trace it, all
they would find was that the deceased agent's chip had
purchased two tickets on the Spirit of America bullet
train from San Francisco to New York City. Any hunters would realize their quarry had three thousand miles
in which to make a discreet exit. It wasn't much, but
it was the best he could do on short notice. Now, before he could allow himself the luxury of collapse, he
must somehow bind this woman to him. For her sake

and for his. Their futures, no matter what he might have wished, were now inextricably entwined.

He pasted another derm beneath his jawbone and began to speak. After a while, she started to cry. Later on, she wept again. They were almost to Reno when she finally slept. Only then did he close his own eyes and let the darkness come.

He awoke to the silver night of the great desert between the High Sierras and the Rocky Mountains. His eyes popped open from a dreamless sleep and he came immediately awake, despite his physical exhaustion. It was almost as if his mind had decreed a time of truce, a vacant place for consideration. Since the accident that had claimed his wife his life had become a long siege of reaction. Things happened to him and he tried to survive them. Now, as the tawny rocks outside his window glistened beneath a horned moon, the time had come for reflection.

It was quiet inside their cabin. Kelly's measured breathing whispered beside him. Almost unnoticed, the deep, thrumming passage of air across the skin of the car sounded an endless musical note. The train rocketed along, suspended by a miracle of technology, and carried them with it, into the east, into the sunrise beyond the mountains.

They would arrive in Denver at eleven o'clock Mountain Standard Time. By then, he would have to decide—what?

He rolled from his stomach to his side, propped his head on his elbow, and tried to ignore the assortment of aches, pains, and minor agonies that still managed to breach his wall of painkillers. Kelly stirred slightly. Her lips moved. A short, unintelligible burst of words leaked out, and he touched her shoulder. She subsided then and turned her face away.

What, precisely, were their options? His mind seemed full of a crystalline clarity, as if the dross had been rendered away in the heat of the previous months. In that clear concentration he saw how much the obsession with Julia's last words, the hope of forgive-

ness, the horror of her death, had driven him blindly
forward. There was no doubt now: Insanity had been
his motivation, no matter how he tried to dress it up
in the chilly raiment of logic. Yet for a rushing desert
moment he knew he was sane again, that whatever
choices he made now would be rational, no matter
what madness might later intervene.

Kelly moved again. Her mingled odors wafted across
him, a weave of roses, and sweat, and dried blood, an
unholy mixture that somehow was not unpleasant but,
in a perverse way, attractive. He felt himself stir
slightly and wondered if that were sanity, too.

He pushed the urge away. Kelly and he were joined
in ways that neither of them might fully understand,
but that was a knot whose untying could wait for the
future. What couldn't wait was the morning, and Denver, and Tagg and Condor and whatever other hidden
menaces might be in store.

He should simply leave her. A very cold part of him
whispered that advice in the dark, and he knew it was
true. All his formal training, everything the military,
Foster, and his other instructors, and even the lessons
of his own experience led to that conclusion. He would
have a better chance of survival without her. She had
helped when he needed it, but his physical wounds
would heal. Leave her, the cold voice whispered. Get
away. Hide. Wait.

He rejected it. He wasn't certain why the voice was
so easy to ignore, but it was. Nor did he understand
the sudden feeling of release he felt, as if the greatest,
most healing decision had now been made and all the
rest was trivia. All he knew was that he felt better in
a loose, undefined way, that true healing had begun,
and that he would survive.

Now a great rocky wall loomed to the north of the
magnetic rails, grim and shadowy against the vast silence of the desert floor. A diadem of light sparkled
at the base of the wall. It seemed a beacon, a marker
of hope.

It was Salt Lake City, the halfway point. For one
instant he thought his whole life teetered on a similar

balance, the weight of the past equalized by the weight of the future. Then the moment slipped away, and the train rushed on, and the lights grew brighter.

Morning was coming.

He began to plan.

The great steel snake of the train erupted from the long burrow of the New Eisenhower Tunnel, fourteen thousand feet in the sky, and began the winding descent toward Denver.

"Oh, God, that's beautiful, Josh."

He'd made this trip before, but the splendor of the Rockies, despite familiarity, still had the power to awe him. Kelly had never seen these needled, snow-crowned fields of ancient stone and couldn't turn away from the vista. Each new wonder brought a soft, exclamatory sound.

He had hunted and fished in these mountains, spent long, sharp-edged nights beneath the cleanest stars in the world. The memories brought an ache—small mental snapshots of the only happiness of his childhood. Now a stand of aspen rushed by, quaking gold in their fall colors, and beyond, brown upland meadows dusted with first snow.

He glanced at his watch. "Another hour."

Something in his voice distracted her from the window. "Josh? What do we do now?"

She had finally begun to understand the peril of their circumstances. He had told her everything, from his original suspicions to his most recent deductions about Tagg. She had absorbed it without much comment, as if the details mattered less than the result. Perhaps she was right about that. The past was prelude. Now they had to survive.

He shrugged. "What I said: We hide."

Two sharp vertical lines grew above her nose. "Is that all, then? We hide? For the rest of our lives?"

She looked so tired, so *defeated* that he reached out and pulled her to him. Her breath was warm on his cheek. "No, it's not that bad. I don't think. Eventually, whatever I've stumbled into will reach an end, a consummation. All conspiracies do. Whatever is happening will succeed, or fail. As for those two dead men, I think that is a secret that Tagg will bury deep. I told you. There's no way it could have been an official operation. Tagg would have had to lie to his own superiors. The bodies will be an embarrassment. He'll find an explanation, and it won't include us.''

She pulled slightly away. ''Then it's over?'' She sounded suddenly hopeful, and he was saddened by the necessary truth.

''No, it's not over. Tagg has his own agenda, his own secrets. Those still remain. And that's why Denver. Unless I can uncover those secrets, and use them to buy us out, then we're in danger. I don't have anything to trade right now. And that's what we need, something to trade. We need leverage.''

He felt her muscles stiffen, but then she relaxed. ''Okay,'' she said. ''Just . . . we have to be very careful, don't we?''

''Yes. Very careful.'' He tilted her chin up so that he gazed directly into her faded eyes. ''You will have to do exactly as I say. There may be times I can't explain, but even then, you have to do it. Can you?''

She didn't hesitate. ''Yes.''

But she was an amateur, and he wondered if she understood what she so readily agreed to. Time would tell. ''Good,'' he said. ''Then we'll be all right.''

She turned back to the window, and he busied himself with concealing the two Clubs beneath freshly purchased clothing. Thank God Calvin Teeters had been a saving man. He wouldn't be able to use the dead agent's credit chip in Denver, but that was okay. He had other resources, older resources, there.

Then we'll be all right?

He hoped it wasn't a lie. But in his world few things remained true. Not over time, they didn't.

They traveled light. Kelly carried their single suitcase, and if she noticed the heavy weight of the two Clubs hidden in the bottom, she didn't mention it. Tower locked the door of their compartment and hung a "Do Not Disturb" sign on it. The sign was in five languages. With any luck the message would be honored, and there would be no memories of the couple—a man, his face muffled with a blue woollen scarf, who limped, and a woman, her face distant and preoccupied—who quietly left the train in Denver, two thousand miles before their official destination.

Tower gasped at the knifelike wind that cut through his thin coat. He'd forgotten the sudden cold snaps that plagued late Colorado autumn. Kelly, however, seemed invigorated by the change in weather. The sky overhead was a crackling, cloudless blue, and though sudden breezy gusts tugged at the bottom of her coat, her face took on a ruddy, healthy glow and her washed out, denim eyes began to sparkle.

They rode a people-mover walkway from the boarding platform, then walked from the terminal out to the bustling streets of Golden. Down below, Denver exploded from the edge of the high plains in wall after wall of glass and steel. The center of the old city had grown beyond what Tower recalled. Hadn't he read about a big new push to revivify that crumbling heart? Something had certainly been done. What he remembered as a dark and chilly slum, where tenements leaned flank to flank like drunken old men while malnourished children scrabbled in their malign shade, now seemed an eruption of pristine towers and broad, spotless pavement. From their vantage point in Golden, which had once been a separate town but was now only another Denver neighborhood, they could see the entire city spread out below them. Beyond the city center were rank on rank of smaller buildings, high rises, wide plazas, and parks, which eventually melted into the great, sprawling north-south wings of the metropolis. The megacity stretched from Colorado Springs in the south to Fort Collins in the north, a river of concrete and humanity fifty miles wide and one hundred and twenty miles long.

In the crisp, gemlike glow of the forenoon the city was a wonder. But for Tower, no matter how the place remade and renewed itself, no matter how clean and ordered it became, it remained a place of shadows. He paused a moment, the wind whipping at his face and making his eyes water, as he gazed on his childhood home for the first time in years.

A small shudder stole through the large muscles of his chest. Home, it was said, was where they had to take you in. But this place had always turned him away. He felt an uneasy foreboding that chance and death should bring him back here.

Finally he put those badly healed, not quite buried memories away. What was done was done. He was a different person than he had been in those days. And Kelly's half-shouted words over the wind—"Josh? You okay?"—reminded him that he had more pressing concerns than the rancid details of his unhappy childhood.

"Come on," he said and took her hand. "This way."

They took a laser cab into the city, and Tower ignored the sly feeling that something huge and heartless had just swallowed them whole.

They landed on the main taxi pad at the head of Sixteenth Street, where it intersected Lincoln below the golden dome of the State Capitol Building. He led her gingerly through the crowds, while she fruitlessly tried to balance the suitcase and shield her ears against the continuous firecracker fusillade of the taxis taking off and landing. Over the terminal the blue sky was alight with a web of nearly invisible beams, the fragile, spectral fingers of power that reached down from rushing satellites overhead to tug the little cars into flight.

It was the smell that got him.

They waited at the top of the down escalator while he keyed their chips for the Colfax Underground, and just as he handed over her chip, the vagrant wind shifted and he smelled the *smell*. He blinked. A clinical kind of horror stole over him. He looked around. Everything was clean and bright and polished, but the *smell* reeked in the spotlessness like an undertaker counting heads. It came from his past, but it was real, it was now. Not his imagination.

"Do you smell that?"

She wrinkled her nose. "Ugh. Nasty. What is it?"

A faint titter burped behind his lips. Why, he thought with greasy jocularity, that's the smell of home. The stink of poverty. The aroma of death. He said, "Slums. That's what slums smell like."

She shook her head. "Let's go down."

But when they went up again, in a colder, danker neighborhood, the smell was stronger. Much stronger. It was all around them.

Kelly, nurse and big-city dweller, stood silent, the color draining from her face. "Oh, my Lord," she said in a soft voice. "Josh, look at *that.*"

That was two emaciated, mocha-colored boys with unkempt black hair, squatting on the opposite corner before a rusting half barrel in which burned a fitful, wind-chopped blaze. One of the boys, the younger, perhaps seven, was scrunched as close to the metal side of the barrel as he could get without actually burning his flesh. The other boy, maybe ten but with the bent back of an old man, held something out over the fire on a stick, like a kid toasting a marshmallow. But it wasn't a marshmallow. It was larger, and a fringe of curling, blackened hair still defined its shape. The head of an animal. Tower thought it was a dog. Hoped it was a dog. Please God, don't let there be *rats* that big.

The stench was unbelievable. It wasn't two scrawny children roasting their . . . dinner, but a more pervasive miasma of which that awful scene was only a part. It was nearly high noon, but here in the wrecked shadows of a neighborhood only a few blocks from the scintillant heart of the city, it was already dark. Already? He smiled thinly. Here it never became dark, because it had never known light.

The unbelievable slum of Capitol Hill remained unchanged. He had the horrid thought that it might be eternal, this soup of wretchedness, but even so, he felt a bizarre kind of comfort.

He took her elbow. "Come on," he said.

She looked up at him, surprised, because then he said the craziest thing of all. "We're home."

Eleven-sixty Ogden, fifty years before, had been a marginal apartment house. Two rectangular buildings, set end to the street, cradled the ruins of a cracked swimming pool between them. The pool was no longer in original use, of course. Flapping lengths of fabric, moldy canvas, moth-eaten rugs signaled the presence of dwellers beneath, as did a thin wisp of greasy smoke which rose a foot or so near the edge of the pool before the wind snatched it away.

A narrow, half-shattered concrete stoop yawned like a broken tooth in front of the left-hand building. The complex—what a grand name, Tower thought, *complex*—sat on ground about ten feet above Ogden Street itself, which sloped down to meet Eleventh. Peering through the skeletal remains of a screen of rotting elms, he could see across the roofs to where the old Safeway had been. Now the building was gone; a charred forest of beams and melted aluminum half fallen into the shallow cellar below was all that remained.

"Is that blood?" Kelly said quietly.

He looked down. A wide, irregular rusty patch disfigured the remains of the stoop. "I don't think it's paint," he told her. He fumbled in his coat pocket for his chip case, then thumbed through the keychips until he found the one he was looking for.

It was strange, he realized abruptly. He had—yes, admit it—mentally flogged Julia for not telling him about their child. But the keychip represented a far older secret of his own. Was it fair, then, that his husbandly secrets should go unpunished? He looked around and tried to imagine Julia in a place like this. He couldn't. The hard wind shifted and brought with it a new blast of sour and rotten stinks. Some secrets deserved to be kept he decided and fitted the chip into the lock on the door. But he needn't have bothered. The lock was for show only. At the pressure of his hand, it creaked open slightly. Kelly tried to peer into the crack, but the darkness inside defeated her.

She clutched his arm tighter and he felt her begin to shiver. Even though the wind was icy and penetrating she hadn't done that before.

"Are we going in there?"

"Yes." He pushed the door open. "Here." He tugged gently at the suitcase. She held it up while he unzipped it and removed one of the Clubs. Her eyes went wider and her tongue darted across her lips, but she didn't say anything.

He stepped in front. "Let's go."

Silently, she followed. Behind them the door slowly creaked shut, gradually extinguishing the gray rectangle of light. After a moment it was pitch black. Tower took her hand and they moved forward. He had no trouble with the darkness. As long as he lived, in that building it would always be dark, and he would never have trouble finding his way.

Colonel Loy Tagg wrestled with the realization of a nightmare that had dogged him ever since he'd first entered into his special relationship—the one that would give him power, allow him control, oh, yes— so long before. Somehow, he had gotten himself caught in the middle, one man sandwiched between two vast systems (he was sure his secret employers represented forces at least as large as his own service), and now he was in mortal danger of being crushed into the pro- verbial grease spot.

The office in which he sat belonged to neither of its occupants. By courtesy, since he was outranked, Tagg allowed the other man the primacy of his seat be- hind the desk. He sat bulky and uncomfortable on a thin metal folding chair in front of the desk and tried to think of something to say. He realized he was sweat- ing. How did it go? Don't ever let them see you sweat? But he couldn't help it, and besides, an animal slyness told him the acrid smell of his body might put the other man off enough to give him a slight advantage.

At this moment, even a slight advantage was not to be
scorned.

Brigadier General Whitney Johnson, stone faced and
ramrod stiff, regarded him coldly. From his short,
white buzz cut to his unflinching black gaze, to the
immaculate way his Savile Row suit hung from his
thin shoulders, Whit Johnson was everything that Loy
Tagg was not. If a man could be said to have a genetic
predisposition for the military, Johnson was such a
man. Third in his class at the Academy, he'd been a
fighting man's officer, serving in six UN police actions
and capping his career with the legendary raid on
Chang Xu. That had been his operation, and though a
stray hit from a pop-up grenade had permanently retired him from field command, it had made him a legend. Now he served with the DIA—always, Tagg
thought, with the line soldier's disdain for those who
never faced tanks or artillery in the line of duty. Even
now, it seemed there was the faintest wrinkle in Johnson's upper lip, the tiniest widening of thin, patrician
nostrils, as he regarded Tagg with all the fondness of
a man preparing to clean up an unfortunate, but ex-
pendable, pile of dog shit.

Good, Tagg thought. Let him be disgusted. Let him
be angry. Let him be downright revulsed, if it would
distract him from the real danger. Tagg had mounted,
with wide latitude but little explanation, a massive operation. Two men were dead. If he were to survive,
those bodies must be explained. He certainly didn't
have anything to show for them. God *damn* Josh Tower.
Who could have had any idea he'd be so lucky?

None of which mattered at all.

"Tell me again," General Johnson said, "how you
got on this Tower fellow."

The armpits of his light tan suit dark with moisture,
his tie awry, the unseemly weight of his gut spilling
over his belt, Tagg began to trot out his lies again.

He kept his voice slow and cool. He might sweat.
A fat man surely could sweat. But he couldn't show
fear. If he did that, this skinny martial aristocrat would

bury him without a trace. And that wouldn't do at all. Not, at least, until he'd taken his revenge.

God, how he looked forward to that.

"Well, here it is."

She waited until he'd shut the door behind them. The sound of it was deeper, heavier than she'd expected, as if the door were made of something more dense than wood. After the slow, repulsive climb up three flights of splintered stairs, feeling rotted, sucking things squish beneath her shoes, hearing small bodies scuttle out of their path, this room was not what she'd expected.

Drapes were drawn across the window on the far edge, but a faint light trickled in. The room was sparsely furnished, though neat as a pin. He found a light switch. An old, cracked plastic fixture overhead buzzed on, illuminating everything in its harsh glare. There was a sofa, old but clean, and from its bulky lines she guessed it folded out into a bed. A small kitchenette was to her right—antique stove, small, scarred refrigerator, porcelain sink with rusty black patches where the white had corroded away. The stench was not so pervasive here, and the general cleanliness was reassuring after the ruin beyond the front door.

"There's a small bath through that door," Tower said, "and that one's a closet." He limped past her to the sofa and collapsed suddenly, like a puppet with its strings cut. She stared at him with alarm. He'd been so competent in getting them from the bullet-train terminal to this place that she'd forgotten just how bad his condition was. She dropped the suitcase.

"Josh, let me check those bandages."

His right hand, resting on the sofa cushion, still loosely grasped the ugly, functional shape of the Club. He raised his left hand tiredly.

"I'm okay. Just run down a little. What I need is a nap and some food."

She stopped and stared uncertainly around. Then she turned and went into the kitchen and began opening cabinet doors. Everything was quite clean but empty, except for some baited traps put out for rodents and insects. Somebody had gone to a lot of trouble to keep this place neat and serviceable.

The refrigerator was warm and vacant. She reached down and turned the cooler knob and listened to the small compressor whine into action.

"Josh, what is this place?"

He grinned sardonically. The harsh light made his face look old, knowing, and more wounded than it already was. "In the parlance, it's called a safe house."

She shook her head. "Safe house? I don't understand."

Now some emotion she couldn't quite read suffused his voice. Something not quite scorn, not quite embarrassment. "You could almost call it a safe home."

She was totally at sea. He stared at her as if he expected her to say something further, but she couldn't think of a thing. The refrigerator clicked sharply, hiccoughed, and settled back down into its unobtrusive whine.

"I should probably go buy something to eat." Then she hefted her purse vaguely. "But I don't have any money. You said we couldn't use . . . that man's . . . chip, or mine, either. Do you have any money?"

Groaning slightly, he heaved himself from the sofa and joined her in the kitchen.

"I don't know," he said. "It depends on whether the thief I pay for this is a good thief or a bad one."

"What's the difference?"

"A good thief stays bought."

He went to the counter next to the sink and tapped one of the tiles. A few tiles were missing, but most were in place. "You got a fingernail file, something to pry with?"

She handed him a small pair of scissors. Wordlessly, he pried up one of the tiles. She stared at the space underneath but saw nothing except a cancerous patch of dried glue.

"Was there . . . something hidden beneath the tiles?"

For the first time, his eyes seemed to twinkle. He took the scissors and scored the bottom of the tile. Oddly, there was no scraping noise. Instead, the tough plastic coating parted, and she saw the yellow gleam of gold.

Robert Hilkind was alone. His body occupied the white room in utter solitude. But he danced upon the face and listened to the whispers of a hundred million ghosts.

''Denver,'' he breathed softly, his eyes blank and empty. ''A little thing. A subway. Denver.''

Then he laughed.

Chapter Twelve

The next day he felt better. The inflammation in his wounded ankle had subsided, and his shoulder, stiffened by elastic tape, seemed safely back in its socket. There was little he could do about his tongue. It was an agony for him to eat, but the mysterious protections against infection that lived in all human mouths had protected him. The tongue would heal, eventually.

He woke up in a single blink, coming from sleep into full waking at once. Next to him, on the lumpy mattress extended from the hide-a-bed, Kelly still lay in deathlike sleep. The muscles of her face were slack. Her breathing was nearly imperceptible. He wondered if she were dreaming.

It was early in the morning. The dim, amber light of the room squeezed around the edges of the cheap, heavy drapes told him that. This had always been a dark place, but there were degrees to the darkness. And after all the years, he could still read those degrees as easily as another might read a netcast.

Somebody in the building was cooking cabbage. Somebody else had finishing taking a morning crap and the old pipes rattled with flushing. He lay still and pondered the submerged meanings. Why had he selected this place, the lair of a man who had called himself a father but who had not loved him? When he had set this up, many years ago, he had wondered over the same question. Couldn't he dissolve the ties to a childhood that had been cold and frightening? Or was this simply an act of defiance, a necessary proving of himself to ghosts long gone but never banished?

Yet he had returned. He had never given up this place, this bolt hole, this island of dangerous safety from the past. Even ten years with Julia had not erased the old habits. Spies and killers needed extraordinary precautions. Perhaps he had needed the psychological idea more than the actual reality, but in any event, in extremity, the place had remained. A tiny, shabby room in a slum next to mountains, where the tiles in the kitchen concealed twenty-four-carat gold and the walls concealed—what?

He shivered, though the room was close and stuffy and full of their mingled body odors. He thought he had come so far, but now everything had collapsed. Inexorably he was sinking back, falling back to the beginning.

He sat up, then moved to the side of the mattress and put his feet on the floor. The bare wood planks were rough and scratchy. Kelly didn't stir. He eased himself up and went to the bathroom. He found a tiny cake of soap, wrapped in desiccated paper with the Marriott logo on top.

The sight cheered him slightly. There was a time in this place when soap had been a luxury. He'd had to steal it then. Now it waited for him.

Some things improved.

RIPPER STRIKES AGAIN read the headline of the *San Francisco Chronicle* on a million video screens. Tagg told his comm unit to shut up, and the brightly lit patch of color winked off.

He finished with the croissant and the two jelly donuts and the eggs and Italian sausage and four pancakes and orange juice and three cups of coffee heavy with cream and sugar.

The Ripper, as the local nets had dubbed him, had become the latest sensation. He had killed two teenagers on the overlook on Twin Peaks. Less than a week later an old woman had been decapitated outside her mansion on Pacific Heights, her stringy white-haired head impaled on a croquet stick facing out toward the

Bay. A few days later, a daze dealer on the fringes of Hunter's NewTown had lost his head, but not for long. That grisly memento had been found shortly after, perched like a squat, wingless bird, on a piling near the Yacht Club.

The Ripper. Tagg smiled. It was amazing what a little publicity could do, but this might be a bit much. It was time to get the Ripper away from his growing public. All this amateur mayhem was tolerable, but it wasn't to the point.

Besides, the Ripper might slip and get himself caught.

That wouldn't do at all.

"You seem to know this place well," Kelly said.

Tower shrugged. "Well enough." He had gotten up before her, gone out—she'd almost awakened at the soft snick of the door closing—and returned. He brought a plastic bag of groceries. The bag sported the 7-Eleven logo. When she looked in the kitchen, she saw that all the tiles on the counter had been pried up. They were stacked in a neat pile in the corner. She couldn't tell if any were missing.

He made instant coffee using hot water from the tap. It was hard to get the powdered cream to dissolve in the lukewarm liquid. Even so, the coffee was good. She felt the caffeine zip through her veins, opening up the cells in her brain.

"I must love you," she said. She dropped the words into the morning silence like an old-fashioned hand grenade. They lay there ticking, ready to explode.

He looked at her. She couldn't decide what his expression meant. "What?" he said.

"I must love you. I mean, none of this makes any sense, otherwise. My life is a mess. No doubt I've lost my job. Men I know nothing about are chasing me. You say they want to kill me. Now I'm in a slum in Denver, drinking instant coffee from a tap. And sleeping on a lumpy bed. And trusting you." She paused. "It must be love. What else could it be?"

He couldn't think of an answer. He sipped his coffee. He didn't have answers for his own questions. How could he find answers for hers?

"I have to go out today."

She nodded. "And you want me to stay here, to keep the door locked, to not even think about leaving."

Her voice was completely serious, but it was the closest thing to humor either of them had shared in days. He felt his lips curve. "That's right."

"And you'll be back, and things will happen."

He finally caught it. He was so stupid, sometimes. "I'm going out to peddle the gold," he said. "I'll look for people who understand these sorts of things. I'll find somebody, because in a place like this there is always somebody." He spoke slowly, carefully. "After I have credit again, I'm going to use it to try to get us out of this. To buy equipment. Phony identification. Bribes. Whatever it takes. Okay? See, I'm not trying to keep secrets from you anymore."

She reached over and patted his hand gravely. "See that you don't."

He nodded. Something else had just been decided, in its own way just as important as his earlier decision not to abandon her. But only time would tell how good a decision it was.

She seemed to like it well enough. She touched his hand again. "When you get back, we go to a real grocery. This dump needs a woman's touch."

After he had gone, she sat in silence at the tiny counter that separated the kitchen from the living area. She drank another cup of lukewarm coffee and wondered why she had said it.

"Oh, Carl. I'm sorry." But she felt ridiculous, speaking into the emptiness of the morning, and she didn't know what she was apologizing for. Carl was dead, so he couldn't tell her either.

It didn't matter. It felt right, and that was all that counted.

* * *

The wind had that kind of nearly visible transparency that often comes to Denver in the late autumn. You could follow its tracks by watching the movement of the things it touched. Black, skeletal branches moved, and rags of paper, bits of refuse, plumes of smoke from the ubiquitous corner trash barrel fires. As he trudged up Thirteenth Street he didn't get the feeling that the young boys and old men gathered round these flames were without homes. It was more that the corners were gathering places, social clubs, the poverty-stricken version of a day at the office.

Which was, of course, exactly what they were. Tower no longer knew specific addresses, but he knew enough to read the advertising. After a couple of hours of searching, he found the right shingle.

He moved close to the barrel and rubbed his hands over the warmth of the flames. His breath plumed out in a long, silver feather as he spoke.

"I want to do some dealing," he said to the huge, fur-wrapped black man who wore thick ropes of gold around a neck like a tree trunk.

The black man showed teeth like the edge of a glacier in the sun and said, "Course you do. But do it quick. You look like you about to fall in that barrel there. You look about to die, man."

Tower grinned slowly. "Not quite yet, banker. Not before we deal."

The banker, who said his name was Banker and who never stopped smiling during their transaction, examined the tile that Tower offered. He turned it over and hefted it in his big hand, and after a while he made an offer. It was about what Tower expected—less than thirty percent of the current value of the gold. They haggled and finally settled on sixty-five percent. Banker promised payment in clean credit drafts, the chips payable to bearer. Tower agreed to the transaction. He didn't particularly worry about being ripped off. He had let Banker see the butt of the Club stuck in the waistband of his jeans, concealed beneath his overcoat. Banker had given no sign, but he had seen. The high-tech weapon was a presentation of bona fides, and a warning. Men who carried weapons like that were not to be trifled with, no matter how weak they might appear. Clubs were hard to come by. Men who possessed them might represent other, more dangerous forces.

When they had agreed Banker smiled an even brighter smile, almost blinding above the leaping flames in the barrel. It made him look like a genie rising from fire.

"Make you a good offer on any other equipment you got," he said.

"Maybe," Tower said. "Maybe later. But first, I need to find some equipment of my own."

Banker nodded. "You came to the right place, man. I be the banker here. I know everything."

And, as it turned out, he did.

Tower knew he had no leverage in Denver, not the kind of leverage he could have once used, when all the resources of the Defense Intelligence Agency had been on call for him. But this was another, more ancient system, and he understood it just as well. The people who lived here had been rejected by the system of credit and exchange and respectability, but they had their own system, their own standards. Their own heroes. Two days after he had turned his hidden gold into sterile credit, he sat down in a small room that hummed and buzzed and clicked and pinged.

The room sounded like an electronic zoo at feeding time. It glittered like the inside of some amazing, convoluted shell. Every inch of the wall, and much of the ceiling, was covered with machines. Video screens shifted and jittered like so many twitching eyes. Chip readers coughed slowly, digesting private codes. Multiscanners monitored the nets. And three big superframes did—what? He sat down in a thickly upholstered chair that seemed to have been stolen from the first-class

section of an LEO shuttle and looked at the ruler of
this constricted realm.

Meister Bee was not at all what he'd expected.

Meister Bee was twelve years old. Tower knew this
because Meister Bee had told him up front. He'd said,
"I'm Meister Bee. I'm twelve years old." And then
he'd shrugged and said, "I'm telling you so you don't
get any stupid ideas. So you think carefully and decide
what kind of twelve-year-old kid could do what I do.
You think about that and you won't make any mistakes
with me."

All this had been said with a slow, deadly serious-
ness, without any expression, which had, in a way,
made it all the more frightening. Tower had understood immediately. There were three groups that
shared the running of the Denver Deep. Meister Bee
headed the most important one of them. That a child—
Meister Bee stretched that definition considerably, but
technically, it was true—could have risen to oversee
such an undercover gold mine as the Deep testified to
skills not normally considered childlike: torture and
murder and extortion, and a number of others that dif-
fered only in kind, not in degree.

Meister Bee's face was unlined, thin, unblemished
by the faintest sign of a beard. His eyes, the color of
lead, waited for an answer. Tower didn't have to lie.

"I won't make any stupid mistakes," he said. "I
know what you have to be. To be what you are."

Meister Bee blinked. He wore sunglasses that were
only faintly smoky, and when he blinked, Tower heard
a quiet, whirring noise. He felt his chest relax. He
hadn't known what the weapon was, or how it was
controlled, but he'd known it was there. Now he understood. Meister Bee's glasses were a miniature
blinkup sensor. The panels monitored his eyelids, and
certain movements were control codes. The whirring
noise had been a gun snout—a Club, a laser, a narrow-
band ripper—anything at all. For the moment, they
understood each other.

"So what," Meister Bee asked, "can I do for you?"

Tower told him.

When he had finished, the child's leaden eyes had turned a different shade, as if the lead had melted and become hot and sparkling.

"Nice shit, man," Meister Bee said. "The equipment will be no problem. Just give me a list."

Tower nodded.

"The rest of it? That will cost."

"Yes," Tower said. "No problem." He tossed one of the bearer chips across the desk. The boy stuck it in a reader, pulled it out, and put it in his pocket.

"Okay." He turned his thin shoulders against the leather of the seat. As he did so, Tower saw faint glimmers of what might have been wires, extending from the back of his head. Connections for the blink glasses, he supposed.

"Don't come back here," Meister Bee said. "I'll give you contact codes after you're set up."

Tower waited, but nothing more was said. The meeting seemed to be over. He stood up, turned, and walked toward the door. He heard the soft whirring again, and the back of his neck itched. When he reached the door, he paused and looked back.

Meister Bee's glasses had gone a bright, reflective silver. His jagged hair, black as an oil slick in the light, seemed to glitter.

He reminded Tower of a small insect, happy in the center of a great, deadly web.

Happy and hungry.

Tower nodded, but Meister Bee ignored him.

Only after he had left, after two scrawny, ratlike boys in their early teens, each armed with new-looking Czech copies of Israeli Uzi Needlers, had escorted him up from the cellar beneath the burned out Safeway, did Tower fully realize he'd been in the court of a prince. Perhaps even a king, in this realm of the poor, this system within the system.

It's all systems, he thought, and something touched him, but he didn't quite know what it was. Not then. Later, though. He was certain of it. Later.

* * *

His code name was Condor, and he had named the operation Condor, and that pleased him a little every time he thought about it. He had been at this game a very long time and had learned that even small things had meaning.

The message had come through the usual sources, diffuse, impinging on his receptors from three different directions at the same time. All this secrecy amused him. It didn't surprise him, for in his line, secrecy was the currency of transaction. The humor of it came from their naivete. They supposed they had hired him, as a mercenary, for a job, but nothing was that simple anymore. He had ferreted them out within a week, despite all their precautions. They still thought they had anonymity, and he hadn't disabused them of that notion. But he knew them, and understood their goals, and so wasn't surprised at all when the new orders came through.

He'd been expecting them, in fact. But it was an interruption. He had hoped to be able to focus, to concentrate on the job, their job and his job; and now he had to arrange for Tagg. Tagg was a fat man, a clown, a buffoon, but there were edges under all the fat. Sharp edges that could cut the unwary.

Condor sighed. It would take a bit of time. Not much, but more than he wanted to spend.

Perhaps if he lured Tagg to him he could finish more quickly.

Condor was a big man, not as young as he'd once been. He had few illusions left. He was old enough to allow himself a few soft spots in the shell around his heart, but not many. Tagg had no claim on such a spot. Tagg was business.

He would lure him and kill him and get back to his own projects. That was best.

That would be easiest.

Colonel Tagg finished packing in his room at the New Mark Hopkins, a sixty-story knife piercing the rock of Nob Hill. He had Newsnet on, idly following the progress of local police in their search for the Rip-

per, while he packed. He topped off his suitcase with
a plastic box containing two pastrami sandwiches made
of local sourdough. One thing about San Francisco
was the food. Washington was a desert compared to
the food of San Francisco. He snapped down the lid
of his suitcase and the net screen began to blat about
the disaster. The newscaster used the word three times
in his first two sentences.

Disaster . . . disaster. A disaster.

Tagg stared at the screen. At first he thought it was
some kind of joke. The scene was so bizarre. He
blinked. Then his memory supplied the right picture,
and he recognized the State of Illinois building. It was
a hundred and seventy-five stories tall, one of the
monuments to the city of Chicago's mania for record-
setting skyscrapers. Halfway up the distinctive cylin-
drical shape a great bloom of black smoke billowed
out, but that wasn't what caught Tagg's interest. Within
the smoke, partially hidden by it, was a long, blunt
shape, as if a giant had hammered a huge spike into
the side of the building.

The announcer's voice-over was tense. Tagg listened. The announcer kept repeating the same facts
again and again, as if he couldn't believe them himself.

The two o'clock shuttle from the Consort transfer in
LEO had somehow lost the grid as it settled toward
touchdown at New O'Hare. Computers had failed, or
satellites, something—it still wasn't certain. At any
rate, the shuttle had plowed into the building and all
the passengers were dead. Fire had exploded through
at least three floors of the tower, where fifteen hundred
people worked. Most likely they were dead, as well.

Chicago firefighters struggled to extinguish the blaze,
but they were hampered by high winds and the danger
of the wreckage of the shuttle falling to the streets
below.

Already lawsuits were being filed.

It was a disaster, Tagg decided. Not so much for the
dead. Tagg didn't care about the dead. But Consort

stock would fall again, just as it had earlier when the laser taxis had crashed near San Francisco.

Consort was having a lot of problems lately. He owned five shares himself. He wondered if now was the time to sell part of his holdings. Before the stock went any lower.

Kennedy Crater must be batshit, he thought.

The announcer came on. His face was white. Tagg couldn't understand it. It wasn't the announcer's problem. Not unless he owned a bundle of Consort.

He picked up his suitcase and headed for the door. He had his own problems. He had stalled General Johnson with lies, but that wouldn't last forever. He needed a body.

At the very least, he needed a body.

Higgins smiled. He sat at the window of his barren apartment and looked out into the sunshine sparkling over the city. It seemed like there was a reflection of the sunshine inside his brain, a small hot yellow spot that blinded his eyes from behind.

He looked down at his hands. He had washed his hands carefully, but he could still see the dark red sludge underneath his fingernails. He thought that maybe nobody else could see the sludge, but he still could.

The sun burned outside and the answering sun burned inside his skull, and he smiled and tried to figure out whether anybody else could see the dried blood beneath his fingernails.

It gave him something to do, while he waited for the fat man to pick him up and take him away from there.

"You wouldn't believe it—he's just a kid," Tower said to her.

She had made him go shopping with her. They had ridden the Colfax Avenue underground clear out to Aurora, to a huge shopping mall there. She had purchased clothing and dishes and pots and pans and arranged for an enormous grocery order to be delivered.

Now she pulled a casserole dish from the small oven and eyed it suspiciously. She was fairly certain the thermostat on the oven didn't work right. The oven was hotter than the dial said it was, and the microwave generator had obviously seen better days. But the casserole seemed to be cooked now, after three tries.

It was chicken and mushrooms and red wine and fresh curlicues of pasta. It was the kind of thing a woman alone cooked for herself, because it was easy and good and could be reheated many times.

"That smells good," he told her.

"What did you say? About just a kid?"

He told her again about Meister Bee.

"That sounds awful," she said.

He dished some of the casserole onto her plate. The plates were nice, heavy ceramic work imported from Malaysia, from the new factories there. "I don't know," he said. "Something has changed from when I was a kid. They're running things now. Not everything. People like Banker are still around. But in that little room, with all those machines. Just kids. They were like very smart rats." He paused. "Smart rats with guns."

"Terrible."

He tasted his food. "That's good," he said. "You're a good cook."

"Children."

He remembered his own childhood. "They don't do so bad," he said at last. She shook her head, but he didn't say anything else for a while. He really did think her casserole was very good.

Two large, unsmiling men dressed in gray work coveralls delivered his equipment the next day. It took them a while to negotiate the dark stairs and the rubbish choking them. They stacked the boxes and crates in the center of the room, and when they were done, the larger of the two said, "Thumbprint here," and he held out a chip with a shiny plate on it.

Tower shook his head. "No. No thumbprints."

The man shrugged and put the chip back in its case. "Your funeral. The guarantee's no good without a print."

Tower didn't say anything. After a moment the man shrugged again. "Come on, Al," he said to his partner. "Let's get out of here."

"You'll have to help me," Tower told Kelly.

She did. His shoulder was getting better, but it was still stiff and weak. It took them five hours to set up everything. He checked for power drain and decided it was all right.

"Now what?" she asked.

He sat down in front of the main entry pad. "Now we find out."

She walked into the kitchen and took a package of flour from the cabinet. "Find out what?"

"Why everybody's trying to kill us."

Her lips moved into a narrow line. "Oh, good."

"Better than what we had before," he assured her.

Colonel Tagg received the message through sources he was not supposed to be able to access any longer. General Johnson had put him on a short leash. That was the way the thin martinet had said it.

"You're on a short leash, Tagg. You don't do anything about this . . . *matter,* until I've completed my investigation. Do you understand me?"

And Colonel Tagg had saluted him as well as he could and read from the disgust in the old man's eyes that it hadn't been good enough. The old man had a puzzle, and the pieces were dead men and missing men. He knew something had gone wrong, but he didn't know what. And maybe, just a little, he was afraid of what he would discover. It wouldn't be the first time some cowboy had gone out of channels and gotten mud all over the Defense Intelligence Agency.

Tagg looked into Johnson's eyes and understood that the leash was very short, indeed. General Johnson thought it was enough. But Tagg knew it wasn't.

The message was cryptic, but it came from good sources, the kind of assets every spy master cultivated, not for any specific reason, but for general awareness. Assets were eyes and ears, and now, somebody had seen something. Heard something.

A man who was damaged had gone to ground with a woman in Denver. That was all, but it would be enough.

The search had narrowed.

He knocked on the shabby door of the apartment and waited until Higgins opened it. The other man stared at him. Tagg thought Higgins looked crazy. His eyes had a bulging, ominous glaze to them, and Tagg wondered how long he would be able to control the man.

The drugs were always chancy, when you dealt with a true psychotic.

"Is it time?" Higgins said. His voice was thick, choked with a welter of emotions that he couldn't name, couldn't understand.

Tagg nodded. "Yes. It's time."

Higgins touched the pocket of his jacket. He felt the comforting weight of the knife there. "Okay," he said. "Let's go."

Tower worked steadily for an entire week. Meister Bee had been able to supply him with software that was even better than the custom stuff he'd lost in Kelly's apartment. He had to modify it some, but when he had finished, he made more progress in three days than he'd made in all the time before.

And he began to understand why Meister Bee controlled the data underground in Denver, why the Deep was his. On screen, fronted by the wizardry of his programs, the deftness of his touch, he was a marvel. His work was not that of a twelve year old. Tower had seen him, and he still didn't believe that he could do the things he did.

The electronic touch of the child was a whisper, a razor of discrimination, a bloodhound. Nothing was safe from his skill. Tower knew that his own technical abilities paled in comparison. But Meister Bee lacked one thing: He didn't truly understand scope. He could dissect fragments with appalling ease, but he couldn't fit pieces into a whole.

He didn't understand systems, not as well as he would later. In a way, Tower was glad of that. If Meister Bee understood systems, Tower thought that he might kill him himself. As a service to humanity.

Meanwhile, he probed and mapped the ramparts of Condor. He made no effort to penetrate the massive protections this time. He merely discovered the limits of Condor's influence. The connections. The systems of which Condor was a part.

When he had finished, late at night seven days after he'd begun, he was bathed in sweat and his stomach bubbled like one of Kelly's casseroles. Whatever Condor was doing was on a scale much larger than a city or a single government. Condor was not a part of one system. Condor was inextricably wired into *all* systems.

Colonel Tagg and Higgins flew into Denver on the direct laserliner from SFO. They arrived at dusk, when the sun was a bloody globe slowly impaling itself on the mountains. Higgins seemed fascinated with the doomsday glow, and even Tagg shivered at the possibility it might be an omen. He didn't believe in omens, but everything that had happened was so weird that, at times, he wondered if somehow the hand of fate might not be involved.

He didn't believe in fate, either, not under that name. He called it good planning. But everything was somewhat wrecked, and he was trying to hold it together with his own wit and a half-crazed murderer. Tower was in Denver somewhere. So was Condor. Was it a coincidence?

Tagg didn't believe in coincidences, either. But he had no choice. So he might as well consider fate, too. And omens.

"Come on, Higgins."

Higgins followed him out, his face burnished beneath the dying heat of the crimson sun. He looked like he was melting.

He thought he was melting, as well.

"Bingo," Tower said softly.

She had napped earlier in the afternoon. Since Tower wouldn't let her leave the apartment alone, and he spent most of his time in front of his computers, she had gradually found herself taking up old rhythms, basic rhythms that she had fought in an effort to lead a normal life.

She slept late in the morning, leaving coffee and breakfast for him. Sometimes, in the afternoon, she napped. At night she read, experimented with cooking, or simply watched the back of his head as he worked. He was much improved. She had given him a list of medicines, and he'd gotten them somewhere, most likely on the black market, which functioned as the slum economy. She'd made him eat regularly, and he'd begun to exercise again—long sets of situps and knee bends and pushups, despite the ache in his shoulder. His tongue had healed, and the gash in his cheek was only a thin, white line, almost invisible against his pallid skin. He'd put on some weight.

I could fatten him up pretty good, she thought, if I had a chance. The day she'd told him she must love him had almost disappeared from her memory. He never mentioned it, and she never pursued it. If she thought of it at all, it was to recall the distinction: She'd said she must love him, but she hadn't said she did love him. It was a fine distinction, but one she thought she appreciated. He would have to help her over the final hurdle. She'd gone as far as she could.

"What, bingo?"

He turned and faced her. She was on the sofa. They didn't fold it out until the early morning, usually.

"I know the shape of it," he said.

"Is that good?"

"I think so."

But even as he said it, another man, in another place, checked some of his defenses and realized that he'd made an error. Not an irremediable error, but the mistake couldn't have come at a worse time.

Condor shook his head. God damn Josh Tower. Why couldn't he ever do what was expected? Now he really *would* have to die.

Chapter Thirteen

It almost didn't happen. As the twentieth century staggered and lurched toward its close, the United States had grown rich and tired. Japan grew rich and wary. And the Soviet Union simply grew tired. But the visionaries had dreamed their dreams, and Lawrence Schollander and Mitsu Fujiwara welded together the great conglomerate of companies and nations that became Consort. At the beginning, Consort had given away stock like prizes in a Crackerjack box, in order to create public legitimacy for the new company. Those had been frightening times, and failure had been always close at hand.

But Schollander and Fujiwara had made their own private peace, and then the first gigawatt laser installation had gone on-line in the Nevada desert. Consort was in the transportation business to stay, and within two decades, Consort moved the earth. One of the places they moved it to was the Moon.

Kennedy Crater and Luna, Incorporated—wholly owned subsidiaries of Consort—together made up the most lucrative business entity the world had ever seen. It was all as Schollander and Fujiwara had foreseen, and it was good.

Now they would make it better. But it was a ticklish business, and Robert Hilkind said the chances of success had lessened to sixty percent. Schollander, his face as bland and smiling as any sweaty Ford salesman, stood on the top floor of the headquarters building of Luna, Incorporated, and gestured at the green fields of Kennedy Crater spread out below.

"This is ours. We built it."

Fujiwara had heard this before. Schollander's constancy was soothing, but his expression of it was sometimes irritating. He shrugged. "If word gets out before we acquire sufficient stock, they will take it away from us."

Schollander nodded. "You hire the best and let them do their job. It's all we can do."

"Is Condor the best?"

"Bobby says he is."

Fujiwara turned slightly, so that he was facing the clean curves of the Shell, where the rock and roll stars came to play sometimes. "Can Bobby help?"

"Yes. When the time comes."

"I don't understand that interface, the way he's connected to the computer. It doesn't seem human."

Schollander's face was open, burning with good humor. "Of course you do," he said. "It's the future."

"Only if we win," Fujiwara said.

Kelly was not exactly worried about him, but he had become strange. She'd never really understood what he did, how he made his living. He'd told her in the hospital. Datahunter. It's what I do, he'd said. But she hadn't really understood.

He spent twelve, sixteen hours a day in front of his screens. He had three now, and each screen was divided into smaller boxes, each with its load of information. He'd tried to show her.

"There." He pointed at a small rectangle on one side of his central screen. "That's the average number of transactions Condor Securities completes each day."

She stared at the numbers. They made no sense to her.

"And here." Another box. "This comes from the SEC. They regulate stock transactions in the United States. They used to be more important, when all the action was here. But now exchanges are open all the time, all over the world. Trading goes on twenty-four hours a day." He raised his eyebrows. She nodded.

"The SEC requires notification if an individual or company purchases more than a certain percentage of any other company. But there are ways around it."

She waited. He glanced at her as if he expected a question, but she didn't say anything.

"You set up dummy companies. Shell corporations. Or you operate on foreign exchanges. Or you combine all of it. Things move so fast, nobody can keep up anymore. It's like trying to empty the ocean with a spoon." He paused, pleased with the idea. "Condor is buying heavily. They have people all over the world, using fronts, phony companies, cut-outs. They are lying to the SEC. An enormous amount of money is going through Condor every day."

She tried to figure it out. She understood that it was his penetration of Condor in the first place that he believed was the cause of everything that had happened later. But she didn't see the connection. Condor was buying a lot of stock. So what?

"So what?" she said.

He tipped his chair back and looked up at her. His face was flushed in the green glow of his screens. "Condor isn't buying just any stocks. They've covered it well, but they are buying a particular stock."

She thought he was stretching it out for drama. She didn't feel in the mood for drama. "Josh, just tell me, please."

The skin at the corner of his eyes crinkled. "Consort. Condor is buying Consort."

She knew what Consort was. Everybody knew. She owned stock. Everybody owned stock in Consort. The citizens of fifteen nations had been *given* stock in Consort, back at the beginning. It had seemed like a publicity stunt, a new kind of advertising, at the time. But the stock was real. Eventually, it paid very high dividends. Some nations even used it as a basis for their welfare plans. But it was a stock, and it could be bought and sold like any other stock.

"Condor is buying Consort," she said.

He waited, but she didn't say anything else. Finally, he let his breath out. He would have to tell her.

"They own thirty percent. Condor has bought thirty percent of Consort. And nobody knows. Except for the people they are buying for. Whoever they are."

Thirty percent. That seemed like a great deal of stock. A lot of money. She saw that far. "It's a lot, isn't it?"

He stared at the screen, at his green shaded boxes, and nodded. "It's more than the worth of Great Britain. It's more than the current holdings of the U.S. government. It's more than anybody in the world has—except Consort itself."

She could feel his tension. Wordlessly, she touched his shoulder.

"No wonder they don't want anybody to know. That they're ready to kill anybody who finds out. Jesus." His voice was soft and full of awe. "Somebody is raiding Consort."

He stood up and turned to face her. He looked down into her face. "Do you understand?"

"I think so," she said. "You've gotten involved in something very big."

He put his hands flat on her shoulders. "Whoever's doing it," he said, "has all the money in the world. Is *risking* all the money in the world."

She tried to imagine that much money. She couldn't. "Does this help us?"

His voice was almost savage. "If I can find out who," he said. "Then I have all the leverage in the world."

She shivered, not at his words, but at the way he said them. He dropped his hands to her waist and pulled her close. His voice was warm in her ear. "All the *leverage* in the world," he whispered.

She made Teo Chu noodles with beef and cabbage for dinner. She had bought a thermometer that hung inside the oven, and now she could adjust the temperature properly. It was as she'd thought. The battered controller on the old oven was wrong by a hundred degrees. But now it was okay, and the rich, salty odor of the noodles filled the small apartment.

One odd thing: She realized she could no longer smell the stench of the building or the neighborhood. She even opened the windows in the daytime to let in a little fresh air. The human olfactory system could become used to anything. What she couldn't acclimate herself to was the ruin outside the door. The darkness and the cold, and the things that oozed and squished beneath her feet when she hauled the trash to the rusting, corroded dumpster at the back of the building. She had the feeling that many people lived in the building, that each door hid a writhing nest of humanity—five, ten people to a room. She heard the noises, faint and muffled by the soft, absorbent refuse that choked the hallways. Babies crying. Drunken shouts. Low, humming conversations. Screams. Cries. Maniacal laughter. But she never saw anybody. Except, of course, for the creatures who rooted through the garbage in the alley, who watched as she tossed her sacks of trash up on the pile, who waited until she had walked away before leaping on the mound and tearing the bags open with yellowed, hooked fingers.

Tower said it had always been that way. He didn't see anything abnormal about it. She wondered what depths his clean, middle-class exterior concealed. She thought about that often, the things she didn't understand about him. Didn't know about the man she must love.

He had been working at a white-heat pace for two days, ever since he'd explained to her about Condor and Consort. He said there was a connection, of course. If the players were that big, then perhaps the government had been suborned. That would explain the DIA. Or maybe it was the government itself, mounting a buyout. But he said that didn't make any sense. He wasn't sure what did make sense, but he was going to find out.

He told her again not to go outside during the day, when she might be seen. She took the trash out at midnight, when it was pitch dark and the stars were occluded by a nasty orange haze and the clawed creatures in the alleys huddled by low, greasy red fires and watched her with the eyes of rats. She pictured them leaping on her, tearing her skin open like a bag, digging around inside with their yellow claws. Finally, she made him get up from his screens and take the trash out himself, and she didn't go beyond the front door at all.

"How much longer?" she said, as she set out plates, flatware, and two wine glasses.

He looked up from the main screen. "Tonight should do it. I have to finish a deal with Meister Bee. With the kid."

She found it marvelous that he should place so much on a child's shoulders. This Meister Bee must be something extraordinary. And then another part of her pointed out that all of this was extraordinary. Just months ago she'd not yet met Josh Tower. She'd lived by herself in a neat little apartment and gone to work every day, and the only thing she'd worried about was her memories. Her guilts.

It all seemed so trivial now.

It all seemed so frightening now. She was wearing out from the tension. He didn't seem to notice that she spoke little, slept a lot, asked no questions. She was within herself, waiting. There was nothing she could do but wait. She couldn't even allow herself hope. Hope implied a reason, knowledge. She didn't know anything. Despite all his explanations, she was still ignorant.

Yes, she must love him.

"It's ready," she said. "Come eat."

Smiling, full of his arcane discoveries, he came. "It's good," he said. "This is very good, these noodles."

She nodded. I'm a cook, she thought. And she wished it would end.

It had begun as a great ocean disturbance, a vast area of low pressure moving down from Alaska, lurking just offshore, gathering its strength. When it had reached the borders of the United States, the jet stream shifted suddenly south and began to drag it over the land, bringing rain up and down the coast from Seattle to San Francisco. By the time it had bulged across the Sierras and come down on Salt Lake City, it was a howling white terror. In Colorado, Aspen and Vail and Steamboat Springs battened down the hatches. The snow bunnies and the tanned professionals looked outside, shook their heads, and were glad that the firewood boxes were full and they were sheltered beneath their expensive condominiums. Above Denver, the perennial pall of smog began to dissipate, blown out toward the eastern plains before the stiffening breeze. And the clouds pushed up behind the mountains like great piles of dirty cotton, thick and heavy and ominous.

In Capitol Hill, the wind began to rise.

Tagg glanced up as the wind buffeted the thick, double-paned windows of his rooms in the Brown Palace Tower. They were large rooms, a suite with two bedrooms. He sat in the main room and tried to ignore the sound of Higgins's video screen tuned to some idiotic game show in the far bedroom. He could have placed Higgins by himself, in his own suite, but recent observations had convinced him that Higgins could not be trusted to control himself. The last thing he needed was the discovery of some hapless bellman's skull impaled on a potted plant in one of the luxurious hotel hallways.

He had already been out twice and was considering a third venture. The storm bothered and reassured him. It might make his journey difficult, but it would conceal whatever he had to do at the end of it.

He rubbed his belly absently. He'd been in Denver five days now. He'd been unable to pursue his information through the original sources, but it didn't matter. He knew where to go to ask the right questions of the right people. It was all very simple, really. And finally, late this afternoon, a huge, fur-swathed black man had told him what he wanted to know. It hadn't even cost very much. Now he had a description and an address.

A man with scars and wounds and a Club stuck in

his belt would always be memorable, even in a place like Capitol Hill. He smiled again. It was just a matter of knowing who to talk to. And Tagg always knew that.

"Higgins, get dressed."

The man lying on the bed in his undershorts grunted something unintelligible. His cybernetic prosthesis, without its sheath of concealing artificial flesh, glinted evilly. Higgins had torn the flesh off with his own hands. He preferred the cold purity of the metal itself. The metal, sharp and simple, like knives.

"Get up. It's time."

This time his grunt was querulous, stupid and angry. An animal sound.

"Tower," Tagg finally said. "It's time for Tower."

Higgins lumbered into the room less than two minutes later, fully clothed.

"Good," Tagg said. He looked down and went on mildly. "Don't carry that knife in your hand. Put it away, you idiot."

The trigger word so carefully implanted months before had done its work. Higgins was drooling, but he didn't seem to notice. Tagg became even more grateful for the coming storm. He wouldn't be so noticeable, leading a monster around.

"Come on, Higgins. Let's go get Tower." At this repetition of the trigger word, Higgins nodded so hard that he sprayed spittle on Tagg's coat. Tagg wiped it off.

He opened the door and Higgins stepped out into the hall. Tagg paused to check the room. Nothing incriminating there, in case he had to leave unexpectedly.

The storm had decided him. Better to do it now, get it over with. He patted Higgins on the shoulder. He was almost fond of him. He wondered if there would be any way to keep him after this.

Probably not, but you could never tell.

It was brutal weather. Snow had begun to fall with the sunset, which had come like a torch doused in icy water. At first there had only been dancing flurries that resembled bunches of small white insects beneath the clear glare of the streetlights. But in this neighborhood the streetlights had been ripped down for their metal, and nobody was foolish enough to spend money to replace them. The snow grew thicker, whipped like cream before the wind.

Coudor tried to protect himself by hugging close to the wall of a house at the intersection of Ogden and Twelfth Street, but the snow was so thick he couldn't see the building across the way. Not that it mattered. He held his bare hands up to his lips and blew on them. His breath was a cloud that turned to ice before it touched his fingers. The night was full of indiscriminate howling, as the gale tore at the tattered bones of the slum. Even the ever-present trash-barrel fires were out, their keepers gone away to burrows less inhospitable. A part of him noted that there were no witnesses.

Another part of him longed for the warmer wildness of his home, for the sea that tossed like liquid pewter and the long calls of the shorebirds. But that was beyond him now, and failure could bar him from it forever.

That thought frightened him, as much as he could be frightened. He regretted the past, regretted the present, and regretted the future most of all, but there was nothing he could do about it. He was a realist. What was necessary would have to be done. It was a shame, though.

He held that thought as he stepped out into the wind and dark, and he began to work his way across the street. The weight of the Magnum was comforting, as much as it could be, in his pocket.

If only his fingers weren't so cold.

Even though he knew the storm was raging outside, he could hear nothing of it. Here, inside, buried beneath charred ruins, the only sounds were of machines. Wheeps and tings and hums and sudden chirps.

Meister Bee regarded him from behind his silvered blinkup glasses. His thin face was still, his lips barely moving. Tower couldn't see his eyes at all, and he was unnerved by how much difference it seemed to make. Without his eyes, Meister Bee might have been some kind of extension, some extrusion from the welter of machines that surrounded him, encased him. The disconcerting visionary flash of a queen ant surrounded by thousands of silicon workers popped up and disappeared. Not human at all, something whispered inside his skull. Not human at all.

"I can't crack the walls," Tower said.

"I can." Utter certainty. "There's nothing I can't crack."

"Do you understand the stakes?"

"I think so." So still, that voice. Quiet. Full of secret powers.

Tower said, "How much?"

The thin lips widened. It might have been a smile. "This one's on the house. There will be enough for everybody. Am I right?"

"You're right," Tower said. He felt very tired. The muscles in the back of his neck ached, and he dreaded going back into the storm.

He got up slowly. Meister Bee's blank gaze tracked him like a gun sight. "Tower," he said.

"Yes?"

"I'll funnel everything to your rig when I'm done."

Tower nodded. "When?" He was exhausted with the waiting. He had hidden, and hunted, and waited, and now his bones felt like they would melt.

"Tonight. It won't take long."

Tower stared at him, astonished.

"I told you," Meister Bee said. "I am very good."

The last thing Tower saw, as he left the snug, hidden room, was the quick, luminescent flash of the blinkup connectors. If that's what they were.

Outside, the wind and the night and the snow swallowed him. He hoped Kelly had cooked something hot. It would take a lot of heat to make him warm again.

She let the flap of drape fall over the window. She could see nothing outside in the white dark. Occasional icy flurries spat against the streaked glass. The small apartment seemed closed in, claustrophobic. She tried not to think about what might have become of the creatures in the alley, who lived on garbage. Had they bored beneath it, into pockets of damp and rotting warmth? The thought made her shiver suddenly.

So cold. She wondered when Tower would get back. He'd gone out, to see Meister Bee, he'd said. He didn't tell her what it was about. She would have listened, but she suspected that he knew the truth. All his information, the things he told her, only confused her further. She felt cast adrift and trapped at the same time. The reality of Colonel Tagg had receded. The blunt, raw pictures of death—the two men in the office, the blood—had gone fuzzy and indistinct, the way bad memories always do. She couldn't reach inside herself to find a sense of urgency anymore. It was all day to day, and now the days blurred into each other, so that it seemed she'd been here forever.

He said it was coming to an end, and the consummation he'd promised was now about to occur. But she was afraid his idea of an ending was different than hers. She didn't believe he wanted what she did: an answer to her question, a help over the final hurdle. A home, children. A life without the old guilts.

He lived in a world where the rules were different, where nothing was certain, and nothing lasted forever. Perhaps we all do, she told herself, but we don't want to admit it.

It was a terrible notion. She stepped around it and refused to look at it anymore.

House crazy, she thought. Snowbound. All the words. I need to *do* something.

What she settled on was the closet. She thought she'd heard a rat, some kind of animal, scratching in there. Faint, clicking sounds. There was a broom in the kitchen. She would sweep and arrange things and put out another trap.

Something to do. Anything.

222   W. T. Quick

Outside the wind shrieked and rattled the glass and
shook the entire building as if it were made of cardboard. The lights flickered. Then they steadied. She
waited. After a moment she shook her head and went
to get the broom.

He fought his way past the ice-coated chainlink fence
around the 7-Eleven. Amazingly the place was still
open. The clerk, an old man with gray skin and watery
eyes, looked at him as he came in and shook the snow
off himself.

"Lousy night out there," the clerk said. His voice
was cracked and scratchy, like an old videotape.

"Ugly," Tower agreed. "Surprised to find you
open."

The old man shrugged. "The TV is saying to stay
off the streets. My place, the goddamned heating is
probably out anyway. Might as well stay here. At least
it's warm."

Tower nodded. He wanted to get something for
Kelly, but he didn't know what. The ludicrousness of
the idea struck him. Pick up a present for his girl—
hey, was that what she was?—so where did he shop?
The 7-Eleven, of course. Romantic right to his bones,
that's what he was. He grinned.

"Blizzard like this, not funny, mister," the clerk said.
"I remember the storm of oh-five, that was a . . ."

Tower wandered down the aisle on his right, half
listening to the clerk's drone. The old man didn't seem
put off by this bit of rudeness. Or perhaps he just liked
to talk, and another warm body in his store gave him
enough illusions of an audience.

He finally settled on a box of See's Chocolates, the
kind with fillings that had colors never seen in nature,
and a quart of Haagen Dazs Butter Brickle ice cream.
He had carried these back to the counter when the
lights flickered, went off, came back on again.

"Just like oh-five," the clerk announced. "What
you want to buy, mister, is some candles. We got a
special, those little white ones you set on saucers. They
burn twelve hours, supposed to."

It made sense. Tower had his own memories of the blizzard of '05, and one of those memories was of his father, blind drunk, chasing him around the apartment in the dark of the storm, after the power had gone, with the general idea of smashing in the side of his skull. He couldn't remember what had set the old man off. Nothing, maybe, except the booze. But he remembered the darkness and the terror, and he had no urge to spend any time in that apartment blacked out in a storm.

"Where are they?"

"Right down that aisle."

It was only a block to the apartment. He turned right, on Eleventh, and headed for the alley. The wind would be milder there, broken up by the backs of the buildings.

The old man watched him go. "Be careful, sonny," he called in his quavering, old man's voice. "You remember the blizzard of oh-five."

But Tower was gone, and the old man never saw him again.

Tower slogged up the alley, leaning first one way, then the other, as the wind smote him from changing, unexpected angles. The snow had turned hard and gritty, and it stung his cheeks like tiny insects. He hugged the small bag to his chest and wished that he'd worn gloves. The blue muffler protected his face somewhat but kept sliding down to his neck. He tried to tug it up, but it wouldn't stay.

He counted his steps as he walked, one two, one two, an old childhood trick. He'd walked this alley before, going to this apartment before, and in that instant he was almost stunned by the circularity of it all. Gone so far to come so far back. Was it any different now than it had been then?

He'd burned. He'd lived with the heat, nurtured it, until it had melted a way out of the dark and cold into a brighter, warmer world. Those kids in the army, kids who looked just like him, but were as different as aliens from the stars. In the DIA Foster had been the first to sense it, to try to understand his contradictions. And when he had, he'd channeled the fire and made Tower understand how to use the hate and the cold, how to strike back.

"You already understand reality," Foster had told him. "All you need are the tools to deal with it. These other kids, they think life is mommy and daddy and a new car for graduation. They will be terribly surprised when some scrawny ten year old blows their balls off with a rusty AK-47. But you won't. You might have been that kid, right?"

So maybe it had been an advantage, and maybe not. He had survived his time in the army, and when he'd come out, he thought it was all behind him. Had convinced himself of it, in fact. But when it had all fallen apart, he hadn't been surprised, not as those nice, middle-class teammates would have been.

He had no expectations. Life was a rotting apartment and a drunken, murderous father and an alley. An alley in a storm, leading to the past.

He reached the rear of his building and paused, even though the wind and the snow had penetrated his collar and he would need to get dry soon. Kelly was afraid of the garbage, of the men and women and children who lived in the alleys and ate the garbage. Maybe it was because they were so strange to her, and that strangeness made her afraid.

He found nothing frightening about them. Even when he was little, they had been there. If anything, they gave him a kind of pride. He had been low, oh yes, but the alley people had been lower still. In the hierarchy of poverty, they were his inferiors. At that time, it had been nice to know that somebody, anybody, was below him on the great ladder of life.

Ladder of life? Jesus Christ, what was he thinking of now?

He grimaced and pushed open the back door and stepped into the warmer dark. He didn't notice the shadow of movement at the garbage pile, and if he had, he wouldn't have thought anything about it.

Some people lived on garbage, and some didn't. At the moment, he didn't, and that was enough for him.

He reached his floor and heard the door down below open and the wind howl louder. He fumbled for his keychip. Somebody was working their way up the stairs. Trying to be quiet and not quite succeeding.

He thought of the way his father had come home sometimes, walking the same way, trying to be quiet.

Be quiet for what? His father had no reason to hide. His son had not given a shit. Not for a long time.

He grinned bitterly at the vagaries of memory and fitted the chip into the lock. He opened the door and stepped inside, and Condor came up behind him and stuck the barrel of the Magnum into the base of his neck.

"Don't do anything," Condor said. "Anything at all."

After a moment, while Tower stood frozen in the bare yellow light of the buzzing overhead fixture, Condor made up his mind. "Forward," he said. "Just a step."

Tower moved into the empty room, still clutching his bag. The snow melted off it and dripped on the splintered wooden floor.

"Good. Put down the bag."

Tower bent over slowly and put the bag on the floor. For one instant the feel of the gun barrel left his neck, but as he straightened, it returned. He could feel the nearness of Condor, knew that if he struck backward with an elbow, he would hit the man.

But the man would kill him. He had no doubt of it. It was cold outside. The man had come from outside, and he would be wearing a heavy coat. The coat would muffle any blow. He couldn't disable the man with one stroke, not before the man killed him.

He stood silent, waiting.

"Down on the floor," Condor said. "On your belly. Hands out."

Tower got down on his hands and knees, then

stretched out flat. He put out his arms, put his palms
flat on the floor. A splinter scratched his cheek.

"Don't look up," Condor said.

Tower felt the hands pat him down, his sides, his
legs, the inside of his thighs, his ankles where a man
might keep a hide-out gun. He felt unutterably sad.
He recognized the voice of Condor. He didn't know it
was Condor, but he recognized the voice, and many
pieces of the larger puzzle slammed into place with a
hollow, echoing sound. Like doors closing.

"Okay," Condor said. "Turn over."

Tower slowly rolled onto his back. Condor loomed
over him, a great dark muffled shape outlined by the
overhead light.

"Hello, Link," Tower said. "Nice to see you
again."

"Stand up. Coat off," Foster said.

Tower knew the drill. Carefully, he removed his coat
and let it fall to the floor. He unbuttoned his shirt and
took it off, to show that he didn't have a belly gun
taped on or a knife in a wrist sheath.

"You already checked the rest," he said. "Unless
you want to see my balls."

Foster grinned. "That's okay, Josh. I know you
never liked to carry anything down there. You always
were afraid of something happening to the family jewels."

Tower nodded. The room was quite hot, but he felt
cold. Goose flesh bloomed on his chest, on the out-
sides of his arms. Foster kept the big Magnum on him
as he stepped around.

"Josh, I—"

The door to the apartment opened silently—Tower
had oiled the hinges—and a fat man with green eyes
walked into the apartment. He had a monster with him.
Both held Clubs.

Foster kept his Magnum on Tower, as the man
slowly climbed to his feet.

"Drop it," Colonel Tagg said.

"You came for him," Foster said. "He's no good to you dead."

"Oh, no, Foster. He's very good to me dead."

Higgins shot Foster twice. The big man slammed against the wall with a heavy sound. His Magnum hit the floor and clattered away under the sofa.

"Who are you?" Tower asked.

"Nobody," Tagg told him.

"I recognize the other one."

Higgins snarled.

"Where's the woman?" Tagg said.

"What woman?"

Higgins came over and hit Tower in the side of the face with his Club. Tower fell down.

"Where is she?"

"I don't know."

"The bathroom, Higgins," Tagg said.

Higgins went to the bathroom, opened the door, looked inside. He closed the door.

He went to the closet and opened it, and Kelly pulled the trigger on the Club she'd taken from the suitcase. She pulled the trigger as fast as she could.

The lights went out.

Chapter Fourteen

On Luna, in Kennedy Crater, in a white room buried beneath the Luna, Incorporated, Headquarters, the man with terrible eyes looked up at the other two.

"Something's happening," he said.

"What?" said Fujiwara. He had never seen Robert Hilkind this upset. It was almost as if he were afraid.

"I don't know. Something big. Something big is moving against us. Trying to crack our shields."

Now Schollander stood. "What? Who? Consort? Is it Consort? Or the government—the United States?"

Hilkind shook his head. "I don't know," he repeated.

Fujiwara said, "What about Condor? Where is Condor?"

"I don't know," Hilkind said a third time. It sounded like a mantra. A mantra for funerals.

The stifling darkness was full of sounds. Tower heard Kelly begin to sob. From the same direction came a low, hoarse, animal moan of pain. And very close to him, floorboards creaked.

Colonel Tagg was a fat man and, like many fat men, was very light on his feet. He could move quickly when he felt like it, although he didn't do so often. It was a good thing to keep your talents secret. Then, when necessary, you could spring a surprise.

He stepped toward where his memory told him Josh Tower should be crouched on the floor. He kicked out hard and almost fell when the tip of his shoe hit nothing but air.

He held the Club tightly in his right hand, held it the right way, close to his body so it couldn't be deflected. He paused, then began to turn in a slow circle, every sense straining for any sound, any hint of movement.

It was all going sour now. Nothing had gone right, not from the very beginning. Chance had ruined him. The omens he hadn't believed in had been correct.

He kept the Club next to him and, as he turned, he pulled the trigger. The high-velocity rockets slammed into the walls, penetrated, blew through the walls beyond the walls.

He would set up a field of fire. Chest high, waist high, and finally toward the floor. He didn't care anymore. Link Foster, Josh Tower, Higgins, the woman—he would kill them all. He savored the thought of it and pulled the trigger again and again.

Four feet away, listening to the pneumatic cough of the weapon, Tower closed his eyes and remembered years in this room. Remembered his alcoholic father clambering like a malevolent insect through the dark with murder on his mind. The recollections burned into his cells told him everything he needed to know. Finally, balancing the tiny squeaks that sounded as Tagg shifted his weight and shifted again, Tower reached forward and caught the plastic bag that contained a box of See's Chocolates and a quart of Haagen Daaz Butter Brickle ice cream. The ice cream weighed almost two pounds. Tower started his swing low; he brought the bag up like a weighted whip, a flexible cudgel. He swung with all his force, aiming for the spot where his memories told him a fat man stood.

He felt the bag slam into something and heard a soft, heavy crunching noise.

Silence.

Rough, snorting sounds. The scrabble of feet.

It seemed the room was full of lurching, lumbering shadows.

Then silence again.

He lay on the floor, listening to the rasp of his own

breathing. Kelly began to cough, a terrible, racking sound. The lights came on.

Tower turned and faced the charge of the monster.

Adrenalin played along his veins in an unholy, screaming minuet. He saw immediately what had happened. Kelly huddled half in, half out of the opened closet door. She slumped forward bonelessly, her face concealed. The Club was hidden beneath her. She had aimed the unfamiliar weapon clumsily, had pulled the trigger without thought. It was sheer luck she'd hit anything at all. Yet she had done terrible damage to Higgins.

A huge slab of the heavy man's face was gone. Blood pulsed in the wound there, flowed down his cheek, soaked his left shoulder, blended into a fist-sized hole beneath the joint. An eyeball hung crazily in the head wound, dangling, staring. Bits of bone and muscle glimmered in both wounds like flecks of meat in a diabolic Christmas pudding. But his leg was the greatest horror. Dot had unwittingly aimed low, then pulled the muzzle of her weapon upward in panic. Her first shots had stitched into Higgins's prosthetic replacement, ripped away his pants leg, and chewed off fist-sized chunks of artificial flesh. Beneath, bent and blistered, the metal bones and dark, glistening ropes of nerve conductors hung exposed like the guts of a bloodless demon.

Higgins lurched forward. Snoring sounds belched from the flap of his nose. More blood and a thick, yellow pus leaked from his mouth. His good eye was red as a cherry. He didn't seem to look at Tower, but he staggered toward him. He had dropped his own Club. Now, in his right hand, he gripped a wickedly edged steel knife. Malignant streaks of rusty red disfigured the shining metal.

Higgins was no longer certain where he was. The bright yellow sun flamed inside his skull, and now the molten worms were coming awake. He could feel them squirm inside his brain, seeking a place to feed. He knew they would eat their way out, tiny voracious teeth snapping together, until finally they burst from his eyes in a swarm of bloated flesh.

But he could stop them. He knew the secret. He knew the word of power. The power was *Tower*. And *Tower* was right in front of him. Colonel Tagg had been right. It was so simple, so easy. So *clean*.

His leg didn't seem to work right, just like in his bad dreams, but he willed himself forward. The pain was terrible, but he didn't care. Once he had hacked off *Tower's* head, everything would be all right. And the woman. Hadn't there been a woman? Yes. Her head, too. They would make a pretty pair.

He ground his teeth together, unaware that he had already gnawed half his tongue off. Blood began to ooze over his thick lips. He smiled at the object of his salvation. At *Tower*. His teeth glistened crimson.

He felt his bladder and bowels let go. The front of his ruined trousers went dark, and a horrible stench filled the room. He didn't care.

He raised his knife and shambled forward.

It would all be over in a moment.

Tower faced him with the bag of groceries in his right hand. He glanced at Kelly, but she was out of it. Her shoulder heaved convulsively. She'd given him a chance, but the rest he would have to do himself. He licked his lips and tasted salt. Higgins danced in his vision, slipped sickeningly away, the returned. He blinked, and he hoped the concussion wouldn't cut him down helplessly before Higgins's attack. Higgins was only a few feet away now, the knife held close to his side, blade flat and edged inward. It was the fighting stance of a professional. Tower pushed his left arm forward in a blocking move as he swung the bag in a quickening circular motion. Higgins might slice up his forearm, but that was better than letting him get in a killing blow.

"Tower!" Higgins said. The word came out softly, a choking sound full of mucus. More fluids leaked from his mouth, drooled down his chin,

Tower stepped back just as Higgins lunged. The long

silver knife flashed out. For Tower, it was as if time
had slowed down. He watched the blade rise in an arc,
its edge glittering in the pitiless light. He saw the metal
cut into the flesh at the side of his forearm, flay it
open, expose white bone.

Higgins grunted and shook his ruined head. Blood
and pus spattered across Tower's face. Higgin's damaged prosthetic clicked suddenly, then clicked again.

Tower swung his makeshift mace as hard as he
could.

The weighted plastic bag crashed into the gaping
hole on the side of Higgins's skull. Gore splashed.
Higgins moaned, and for a moment Tower felt a triumph. But before he could follow up his first strike
the larger man, agile as a hunting cat, leaned back and
brought his artificial leg up and around in a karate
kick.

The heavy metal caught Tower on his upper thigh,
and all feeling below disappeared. His leg went out
from under him, and he collapsed to the floor.

It saved his life. Higgins's knife passed over his head
with a vicious hiss. Two inches lower and he would
have buried it to the hilt in his left eye.

Tower rolled.

Higgins snorted and turned slowly to follow. Blood
streaked across the wooden floor as Tower scrabbled
like a wounded crab to escape. Now Higgins brought
his prosthetic up and slammed it down.

Crunch!

Each blow left a fragmented gash in the wood.
Tower pushed himself backward, barely keeping ahead
of Higgins's inexorable advance. Above him, the big
man's single red eye blared with baleful intensity. Higgins's knife whickered and slashed at thin air. Tower
bumped into the edge of the sofa. There was no more
retreat. No place to go.

Higgins gagged up a great clot of blood and leaned
forward.

"*Tower,*" he crooned. "*The Power!*"

Tower's right hand touched something slick and cold

and hard, and he remembered. His fingers curled around the grip of Foster's .44 Magnum.

He jerked the weapon from beneath the sofa, twisted it up, aimed.

Higgins smiled, as if he couldn't see the weapon, or didn't care. *"Tower!"* he belched one final time.

"No," Tower said, And he pulled the trigger until the big Magnum was hot and empty. The sound of the shots came so rapidly they filled the room with a single peal of cracking thunder.

Higgins's head exploded.

The force of the massive bullets destroyed his chest, punched him back, slammed him against the kitchen counter.

His brains left a long, glistening tail on the wood as he slid to the floor. Twitched once.

Died.

Tower dropped the pistol. It made a hard, metallic clunk on the wood. He crawled over to Kelly and put his arms around her. He touched her hair.

"It's over," he whispered, and he felt her body heave. "It's over. It's over. . . ."

Later, he dragged Higgins's body into the night and threw it on the garbage heap. He watched the snow cover it. It took only a moment.

No police had come. He didn't expect any. In the slums, bodies became garbage with little notice. That was the way of things.

He went back upstairs and talked to her. She had gone beyond hysteria to a blank, dead acceptance.

Once, she said, "Be sure to take the roast out of the oven." She looked at him as she said it, but she didn't see him. "It will burn," she said.

He nodded, and he searched in her purse until he found the right derms. He put two on her neck and held her until she fell asleep. Then he put her on the sofa and covered her with a blanket. He touched her forehead. It was cold and clammy. He looked at his fingers.

What had she said? That she *must* love him? Yes.

Now he understood. He wondered if he could help
her.

He wrapped the slash on his arm with a towel as
well as he could. It wasn't a perfect job, but it would
hold long enough. He looked at the Magnum on the
floor and left it there. He had no ammunition for it.
He put a Club in each coat pocket. A lot of firepower.

Tagg was gone. Foster was gone.

It didn't matter. He knew what he had to do. He
called Meister Bee to arrange for her protection. As
he was leaving, he glanced at her one last time, at her
face, at the slack muscles. He bent down and kissed
her cheek. Then he left the apartment and went out
into the storm.

Condor Securities had never been difficult to find.
It was even listed in the Denver net book. Tower took
the Colfax Underground as far as he could, and then
he walked down the Sixteenth Street Mall, letting the
snow fall on him. The pavement of the mall was
heated, and the snow did not stick. Outside the mall,
drifts were piling in great white mounds, but inside,
there was only the slickness of dark water.

He came to the building and went inside. There was
a vast lobby, two stories high, and a desk with a single
security guard. He went up to the guard, who eyed
him with amazement.

"Condor Securities, please. I'm expected."

The guard didn't say anything. He nodded and
punched a button and spoke softly into the air. After
a moment, he nodded.

"Go on up. Twelfth floor. Turn right off the elevator."

He felt the guard's eyes on him until he stepped into
the elevator and the door closed. He rode up, got off,
turned right.

The long hallway was studded with blank doors. The
lights overhead were harsh, clinical. It was very quiet.

He came to the door that read "Condor Securities."
He stopped a moment, his hand lightly touching the
knob. Then he turned, and pushed, and went in.

There was a spare, clean, anteroom, occupied by an empty desk. On the desk was a vase of silk flowers, roses, tulips, marigolds. The air smelled clean and dusty at the same time.

He went through the door behind the desk and entered a large office. Several desks were divided by low, portable walls. Each desk held a screen and touchpad. The room was empty, but the lights were on.

He stopped and looked around. At the far end of the office was another door. It was partly open. There was light and the thin sound of music. Chopin, he guessed. He walked down an aisle between the desks and opened the door all the way. He stepped into the room.

There was a large, mahogany desk. Its top was bare and polished. A thick, padded, black leather chair was behind it, its back turned toward him. The drapes in the office were open, looking out on the storm, the snow.

"I'm here," Tower said.

The chair turned. Lincoln Foster stared at him. "Sit down," Foster said. He pointed at a chair in front of the desk.

Tower took the Club from his right-hand pocket. He pointed it at Foster. "No," he said. "It's over.'

Foster nodded. "I know it's over. Sit down. You can kill me later."

Tower shook his head. He extended the Club slightly. He felt the muscles of his right hand begin to contract.

"No," he said again.

"I have the tapes," Foster said. "The tapes you wanted. From the laser taxi. What Julia said, at the end."

Sweat flooded across his forehead. It ran down into his eyes. His hand felt suddenly loose, weak. He licked his lips. He lowered the Club. "Tell me."

"Sit down," Foster said.

Tower sat down and put the Club in his lap, folding his hands over it. "Tell me," he said again.

Foster was bare chested. There was gray and white in the patch of hair on his chest. Only a few streaks of black. Two livid bruises glistened on his chest, black and purple fading to yellow. He touched one bruise lightly. "I wore a vest, of course."

"What if Higgins had shot you in the head?"

"I would be dead. But he didn't." Foster shrugged. "I wasn't counting on Higgins anyway. Or Tagg, either. Not then. Higgins was only Tagg's wild card." They stared at each other, contemplating the breaks of the game they both understood perfectly well.

"There were a lot of wild cards," Tower said. "I guess I knew all along, or almost. I just didn't want to admit it."

Foster's furry eyebrows crawled up his forehead. "Knew what?"

"About you. That it was you. But I didn't want to believe it."

"How could you have known?"

"The white room," Tower said.

"The big man shook his head. "I don't understand."

"My computer room. The one I supposedly wrecked. I didn't figure it out until later. A lot later. But when I did, everything started to make sense. Everything. Link, how could you do it to me?"

Foster leaned forward, winced, then leaned back. "Josh, what are you talking about? What about your computer room?"

"It was *spotless!* No blood. There was blood everywhere else. Even when I was cleaning the place out, the scabs on my hands were still fresh enough to break and leave blood. So how did I smash the computers the night before, blind drunk, without leaving *some* marks?"

"Oh, Josh. You always were too smart for your own good."

Tower's voice was low and savage. He didn't seem to have heard Foster's interjection. "So once I realized that, then other things began to make sense. Like how you got out of your house when the whole God damned navy rolled up on your beach. Did you know I thought you were dead? That I actually *worried* about you. Felt *guilty?*''

A faint grin flickered across Foster's features. ''That one was real, Josh. I did get away. The day I can't break out of a trap . . . He shook his head.. ''The blood on the kitchen floor wasn't mine. If that's what you thought.''

Tower touched the Club in his lap. ''Why bother? Tagg was yours, somehow, wasn't he?''

''Oh, yeah, he was mine. But he didn't know it. Tagg was meat. And he went off the leash.''

The room seemed surreal to Tower. They faced each other and spoke in low, conversational tones. As friends might speak. But now the full sad betrayal of what Foster had done began to seep through his bones, as yet another part of his life slowly crumbled.

Dead, gray weight began to crush his chest. He chuckled. The sound was hollow. ''You always said that when there wasn't a reason, the reason was money. Was that your reason, Link? Money? Was that all there was?''

For the first time, Foster grimaced uncomfortably. ''I'm an old man, Josh. For this business. You think I liked it, being out of the game, out to pasture? Data-hunter!'' His voice went thick with scorn. ''Piddling around in other people's trivial problems, going half blind in front of a screen for nickels and dimes. And then . . . *this* came along, and I—I took it. It had nothing to do with you.''

''It must have been a surprise. When I came into the picture, I mean.''

Foster's eyes widened. His pallid skin grew brighter. ''Oh, hell yes. I didn't want to hurt you, Josh. And when I found out about Julia—''

At his dead wife's name, Tower couldn't hold it in any longer. The knot of surging rage inside him balled up in his throat and exploded in a torrent of words. ''Don't use her name. I figured out that part, too. You killed her, you son-of-a-bitch. *You!* My old *buddy!* Like a *father* to me, you *bastard!*''

Foster sagged back beneath Tower's naked anger.

He raised his big hands, palms out. "Josh . . . Josh, I had nothing to do with that."

Tower's lips twitched. The skin on his cheeks, white as bone, showed two sudden spots of color. His pupils contracted to tiny dots. "Not specifically," he said softly. "But you set it up, didn't you? You were behind the accidents, weren't you? And tell me something, old buddy, if you *had* known. If you had *known* she would die, what then? Would you have called it off? Tell me, Mister Money-is-the-answer, *would you have called it off?*"

The room went dead silent. Tower waited, but the other man didn't answer. He sat behind his desk, looking gray and old and tired, but he didn't answer.

He didn't need to. They both knew the answer already.

"The tapes," Tower said. "I want to hear them."

"In a minute. After you hear them I think you might kill me, and I want to finish my side of it."

Tower inclined his head slightly, as if listening to a voice coming from far away. The wind whispered against the dark glass. He didn't know how he felt. Cold, certainly, and dead. But he wanted to hear all the loose ends. Tie everything up.

His friend had become his enemy. But they shared a past, they were comfortable with each other. There were no surprises, only revelations. You might have been that ten year old, he thought.

"Go on."

"They came to me because I was the best. Am the best. They presented their problem, and I told them how to handle it. It would have been my last job. Going out in style, you might say. The big score."

Tower understood. He couldn't help it. He remembered the long cold years spying, betraying, killing. Everybody had the dream. The big score. An end to the coldness. Warmth and security and a place out of the storm.

"You killed Julia," he said. "For your big score."

"I didn't mean to."

Foster stared at him but didn't say anything for a moment. Finally he sighed. "They are too big. You haven't met them. Hilkind, the mechanical monster. Fujiwara. Schollander. It's gone too far now. Even if you kill me, it's gone too far."

"Has it?"

"They'll hunt you down. Hilkind, he . . ." Foster shook his big head. "You don't know Hilkind."

"Did you come to my place to kill me?"

"I don't know. I think so. I could have done it earlier."

"That's what I didn't understand. Why you didn't do it then, when I was drunk. You ruined my machines instead."

Foster stubbed out his cigarette, opened the drawer, and lit another. "I felt sorry for you. There was a time . . . Like you said, father and son, maybe. You reminded me of myself."

Tower looked out at the night and shuddered inside. He knew Foster was telling the truth. He saw the closeness, the connection. Reminded him of himself. Oh, God.

"I thought I could ease you out of it, but you wouldn't give it up. I didn't think you'd get as far as you did."

Tower said, "Can I have one of those cigarettes?"

"Sure." Foster pushed the pack across the desk, along with the lighter. Tower lit up. His hand didn't shake at all. He inhaled and watched the spark glow. He ashed the cigarette on the floor, on the expensive blue carpet, and inhaled again.

"The bomb in your computer. That was you, right?"

"I couldn't let anybody get in there. Not you, not Tagg, not . . . anybody else. It was my ace, my insurance. All the data. My protection, if anything went wrong." As he said this, his face grew strained and pleading, as if he wished for another human to understand why he'd done what he'd done. Perhaps he sought absolution. Perhaps he didn't.

"Josh, I'm old. An old man. All I wanted was time, a long time. My place at the beach. My home."

Tower regarded him stonily. The big score. Everybody wanted, needed, the big score. He asked, "Did Tagg know?"

"No. Although I think he was beginning to get my number, there at the end. But, like I said, he was just meat."

"And you controlled him. You sent him after me." His voice was flat and empty. He dropped his half-smoked cigarette and ground it out. It left an ugly black scar. "I want to hear the tapes," he said.

"All right."

Foster ran his thick fingers across the touchpad on his desktop. The Chopin disappeared. In its place was the sound of wind.

"Oh, God!" It was a man's voice. His own voice, though it didn't sound like his own. It never does, a tape recording.

A long, cracking scream, a woman. Then a roar. The shriek of metal tearing. A single sharp hiss. The pinging of overheated steel contracting.

Tower leaned forward.

"Oh, my God! Oh, God!" Julia's voice was low, bubbling. It didn't sound fully human. It sounded damaged. *Oh, God!"*

A long moment of silence. Then wordless moans. Then silence again.

The sliding wheeze of the tape ended. Tower looked up. His eyes were empty, dazed.

"That's all? That's it?"

"I'm sorry. There wasn't anything more."

Then Tower knew there was to be no mercy. Nor forgiveness. Only an end. "I wish you'd killed me," he said.

He raised the Club.

Colonel Tagg came into the office. His face was badly bruised, and blood oozed from his right eye. He said, "I killed the guard. Now you, you son-of-a-bitch."

"No, Tagg, wait!" Foster roared. "It's not—"

Tower turned and shot Tagg five times with the Club. Then he leaned over and vomited. After a moment, Foster came around the desk and took the weapon from him and helped him sit up.

"I'm not like you," Tower said.

"Yes, you are," Foster told him.

"Go ahead," Tower said. "Kill me."

Foster hefted the Club. Then he said, "No. I can't do that."

"Sure you can. You were going to."

Foster exhaled slowly. He looked a thousand years old. "No," he said. "I don't think I was."

After a time Tower raised his head. Beyond the dark windows, the storm hammered insistently. "Then what?"

Foster smiled. "Save our asses, I guess. One more time. For old times' sake."

Tower nodded. "I know how to do that. If the war is between Luna and Consort."

"You figured that out, too?"

"Yes."

"You're something. I taught you everything you know, but . . ."

"You don't get it, do you?"

"Get what?"

Tower's smile made his face resemble a skull. "The child is father to the man, Link. And I'm a man now." Suddenly his shoulders shook. "Finally, I'm a man."

Chapter Fifteen

Tower led the way, picking a careful path through the wreckage of the Safeway. The storm had transformed the neighborhood. It hid the ugliness and desperation beneath great white humps of snow. The wind whipped off the tops of the drifts and flung them into his face, but he didn't notice. He put one foot in front of the other and wondered why he felt nothing.

Two boys came out of the whirling screens of snow-flakes and pointed Uzis at them. Foster raised his hands.

"Friends of yours?"

"Yes."

They went down.

Meister Bee looked up at them as they entered his room. His thin face twisted in surprise. "Who's he?"

"Link Foster," Tower said.

The two guards crowded into the room. Meister Bee grinned.

"I know who you are," he said to Foster.

Foster looked at Tower. "A kid?"

"Don't call me that!" Meister Bee said.

"Oh? What should I call you?"

"Whatever you usually call somebody who can have your head blown off if you twitch funny."

Foster stared at the computer master. "Can you do that?"

The whir of hidden gun emplacements swinging into position suddenly filled the room. "Bet your tired old balls I can."

Foster's faintly bemused expression didn't change. He seemed buoyant, almost happy. "Well then, give me a name."

"Meister Bee."

"That seems moderately impossible."

"Why? You've heard the name, then?"

"Meister Bee," Foster said carefully, "runs the Denver Deep."

The youth grinned. It was a nasty expression. "Then consider the introductions made. Like I said, I already know you. Sit down."

They took the two chairs in front of his console desk.

"Where do you know me from?" Foster asked mildly.

"You're the bonehead that lashed together the Consort buyout. Not bad work, for an amateur."

Finally Foster's composure cracked. "How did you . . ." He stopped and shook his head.

Meister Bee nodded. "I cracked your stuff, and then I cracked Luna's. Luna was harder than you. They've got a real jock up there. Somebody who actually knows what he's doing." He sounded surprised.

He licked his lips and continued. "Neat plan, though. Luna was going to buy out Consort, use the leverage to break themselves away. And you set up the front. Condor. I caught your linkages into Consort's transport-control banks. Like I said, fairly sneaky."

"I'm glad you think so."

"I could have done better," Meister Bee said flatly. He turned to Tower. "You checked my dump to your rig?"

He nodded. "Earlier this evening."

"So, is that it? Our contract is even. You've got what you paid for."

Tower thought about Julia. About Higgins and Tagg and Foster. About the faceless dead in other "accidents." About all the blood and death. He said, "I got what I paid for, but not what I want."

"What do you want?"

"Revenge," he said.

* * *

"You just put the ring around your head. Like this."
Meister Bee was even skinnier than he appeared. When
he came from behind his desk to help Tower into the
auxiliary rig, it was obvious he barely weighed a hundred pounds. But he vibrated with some exotic energy
and, slight as he was, he filled the room.

Foster remained seated in his original chair. The
two guards had left, after relieving the big man of his
Club. "You got a three-foot buffer zone," Meister Bee
had told him. "Come out of that chair any more than
that and you get fried. You understand?"

Now Foster watched as Tower settled himself before
a triple screen bank of machines. Meister Bee finished
placing the induction ring around Tower's skull. Tower
looked terrible. His skin was beyond pale, almost
translucent, as if all the blood had drained out of him.
A crust of dried scab ringed one eye. Blood stained
the rude bandage on his arm. But he was still functioning.

"This setup won't let you dance on the face yourself. But you can sort of go along for the ride. You
don't have direct input, and you don't have anything
like my resolution. But you can keep track, and you
can input manually to me from your touchpad. You
got it?"

Meister Bee went back behind his desk. He reached
down and pulled a long spray of thin, shiny cable,
connected to a silvery plug. He plugged this into a
dark socket beneath his ear.

"Face dancer," Foster said softly.

Now Meister Bee looked surprised. "That's right.
How do you know about it?"

"Robert Hilkind," Foster said. "On Luna they call
him Bullet Bobby. He does the same thing."

Meister Bee looked down at his desk. "No wonder."

"What?"

"I said they had somebody good up there. Now I
know why."

"It doesn't bother you?"

Meister Bee stared directly into his eyes. "It's not the machines," he said. "It's what you do with them."

Tower said, "Can you do what I want?"

Meister Bee said, "Yes."

"Jesus Christ," Larry Schollander said. "What the hell's going on?"

Mitsu Fujiwara shrugged. "Ask Bobby."

But Bobby Hilkind, his narrow face drawn and mapped with thin lines of tension, didn't reply. His eyes were closed. Every once in a while, his bony fingers clenched, like a high-wire artist grabbing for balance.

"Can't we wake him up?" Schollander blurted suddenly.

"You know we can't. Not until he's ready."

Schollander made an exasperated sound deep in his throat. "Who knows when that will be?"

"Ask him. He's the dancer."

The two men watched as Bullet Bobby Hilkind struggled to save their dreams.

The drugs were a blessing. Meister Bee attached the derms himself. "Synthetic curare derivatives. Other stuff. The idea is to shut down any senses you don't need. It's hard enough to sort out the input you'll get through the ring. I'm leaving you enough control to handle the touchpad if it's necessary, but it will be slow. That's okay, though. I don't want you bothering me unless you have to."

Tower nodded. Already, the feeling was going from his skin. The pain washed away. He felt as if he were beginning to float. He realized that his sense of smell had disappeared. Finally, his aural facilities began to go. The last thing he heard was Meister Bee's voice, so incongruously young.

"Close your eyes," he said. "Just close them and wait."

Tower closed his eyes.

For a moment panic gripped him. Then he relaxed. It was very strange. He bobbed like an invisible cork

within the confines of his skull. Then the colors and
the shapes began to appear.

Slowly, so slowly at first. Just a hint, a flick of blue,
a long wash of green. Shapeless, indistinct.

He didn't know how he sensed it, but he knew when
Meister Bee kicked on the power. Now the colors came
faster, an ever-shifting kaleidoscope of shades and
forms. Something vast and sharp edged rumbled past
him. He heard a long, rolling, thunderous sound, and
he wondered how he could hear with his aural nerves
blocked. Then he understood. The sound was taking
place inside his own brain. That was what the induction ring did.

More shapes, more colors. Red and blue and orange. The smell of baked potatoes. Cucumbers. A
harsh, tearing sound, as if the fabric of thought had
been ripped apart.

Something that looked like a cartoon stick figure
danced before his closed eyes. It waved its arms. It
disappeared, to be replaced by a smiley face drawn in
neon purple.

Meister Bee.

Now another figure entered, dark and sinister. Another smiley face, but on this image, the smile was
full of teeth. A huge black shape rumbled up from
below. It was immediately answered by another form,
as big as a skyscraper, settling down.

Analogs, he thought. This is the interface between
man and machine. Where the face dancers dance.

He felt detached. Gigantic structures formed, dissolved. Then, with no warning, the whole pastiche of
images shattered before a sudden fusillade of lightning
bolts.

The shivers of light were terrifying. Dimly, he
sensed their power as the two dancers sought to destroy each other. He couldn't comprehend the forces
at play here, but he knew that time was deceptive.
Somehow, all of this was taking place in a few split
instants. It was awesome, it was frightening, it was
inhuman.

The future of man, he thought.

His side was losing.

The strategy had been simple. Use Meister Bee's talents, his machines, to take over the Condor network. Use the gargantuan pool of stock Foster had acquired as leverage to purchase more Consort stock. If they could gain control of enough stock, they could control Luna, Consort's principal subsidiary. For that was the weakness Tower had perceived. That was the vulnerability of that particular group of systems. Luna had not been able to function on their own. In order for their plan to succeed, they had to set up a separate system to hold the stock. That system had been Condor, and legally, nobody owned Condor. It had all depended on Link Foster's loyalty to his employers.

I could have told them, Tower thought. About his loyalty.

Now none of it mattered. Luna was winning. Their computer ace was about to take control of Condor for himself. It was a dangerous ploy, but Condor had already bought so much stock that Consort would not be able to defend itself. Particularly when Hilkind could penetrate their most sensitive databanks.

Luna would have done that in the first place, Tower thought, if the danger hadn't been so great. At the beginning, their plot could have been crushed. Now, it was questionable whether anything could stop them.

Even Meister Bee.

The scene inside his skull had turned into a maelstrom. Now the shapes were gone. There was nothing but the lightning, as each face dancer thrust and stabbed at the other.

Meister Bee wielded blue lightning, and his enemy struck back with red. Slowly, but inevitably, red lightning was wiping away the field of blue.

Meister Bee was valiant, but it was only a matter of moments, until the end.

Tower opened his eyes.

An inch at a time, he forced his fingers to move. It seemed to take an eternity. Symbol by symbol, he tapped out his message.

"Buy Luna." He finished and began again. Over

and over. *"Buy Luna."* Until he closed his eyes at last
and toppled forward into the darkness and the light.

Robert Hilkind looked up at the other two men from
his nest of glittering wires. His face was pale as a fish
belly. His eyes were puffed in rings of gray flesh. His
teeth chattered and he stopped them. His lips moved,
but nothing came out. He tried again.

"A deal. They want to make a deal."

Schollander glanced at Fujiwara. His face was grim,
unsmiling. He wondered if he would ever smile again.
"Make it," he said.

Tower sat in the chair next to Foster. He wondered
if he would ever forget the dim approximation of dancing on the face. That a frail twelve-year-old boy could
survive it filled him with awe.

Then Meister Bee grinned at Tower. "I made a deal,
of course." He seemed faintly embarrassed. "Not part
of our deal, but in the real world—"

"Of course," Tower said. He didn't know why he
hadn't killed Foster. Maybe he just couldn't do it anymore. Couldn't kill. I'm not like you, he swore to himself.

"You'll come out okay. I bought you safe conduct.
You are off their list. And I took points." Meister Bee
paused. "And I go up. They want my tech. They want
me." For a moment, his voice was filled with soft
wonder, that somebody wanted him. "I'll be up there,
where the future is happening. Not down here in the
garbage."

The big score, Tower thought.

We do it differently than they planned. No run on
Consort. Not anymore. Why stir up the groundhogs?"
Already, Meister Bee talked as if he were a Lunie.
The new, high frontier. The future.

"We have enough stock. A straight trade. The Consort stock for a leveraged buyout. Consort finances,
but nothing for them. No new stock. Junk bonds se-
cured by future revenues. Luna becomes the new company and answers to nobody. Consort understood. It

was inevitable, anyway. This way, they get a lot of cash and friends they will need later.''

It meant nothing to him. Just words.

Meister Bee sighed. ''Your idea pulled it out, Josh. Their guy, he was about to take me.'' His voice sounded full of shadows. ''But when I leveraged Consort stock into the subsidiary buyout, I had them. And they knew it.''

Tower nodded. ''Why didn't you, then?''

''Because . . .'' Meister Bee paused. ''Because they're right, Josh. You may not like their methods, but what they want is right. Luna can't be tied to Earth anymore. They're tomorrow, and Earth is yesterday.''

Tower looked down at his hands. He knew it was true. The man who said ends never justified means had never confronted a Hitler or a Hiroshima. To prevent or accomplish some things, anything was justifiable.

Perhaps Luna fell into that category. Meister Bee thought so, and it was too late to gainsay him.

It was over.

Tower looked up. He realized he was glad.

''Okay,'' he said.

Foster stared at him. He hadn't expected this. Now he had no expectations at all. Meister Bee glanced at him.

''If I were you, I'd find a hole and pull it in after me. They have to blame somebody.''

Foster understood. He nodded. ''I'll be going, then.''

''I'd wish you luck, but I might have to come after you myself. So I'll just say good-bye.''

Foster nodded again. ''Do I get out of here?''

''Yeah. I give you that much.''

''Thanks,'' Foster said. As he turned, Tower thought he looked smaller, older. There would be no warm place for him. Not ever again.

Foster touched his shoulder. ''Josh?''

Tower felt air leak from his lungs. His face was hot. His bones ached. The big man gave off waves of cold, as if he were already dead. Perhaps he was.

Tower wouldn't look at him. After a moment, the hand lifted. Foster moved toward the door.

"Link?"

"What?"

"Good luck."

A long interval of silence. Then, "Thanks." And he was gone.

Tower stood up.

"Where are you going?"

"Home," Tower said. "I'm going home."

Meister Bee nodded, as if he understood. But Tower stared into his blank, glittering eyeshades, and he knew that Meister Bee, with all his machine dreams of Luna, of the big score, was only shifting from one system to another. From the systems of the past to the systems of the future. Yet everything remained, intricate and mysterious, a great spinning construction moving blindly on, always onward, always into tomorrow.

"Systems," Tower said.

"What?"

Tower reached the door, where he listened to the whine of the hidden weapons. "You'll understand," he said. "Someday."

Epilogue

Three boys with glittering, feral eyes aimed weapons at him as he came into the apartment.

"Get out," he told them.

They left.

She waited on the sofa. She was sitting up, wrapped in the blanket. It was very warm in the room.

He sat down next to her.

"You must love me," he said.

Something that might have been hope clothed her voice. "Why?"

"Because I can try to love you."

Because I'm not like him. Because there are never any final answers. Because I'm cold, and I want to be warm.

"Will that be enough?" he asked.

"It will have to be," she told him.

Even two, he thought. Even two make a system. Even two. Outside the snow stopped falling and the wind died. With slow, ambiguous joy, they held each other and waited for the dawn.

About the Author

W.T. Quick was born in Muncie, Indiana, and now lives in San Francisco. He was educated at the Hill School and Indiana University. He is fond of single-malt scotch and writing about the near-infinite possibilities of technology. He is not fond of Senator William Proxmire. He has been publishing science fiction since 1979 and intends to continue.

27 million Americans can't read a bedtime story to a child.

It's because 27 million adults in this country simply can't read.

Functional illiteracy has reached one out of five Americans. It robs them of even the simplest of human pleasures, like reading a fairy tale to a child.

You can change all this by joining the fight against illiteracy.

Call the Coalition for Literacy at toll-free **1-800-228-8813** and volunteer.

Volunteer Against Illiteracy. The only degree you need is a degree of caring.